MORNING STAR

by

H. Rider Haggard

TOM STACEY

First published in Great Britain 1910
Copyright

This edition published 1972 by
Tom Stacey Reprints Ltd.
28–29 Maiden Lane, London WC2E 7JP
England

ISBN 0 85468 174 4

Printed in Great Britain by
C. Tinling & Co. Ltd, Prescot and London

MORNING STAR

MORNING STAR

Rider Haggard, author of *She*, *King Solomon's Mines* and many other world-famous romances, had an extraordinary insight into the mysteries and magic of Ancient Egypt. With sweeping imagination and vivid pen, he recreates the adventures and perils, the loves, the hopes, the fears of that far-off time: far-off and yet not really so distant, for men and women were much what they are today, and who knows but that the gods, in whom mankind has believed for so many thousands of years, may not sometimes intervene—as the Egyptians believed they did—in the affairs of this world?

The girl named Neter-Tua, or Morning Star, was the Pharaoh's only daughter. One day she would wear the double crown herself. And she was High Priestess of Amen.

The man she loves is Rames, captain of her father's guard. When Rames slays a man to protect his honour and that of the lady he can never wed, he is sent into exile, leaving her unprotected against the treachery and sorcery of her enemies.

Unprotected, that is, by human aid. But there were powers in Ancient Egypt which were more than human . . .

Morning Star is a love story and an adventure story, but, behind its colourful pageant, its turbulent scenes of action, its historical authenticity, lies a theme to provoke thought, to make us wonder.

Dedication

My dear Budge,—

Only a friendship extending over many years emboldened me, an amateur, to propose to dedicate a Romance of Old Egypt to you, one of the world's masters of the language and lore of the great people who in these latter days arise from their holy tombs to instruct us in the secrets of history and faith.

With doubt I submitted to you this story, asking whether you wished to accept pages that could not, I feared, be free from error, and with surprise in due course I read, among other kind things, your advice to me to "leave it exactly as it is." So I take you at your word, although I can scarcely think that in paths so remote and difficult I have not sometimes gone astray.

Whatever may be the shortcomings, therefore, that your kindness has concealed from me, since this tale was so fortunate as to please and interest you, its first critic, I offer it to you as an earnest of my respect for your learning and your labours.

Very sincerely yours,

H. Rider Haggard.

Ditchingham.

To Doctor Wallis Budge,
Keeper of Egyptian and Assyrian
Antiquities, British Museum.

AUTHOR'S NOTE

It may be thought that even in a story of Old Egypt to represent a " Ka " or " Double " as remaining in active occupation of a throne, while the owner of the said " Double " goes upon a long journey and achieves sundry adventures, is, in fact, to take a liberty with Doubles. Yet I believe that this is scarcely the case. The *Ka* or Double which Wiedermann aptly calls the " Personality within the Person " appears, according to Egyptian theory, to have had an existence of its own. It did not die when the body died, for it was immortal and awaited the resurrection of that body, with which, henceforth, it would be re-united and dwell eternally. To quote Wiedermann again, " The *Ka* could live without the body, but the body could not live without the *Ka*. Yet . . . . . it was material in just the same way as the body itself." Also it would seem that in certain ways it was superior to and more powerful than the body, since the Egyptian monarchs are often represented as making offerings to their own *Kas* as though these were gods. Again, in the story of " Setna and the Magic Book," translated by Maspero and by Mr. Flinders Petrie in his " Egyptian Tales," the *Ka* plays a very distinct part of its own. Thus the husband is buried at Memphis and the wife in Koptos, yet the *Ka* of the wife goes to live in her husband's tomb hundreds of miles away, and converses with the prince who comes to steal the magic book.

Although I know no actual precedent for it, in the case of a particularly powerful Double, such as was given in this romance to Queen Neter-Tua by her spiritual father, Amen, the greatest of the Egyptian gods, it seems, therefore, legitimate to suppose that, in order to save her from the abomination of a forced marriage with her uncle and her father's murderer, the *Ka* would be allowed to anticipate matters a little, and to play the part recorded in these pages.

It must not be understood, however, that the fact of marriage with an uncle would have shocked the Egyptian mind, since these people, and especially their royal Houses, made a habit of wedding their own brothers and sisters, as in this tale Mermes wed his half sister Asti.

I may add that there is authority for the magic waxen image which the sorcerer Kaku and his accomplice used to bewitch Pharaoh. In the days of Rameses III., over three thousand years ago, a plot was made to murder the king in pursuance of which such images were used. "Gods of wax . . . . . . for enfeebling the limbs of people," which were "great crimes of death, the great abomination of the land." Also a certain "magic roll" was brought into play which enabled its user to "employ the magic powers of the gods."

Still, the end of these wizards was not encouraging to others, for they were found guilty and obliged to take their own lives.

But even if I am held to have stretched the prerogative of the *Ka*, or of the waxen image which, by the way, has survived almost to our own time, and in West Africa, as a fetish, is still pierced with pins or nails, I can urge in excuse that I have tried, so far as a modern may, to reproduce something of the atmosphere and colour of Old Egypt, as it has appeared to a traveller in that country and a student of its records. If Neter-Tua never sat upon its throne, at least another daughter of Amen, that mighty queen, Hatshepu, wore the crown of the Upper and the Lower Lands, and sent her embassies to search out the mysteries of Punt. Of romance also, in high places, there must have been abundance, though the short-cut records or the religious texts of the priests do not trouble themselves with such matters.

At any rate, so believing, in the hope that it may interest readers of to-day, I have ventured to discover and present one such romance, whereof the motive, we may be sure, is more ancient, by far, than the old Egyptians, namely, the triumph of true love over great difficulties and dangers. It is pleasant to dream that the gods are on the side of such lovers, and deign for their sakes to work the miracles in which for thousands of years mankind has believed, although the scientist tells us that they do not happen.

A*

How large a part marvel and magic of the most terrible and exalted kind played in the life of Old Egypt and of the nations with which she fought and traded, we need go no further than the Book of Exodus to learn. Also all her history is full of it, since among the Egyptians it was an article of faith that the Divinity, which they worshipped under so many names and symbols, made use of such mysterious means to influence or direct the affairs of men and bring about the accomplishment of Its decrees.

H. R. H.

CONTENTS

MORNING STAR

CHAPTER I

THE PLOT OF ABI

It was evening in Egypt, thousands of years ago, when the Prince Abi, governor of Memphis and of great territories in the Delta, made fast his ship of state to a quay beneath the outermost walls of the mighty city of Uast or Thebes, which we moderns know as Luxor and Karnac on the Nile. Abi, a large man, very dark of skin, for his mother was one of the hated Hyksos barbarians who once had usurped the throne of Egypt, sat upon the deck of his ship and stared at the setting sun which for a few moments seemed to rest, a round ball of fire, upon the bare and rugged mountains, that ring round the Tombs of the Kings.

He was angry, as the slave-women, who stood on either side fanning him, could see well enough by the scowl on his coarse face and the fire in his large black eyes. Presently they felt it also, for one of them, staring at the temples and palaces of the wonderful city made glorious by the light of the setting sun, that city of which she had heard so often, touched his head with the feathers of her fan. Thereon, as though glad of an excuse to express his ill-humour, Abi sprang up and boxed her ears so heavily that the poor girl fell to the deck.

" Awkward cat," he cried, " do that again and you shall be flogged until your robe sticks to your back ! "

" Pardon, mighty Lord," she said, beginning to weep, " it was an accident ; the wind caught my fan."

" So the rod shall catch your skin, if you are not more careful, Merytra. Stop that snivelling and go send Kaku the Astrologer here. Go, both, I weary of the sight of your ugly faces."

The girl rose, and with her fellow slave ran swiftly to the ladder that led to the waist of the ship.

" He called me a cat," Merytra hissed through her white teeth to her companion. " Well, if so, Sekhet the cat-headed is my godmother, and she is the Lady of Vengeance."

" Yes," answered the other, " and he said that we were both ugly—we, whom every lord who comes near the Court admires so much ! Oh ! I wish a holy crocodile would eat him, black pig ! "

" Then why don't they buy us ? Abi would sell his daughters, much more his fan-bearers—at a price."

" Because they hope to get us for nothing, my dear, and what is more, if I can manage it one of them shall, for I am tired of this life. Have your fling while you can, I say. Who knows at which corner Osiris, Lord of Death, is waiting."

" Hush ! " whispered Merytra, " there is that knave of an astrologer, and he looks cross, too."

Then, hand in hand they went to this lean and learned man and humbly bowed themselves before him.

"Master of the stars," said Merytra, "we have a message for you. No, do not look at my cheek, please, the marks are not magical, only those of the divine fingers of the glorious hand of the most exalted Prince Abi, son of the Pharaoh happily ruling in Osiris, etc., etc., etc., of the right, royal blood of Egypt—that is on one side, and on the other of a divine lady whom Khem the Spirit, or Ptah the Creator, thought fit to dip in a vat of black dye."

"Hem!" said Kaku glancing nervously over his shoulder. Then, seeing that there was no one near, he added, "you had better be careful what you say, my dear. The royal Abi does not like to hear the colour of his late mother defined so closely. But why did he slap your face?"

She told him.

"Well," he answered, "if I had been in his place I would rather have kissed it, for it is pretty, decidedly pretty," and this learned man forgot himself so far as to wink at Merytra.

"There, Sister," said the girl, "I always told you that rough shells have sweet nuts inside of them. Thank you for your compliment, Master of learning. Will you tell us our fortune for nothing?"

"Yes, yes," he answered; "at least the fee I want will cost you nothing. Now stop this nonsense," he added anxiously, "I gather that *he* is cross."

"I never saw him crosser, Kaku. I am glad it is you who read the stars, not I. Listen!"

As she spoke an angry roar reached them from the high deck above.

" Where is that accursed astrologer ? " said the
roar.

" There, what did I tell you ? Oh ! never mind
the rest of the papers, go at once. Your robe is full
of rolls as it is."

" Yes," answered Kaku as he ran to the ladder,
" but the question is, how will he like what is in the
rolls ? "

" The gods be with you ! " cried one of the girls
after him, " you will need them all."

" And if you get back alive, don't forget your
promise about the fortunes," said the other.

A minute later this searcher of the heavens, a
tall, hook-nosed man, was prostrating himself before
Abi in his pavilion on the upper deck, so low that
his Syrian-shaped cap fell from his bald head.

" Why were you so long in coming ? " asked
Abi.

" Because your slaves could not find me, royal
Son of the Sun. I was at work in my cabin."

" Indeed, I thought I heard them giggling with
you down there. What did you call me ? Royal
Son of the Sun ? That is Pharaoh's name ! Have
the stars shown you —— ? " and he looked at him
eagerly.

" No, Prince, not exactly that. I did not think
it needful to search them on a matter which seems
established, more or less."

" More or less," answered Abi gloomily. " What
do you mean by your ' more or less ' ? Here am I
at the turning-point of my fortunes, not knowing
whether I am to be Pharaoh of the Upper and Lower
Lands, or only the petty lord of a city and a few

provinces in the Delta, and you satisfy my hunger
for the truth with an empty dish of ' more or less.'
Man, what do you mean ? "

" If your Majesty will be pleased to tell his servant exactly what you desire to know, perhaps I
may be able to answer the question," replied Kaku
humbly.

" Majesty ! Well, I desire to know by what
warrant you call me ' Majesty,' who am only Prince
of Memphis. Did the stars give it to you ?
Have you obeyed me and asked them of the
future ? "

" Certainly, certainly. How could I disobey ?
I observed them all last night, and have been working
out the results till this moment ; indeed, they are
not yet finished. Question and I will answer."

" You will answer, yes, but what will you answer ?
Not the truth, I fancy, because you are a coward,
though if anyone can read the truth, it is you. Man,"
he added fiercely, " if you dare to lie to me I will cut
your head off and take it to Pharaoh as a traitor's ;
and your body shall lie, not in that fine tomb which
you have made, but in the belly of a crocodile whence
there is no resurrection. Do you understand ?
Then let us come to the point. Look, the sun sets
there behind the Tombs of the Kings, where the
departed Pharaohs of Egypt take their rest till the
Day of Awakening ? It is a bad omen for me, I
know, who wished to reach this city in the morning
when Ra was in the House of Life, the East, and not
in the House of Death, the West ; but that accursed
wind sent by Typhon, held me back and I could
not. Well, let us begin at the end which must come

after all.   Tell me, you reader of the heavens, shall
I sleep at last in that valley ? "

"I think so, Prince ; at least, so says your planet.
Look, yonder, it springs to life above you, " and he
pointed to an orb that appeared at the topmost edge
of the red glow of the sunset.

"You are keeping something back from me," said
Abi, searching Kaku's face with his fierce eyes.
"Shall I sleep in the tomb of Pharaoh, in my own
everlasting house that I shall have made ready to
receive me ? "

"Son of Ra, I cannot say," answered the astrologer.   "Divine One, I will be frank with you.   Though
you be wrath, yet will I tell you the truth as you
command me.   An evil influence is at work in your
House of Life.   Another star crosses and re-crosses
your path, and though for a long time you seem to
swallow it up, yet at the last it eclipses you—it and
one that goes with it."

"What star ? " asked Abi hoarsely, "Pharaoh's ? "

"Nay, Prince, the star of Amen."

"Amen ! What Amen ? "

"Amen the god, Prince, the mighty father of the
gods."

"Amen the god," repeated Abi in an awed voice.
"How can a man fight against a god ? "

"Say rather against two gods, for with the star
of Amen goes the star of Hathor, Queen of Love.
Not for many periods of thousands of years have
they been together, but now they draw near to each
other, and so will remain for all your life.   Look,"
and Kaku pointed to the Eastern horizon where a

faint rosy glow still lingered reflected from the western sky.

As they watched this glow melted, and there in the pure heavens, lying just where it met the distant land, seeming to rest upon the land, indeed, appeared a bright and beautiful star, and so close to it that, to the eye, they almost touched, a twin star. For a few minutes only were they seen ; then they vanished beneath the line of the horizon.

" The morning star of Amen, and with it the star of Hathor," said the astrologer.

" Well, Fool, what of it ? " exclaimed Abi. " They are far enough from my star ; moreover, it is they that sink, not I, who ride higher every moment."

" Aye, Prince, but in a year to come they will certainly eclipse that star of yours. Prince, Amen and Hathor are against you. Look, I will show you their journeyings on this scroll, and you shall see where they eat you up yonder, yes, yonder over the Valley of dead Kings, though twenty years and more must go by ere then, and take this for your comfort, during those years you shine alone," and he began to unfold a papyrus roll.

Abi snatched it from him, crumpled it up and threw it in his face.

" You cheat ! " he said. " Do you think to frighten me with this nonsense about stars ? Here is my star," and he drew the short sword at his side and shook it over the head of the trembling Kaku. " This sharp bronze is the star I follow, and be careful lest it should eclipse *you*, you father of lies."

" I have told the truth as I see it," answered the poor astrologer with some dignity, " but if you wish,

O Prince, that in the future I should indeed prophesy pleasant things to you, why, it can be done easily enough. Moreover, it seems to me that this horoscope of yours is not so evil, seeing that it gives to you over twenty years of life and power, more by far than most men can expect—at your age. If after that come troubles and the end, what of it ? "

" That is so," replied Abi mollified. " It was my ill-temper, everything has gone cross to-day. Well, a gold cup, my own, shall pay the price of it. Bear me no ill-will, I pray you, learned scribe, and above all tell me no falsehood as the message of the stars you serve. It is the truth I seek, the truth. If only she may be seen, and clasped, I care not how ill-favoured is her face."

Rejoicing at the turn which things had taken, and especially at the promise of the priceless cup which he had long coveted, Kaku bowed obsequiously. He picked up his crumpled roll and was about to retire when through the gloom of the falling night, some men mounted upon asses were seen riding over the mud flats that border the Nile at this spot, towards that bank where the ship was moored.

" The captain of my guard," said Abi, who saw the starlight gleam upon a bronze helmet, " who brings me Pharaoh's answer. Nay, go not, bide and hear it, Kaku, and give us your counsel on it, your true counsel."

So the astrologer stood aside and waited, till presently the captain appeared saluting.

" What says Pharaoh, my brother ? " asked the Prince.

" Lord, he says that he will receive you, though

as he did not send for you, he thinks that you can
scarcely come upon any necessary errand, as he has
heard long ago of your victory over the desert-dwell-
ing barbarians, and does not want the offering of the
salted heads of their officers which you bring to
him."

"Good," said Abi contemptuously. "The divine
Pharaoh was ever a woman in such matters, as in
others. Let him be thankful that he has generals
who know how to make war and to cut off the heads
of his enemies in defence of the kingdom. We will
wait upon him to-morrow."

"Lord," added the captain, "that is not all
Pharaoh's message. He says that it has been reported to him that you are accompanied by a guard
of three hundred soldiers. These soldiers he refuses
to allow within the gates. He directs that you shall
appear before his Majesty attended by five persons
only."

"Indeed," answered Abi with a scornful laugh.
"Does Pharaoh fear, then, lest I should capture him
and his armies and the great city with three hundred
soldiers ? "

"No, Prince," answered the captain bluntly;
"but I think he fears lest you should kill him and
declare yourself Pharaoh as next in blood."

"Ah ! " said Abi, "as next of blood. Then I
suppose that there are still no children at the
Court ? "

"None, O Prince. I saw Ahura, the royal wife,
the Lady of the Two Lands, that fairest of women,
and other lesser wives and beautiful slave girls without number, but never a one of them had an infant

on her breast or at her knee. Pharaoh remains childless."

"Ah!" said Abi again. Then he walked forward out of the pavilion whereof the curtains were drawn back, and stood a while upon the prow of the vessel.

By now night had fallen, and the great moon, rising from the earth as it were, poured her flood of silver light over the desert, the mountains, the limitless city of Thebes, and the wide rippling bosom of the Nile. The pylons and obelisks, glittering with copper and with gold, towered to the tender sky. In the window places of palaces and of ten thousand homes lamps shone like stars. From gardens, streets and the courts of temples floated the faint sound of singing and of music, while on the great embattled walls the watchmen called the hour from post to post.

It was a wondrous scene, and the heart of Abi swelled as he gazed upon it. What wealth lay yonder, and what power. There was the glorious house of his brother, Pharaoh, the god in human form who for all his godship had never a child to follow after him when he ascended to Osiris, as he who was sickly probably must do before so very long.

Yes, but before then a miracle might happen; in this way or in that a successor to the throne might be found and acknowledged, for were not Pharaoh and his House beloved by all the priests of Amen, and by the people, and was not he, Abi, feared and disliked because he was fierce, and the hated savage blood flowed in his veins? Oh! what evil god had put it in his father's heart to give him a princess of the Hyksos for a mother, the Hyksos, whom the Egyptians loathed, when he had the fairest women of the world from whom to choose ? Well, it was done and could not be undone, though because of it he might lose his heritage of the greatest throne in all the earth. Also was it not to this fierce Hyksos blood that he owed his strength and vigour ?

Why should he wait ? Why should he not set his fortune on a cast ? He had three hundred soldiers with him, picked men and brave, children of the sea and the desert, sworn to his House and interests. It was a time of festival, those gates were ill-guarded. Why should he not force them at the dead of night, make his way to the palace, cause Pharaoh to be gathered to his fathers, and at the dawn discover himself seated upon Pharaoh's throne ? At the thought of it Abi's heart leapt in his breast, his wide nostrils spread themselves, and he erected his strong head as though already he felt upon it the weight of the double crown. Then he turned and walked back to the pavilion.

"I am minded to strike a blow," he said. "Say now, my officer, would you and the soldiers follow me into the heart of yonder city to-night to win a throne—or a grave ? If it were the first, you should be the general of all my army, and you, astrologer, should become vizier, yes, after Pharaoh you two should be the greatest men in all the land."

They looked at him and gasped.

"A venturesome deed, Prince," said the captain at length ; "yet with such a prize to win I think that I would dare it, though for the soldiers I cannot speak. First they must be told what is on foot,

and out of so many, how know we that the heart of
one or more would not fail ? A word from a traitor
and before this time to-morrow the embalmers, or
the jackals, would be busy."

Abi heard and looked from him to his companion.

" Prince," said Kaku, " put such thoughts far
from you. Bury them deep. Let them rise no more.
In the heavens I read something of this business, but
then I did not understand, but now I see the black
depths of hell opening beneath our feet. Yes, hell
would be our home if we dared to lift hand against
the divine person of the Pharaoh. I say that the
gods themselves would fight against us. Let it be,
Prince, let it be and you shall have many years of rule,
who, if you strike now, will win nothing but a crown
of shame, a nameless grave, and the everlasting torments of the damned."

As he spoke Abi considered the man's face and
saw that all craft had left it. This was no charlatan
that spoke to him, but one in earnest who believed
what he said.

" So be it," he answered. " I accept your judgment, and will wait upon my fortune. Moreover,
you are both right, the thing is too dangerous, and
evil often falls on the heads of those who shoot arrows
at a god, especially if they have not enough arrows.
Let Pharaoh live on while I make ready. Perhaps
to-morrow I may work upon him to name me his
heir."

The astrologer sighed in relief, nor did the captain
seem disappointed.

" My head feels firmer on my shoulders than it
did just now," he said ; " and doubtless there are

payment do you ask for this service, my brother,
for with great gifts would I reward you, who have
done so well for me and Egypt ? "

Before he answered Abi looked at the beautiful
queen, Ahura, who sat at Pharaoh's side, and at the
other royal consorts and women.

" Your Majesty," he said, " I see here many wives
and ladies, but the royal children I do not see.   Grant
—for doubtless they are in their own chambers—
grant, O Pharaoh, that they may be led hither that
my eyes may feed upon their loveliness, and that I
may tell of them, each of them, to their cousins
who await me at Memphis."

At these words a flush as of shame spread itself
over the lovely face of Ahura, the royal wife, the Lady
of the Two Lands ; while the women turned their
heads away whispering to each other bitterly, for the
insult hurt them.   Only Pharaoh set his pale face
and answered with dignity.

" Prince Abi, to affront those whom the gods have
smitten, be they kings or peasants, is an unworthy
deed which the gods will not forget.   You know well
that I have no children.   Why then do you ask me
to show you their loveliness ? "

" I had heard rumours, O Pharaoh," answered
the Prince, " no more.   Indeed, I did not believe
them, for where there are so many wives I was certain
that there would be some mothers.   Therefore I asked
to be sure before I proffered a petition which now
I will make to you not for my own sake but for
Egypt's and yours, O Pharaoh.   Have I your leave
to speak here in public ?

" Speak on," said Pharaoh sternly.   " Let aught

that is for the welfare of Egypt be heard by
Egypt "

" Your Majesty has told me," replied Abi bowing,
" that the gods, being wrath, have denied you children.
Not so much as one girl of your blood have they given
to you to fill your throne after you when in due
season it pleases you to depart to Osiris. Were it
otherwise, were there even but a single woman-
child of your divine race, I would say nothing, I
would be silent as the grave. But so it is, and though
your queens be fair and many, so it would seem that
it must remain, since the ears of the gods having been
deaf to your pleadings for so long, although you have
built them glorious temples and made them offerings
without count, will scarcely now be opened. Even
Amen your father, Amen, whose name you bear,
will perform no miracle for you, O Pharaoh, who are
so great that he has decreed that you shall shine
alone like the full moon at night, not sharing your
glory with a single star."

Now Ahura the Queen, who all this while had
been listening intently, spoke for the first time in a
quick angry voice, saying,

" How know you that, Prince of Memphis ?
Sometimes the gods relent and that which they
have withheld for a space, they give. My lord
lives, and I live, and a child of his may yet fill the
throne of Egypt."

" It may be so, O Queen," said Abi bowing,
" and for my part I pray that it will be so, for who
am I that I should know the purpose of the kings of
heaven ? If but one girl be born of you and Pharaoh,
then I take back my words and give to you that

title which for many years has been written falsely upon your thrones and monuments, the title of Royal Mother."

Now Ahura would have answered again, for this sneering taunt stung her to the quick. But Pharaoh laid his hand upon her knee and said,

" Continue, Prince and brother. We have heard from you that which we already know too well—that I am childless. Tell us what we do not know, the desire of your heart which lies hid beneath all these words."

" Pharaoh, it is this—I am of your holy blood, sprung of the same divine father——"

" But of a mother who was not divine," broke in Ahura ; " of a mother taken from a race that has brought many a curse upon Khem, as any mirror will show you, Prince of Memphis."

" Pharaoh," went on Abi without heeding her, " you grow weak ; heaven desires you, the earth melts beneath you. In the north and in the south many dangers threaten Egypt. Should you die suddenly without an heir, barbarians will flow in from the north and from the south, and the great ones of the land will struggle for your place. Pharaoh, I am a warrior ; I am strong ; my children are many ; my house is built upon a rock ; the army trusts me ; the millions of the people love me. Take me then to rule with you and in the hearing of all the earth name me and my sons as your successors, so that our royal race may continue for generation after generation. So shall you end your days in peace and hope. I have spoken."

Now, as the meaning of this bold request sank

B

into their hearts, all the court there gathered gasped
and whispered, while the Queen Ahura in her anger
crushed the lotus flower which she held in her hand
and cast it to the floor. Only Pharaoh sat still and
silent, his head bent and his eyes shut as though in
prayer. For a minute or more he sat thus, and
when he lifted his pale, pure face, there was a smile
upon it.

" Abi, my brother," he said in his gentle voice,
" listen to me. There are those who filled this
throne before me, who on hearing such words would
have pointed to you with their sceptres, whereon,
Abi, those lips of yours would have grown still for
ever, and you and your name and the names of all
your House would have been blotted out by death.
But, Abi, you were ever bold, and I forgive you for
laying open the thoughts of your heart to me. Still,
Abi, you have not told us all of them. You have
not told us, for instance," he went on slowly, and in
the midst of an intense silence, " that but last night
you debated whether it would not be possible with
that guard of yours to break into my palace and
put me to the sword and name yourself Pharaoh—
by right of blood, Abi; yes, by right of blood—my
blood shed by you, my brother."

As these words left the royal lips a tumult arose
in the hall, the women and the great officers sprang
up, the captains stepped forward drawing their
swords to avenge so horrible a sacrilege. But Pharaoh
waved his sceptre, and they were still, only Abi
cried in a great voice,

" Who has dared to whisper a lie so monstrous ? "
And he glared first at Kaku and then at the captain

of his guard who stood behind him, and choked in wrath, or fear, or both.

" Suspect not your officers, Prince," went on the Pharaoh, still smiling, " for on my royal word they are innocent. Yet, Abi, a pavilion set upon the deck of a ship is no good place to plot the death of kings. Pharaoh has many spies, also, at times, the gods, to whom as you say he is so near, whisper tidings to him in his sleep. Suspect not your officers, Abi, although I think that to yonder Master of the Stars who stands behind you, I should be grateful, since, had you attempted to execute this madness, but for him I might have been forced to kill you, Abi, as one kills a snake that creeps beneath his mat. Astrologer, you shall have a gift from me, for you are a wise man. It may take the place, perhaps, of one that you have lost ; was it not a certain woman slave whom your master gave to you last night—after he had punished her for no fault ? "

Kaku prostrated himself before the glory of Pharaoh, understanding at last that it was the lost girl Merytra who had overheard and betrayed them. But heeding him no more, his Majesty went on,

" Abi, Prince and brother, I forgive you a deed that you purposed but did not attempt. May the gods and the spirits of our fathers forgive you also, if they will. Now as to your demand. You are my only living brother, and therefore I will weigh it. Perchance, if I should die without issue, although you are not all royal, although there flows in your veins a blood that Egypt hates ; although you could plot the murder of your lord and king, it may be

well that when I am gone you should fill my place,
for you are brave and of the ancient race on one side,
if base-born on the other. But I am not yet dead,
and children may still come to me. Abi, will you
be a prisoner until Osiris calls me, or will you swear
an oath ? "

"I will swear an oath," answered the Prince
hoarsely, for he knew his shame and danger.

"Then kneel here, and by the dreadful Name
swear that you will lift no hand and plot no plot
against me. Swear that if a child, male or female,
should be given to me, you will serve such a child
truly as your lord and lawful Pharaoh. In the
presence of all this company, swear, knowing that
if you break the oath in letter or in spirit, then all
the gods of Egypt shall pour their curse upon your
head in life, and in death shall give you over to the
everlasting torments of the damned."

So, having little choice, Abi swore by the Name
and kissed the sceptre in token of his oath.

It was night. Dark and solemn was the inner-
most shrine of the vast temple, the " House of Amen
in the Northern Apt," which we call Karnak, the very
holy of holies where, fashioned of stone, and with the
feathered crown upon his head, stood the statue of
Amen-ra, father of the gods. Here, where none but
the high-priest and the royalties of Egypt might enter,
Pharaoh and his wife Ahura, wrapped in brown cloaks
like common folk, knelt at the feet of the god and
prayed. With tears and supplications did they pray
that a child might be given to them.

There in the sacred place, lit only by a single lamp

which burned from age to age, they told the story of
their grief, whilst high above them the cold, calm
countenance of the god seemed to stare through the
gloom, as for a thousand years, in joy or sorrow, it
had stared at those that went before them. They told
of the mocking words of Abi who had demanded to see
their children, the children that were not ; they told
of their terror of the people who demanded that an
heir should be declared ; they told of the doom that
threatened their ancient house, which from Pharaoh
to Pharaoh, all of one blood, for generations had
worshipped in this place. They promised gifts and
offerings, stately temples and wide lands, if only their
desire might be fulfilled.

"Let me no more be made a mock among men,"
cried the beautiful queen, beating her forehead upon
the stone feet of the god. "Let me bear a child to
fill the seat of my lord the King, and then if thou
wilt, take my life in payment."

But the god made no answer, and wearied out at
length they rose and departed. At the door of the
sanctuary they found the high-priest awaiting them,
a wizened, aged man.

"The god gave no sign, O High-priest," said
Pharaoh sadly ; "no voice spoke to us."

The old priest looked at the weeping queen,
and a light of pity crept into his eyes.

"To me, watching without," he said, "a voice
seemed to speak, though what it said I may not
reveal. Go to your palace now, O Pharaoh, and O
Queen Ahura, and take your rest side by side. I
think that in your sleep a sign will come to you,
for Amen is pitiful, and loves his children who love

him.   According to that sign so speak to the Prince
Abi, speak without fear or doubt, since for good or
ill it shall be fulfilled."

Then like shadows, hand in hand, this royal pair
glided down the vast, pillared halls till at the pylon
gates, which were opened for them, they found their
litters, and were borne along the great avenue of
ram-headed sphinxes back to a secret door in the
palace wall.

It was past midnight.   Deep darkness and heavy
silence lay upon Thebes, broken only by dogs howling
at the stars and the occasional challenge of soldiers
on the walls.   Side by side in their golden bed
the wearied Pharaoh and his queen slept heavily.
Presently Ahura woke.   She started up in the bed ;
she stared at the darkness about her with frightened
eyes ;   she   stretched   out   her   hand   and   clasping
Pharaoh by the arm, whispered in a thrilling voice,

" Awake, awake !   I have that which I must
tell you."

Pharaoh roused himself, for there was something
in Ahura's voice which swept away the veils of sleep.

" What has chanced, Ahura ? " he asked.

" O Pharaoh, I have dreamed a dream, if indeed
it were but a dream.   It seemed to me that the
darkness opened, and that standing in the darkness
I saw a Glory which had neither shape nor form.
Yet a voice spoke from the Glory, a low, sweet voice :
' Queen Ahura, my daughter,' it said, ' I am that
Spirit to whom thou and thy husband did pray this
night in the sanctuary of my temple.   It seemed
to both of you that your prayers remained unheard,

yet it was not so, as my priest knew well. Queen
Ahura, thou and Pharaoh thy husband have put
your trust in me these many years, and not in vain.
A daughter shall be given to thee and Pharaoh,
and my Spirit shall be in that child. She shall be
beautiful and glorious as no woman was before her,
for I clothe her with health and power and wisdom.
She shall rule over the Northern and the Southern
Lands ; yea, for many years the double crown shall
rest upon her brow, and no king that went before her,
and no king that follows after her, shall be more
great in Egypt. Troubles and dangers shall threaten
her, but the Spirit that I give to her shall protect
her in them all, and she shall tread her enemy beneath
her feet. A royal lover shall come to her also, and
she shall rejoice in his love and from it shall spring
many kings and princes. Neter-Tua, Morning Star,
shall be her name, and high-priestess of Amen—no
less—shall be her office, for she is my child whom
I have taken from heaven and sent down to earth ;
the child that I have given to Pharaoh and to thee,
and I love her and appoint the good goddesses to be
her companions, and command Osiris to receive her
at the last.

" ' Behold, in token of these things I lay my
symbol on thy breast, and on her breast also shall
that symbol be. When I lift it from thee and thou
dost open thine eyes, then awaken Pharaoh at thy
side and let these my words be written in a roll, so
that none of them are forgotten.'

"Then, O Pharaoh," went on Ahura, " from the
Glory there came forth a hand, and in the hand was
the Symbol of Life shining as though with fire, and

the hand laid it upon my breast and it burned me
as though with fire, and I awoke and lo! darkness
was all about me, nothing but darkness, and at my
side I heard you sleeping."

Now when Pharaoh had listened to this dream,
he kissed the queen and blessed her because of its
good omen, and clapped his hands to summon the
women of honour who slept without. They ran in
bearing lights, and by the lights he saw that beneath
the throat of the Queen upon her fair skin, appeared
a red mark, and the shape of it was the shape of the
Sign of Life ; yes, there was the loop, and beneath the
loop the cross.

Then Pharaoh commanded that the chief of his
scribes should come to him with papyrus and writing
tools, and that the high-priest of Amen should be
brought swiftly from the temple. So the scribe came
to the bed-chamber of the King, and in the presence
of the high-priest all the words of Amen were written
down, not one of them was omitted, and Pharaoh
and the Queen signed the roll, and the high-priest
witnessed it and, copies having been made, bore it
away to hide it in the secret treasury of Amen. But
the mark of the Cross of Life remained upon the
breast of the Queen Ahura till the day that she
died.

Now in the morning Pharaoh summoned his
Court and commanded that the Prince Abi should
be brought before him. So the Prince came and
Pharaoh addressed him kindly.

" Son of my father," he said, " I have considered
your request that I should take you to rule with

me on the throne of Egypt, and name you and your
sons to be Pharaohs after me, and it is refused.
Know that it has been revealed to me and to the
royal wife, Ahura, by the greatest of the gods, that
a daughter shall be born to us in due season, who
shall be called Morning Star of Amen, and that she
and her seed shall be Pharaohs after me.   Therefore
rejoice with us and return to your government,
Prince Abi, and be happy in our love, and in the
goods and greatness that the gods have given you."

Now Abi shook with anger, for he thought that
all this tale was a trick and a snare.   But knowing
that his peril was great there in the hand of Pharaoh,
he answered only that when this Morning Star arose,
his star should do it reverence, though as the words
passed his lips he remembered the prophecy of his
astrologer Kaku, that the Morning Star of Amen
should blot out that star of his.

"You think that I speak falsely, Prince Abi,
yes, that I stain my lips with lies," said Pharaoh
with indignation.   "Well, I forgive you this also.
Go hence and await the issue and know by this sign
that truth is in my heart.   When the Princess Neter-
Tua is born, upon her breast shall be seen the symbol
of the Sign of Life.   Depart now, lest I grow angry.
The gifts I have promised shall follow you to Memphis."

So Abi returned to the white-walled city of
Memphis and sat there sullenly, putting it about
that a plot was on foot to deprive him of his heritage.
But Kaku shook his head, saying in secret that the
Star, Neter-Tua, would arise, for so it was decreed by
Amen, father of the gods.

B*

CHAPTER III

RAMES, THE PRINCESS, AND THE CROCODILE

AT the appointed time to Ahura, the royal wife, was born a child, a girl with a fresh and lovely face and waving hair and eyes that from the first were blue like the summer sky at even. Also on her breast was a mole of the length of a finger nail, which mole was shaped like the holy Sign of Life.

Now Pharaoh and his house and the priests in every temple, and indeed all Egypt went mad with joy, though there were many who in secret mourned over the sex of the infant, whispering that a man and not a woman should wear the Double Crown. But in public they said nothing, since the story of this child had gone abroad and folk declared that it was sent by the gods, and divine, and that the goddesses, Isis, Nepthys and Hathor, with Khemu, the Maker of Mankind, were seen in the birth chamber, glowing like gold.

Also Pharaoh issued a decree that wherever the name of the Queen Ahura was graven in all the land, to it should be added the title " By the will of Amen, Mother of his Morning Star," and that a new hall should be built in the temple of Amen in the Northern Apt, and all about it carved the story of the coming of Prince Abi and of the vision of the Queen.

But Ahura never lived to see this glorious place, since from the hour of her daughter's birth she began

30

to sink. On the fourteenth day, the day of purification, she bade the nurse bring the beautiful babe, and gazed at it long and blessed it, and spoke with the Ka or Double of the child, which she said she saw lying on her arm beside it, bidding that Ka protect it well through the dangers of life and death until the hour of resurrection. Then she said that she heard Amen calling to her to pay the price which she had promised for the gift of the divine child, the price of her own life, and smiled upon Pharaoh her husband, and died happily with a radiant face.

Now joy was turned to mourning, and during all the days of embalming Egypt wept for Ahura until, at length, the time came when her body was rowed across the Nile to the splendid tomb which she had made ready in the Valley of the Queens, causing masons and artists to labour at it without cease. For Ahura knew from the day of her vision that she was doomed to die, and remembered that the tombs of the dead remain as the live hands leave them, since few waste gold and toil upon the eternal house of one who is dead.

So Ahura was buried with great pomp and all her jewels, and Pharaoh, who mourned her truly, made splendid offerings in the chapel of her tomb, and having laid in the mouth of it the funeral boat in which she was borne across the Nile, he built it up for ever, and poured sand over the rock, so that none should find its place until the Day of Awakening.

Meanwhile, the infant grew and flourished, and when it was six months old, was taken to the college of the priestesses of Amen, there to be reared and taught.

Now on the day of the birth of the Princess Neter-Tua, there happened another birth with which our story has to do. The captain of the guard of the temple of Amen was one Mermes, who had married his own half-sister, Asti, the enchantress. As was well known, this Mermes was by right and true descent the last of that house of Pharaohs which had filled the throne of Egypt until their line was cast down generations before by the dynasty that now ruled the land, whereof the reigning Pharaoh and his daughter Neter-Tua alone remained. A long while past, in the early days of his reign, his council had whispered in Pharaoh's ear that he should kill Mermes and his sister, lest a day should come when they rebelled against him, proclaiming that they did so by right of blood. But Pharaoh, who was gentle and hated murder, instead of slaying Mermes sent for him and told him all.

Then Mermes, a noble-looking man as became the stock from which he sprang, prostrated himself and said,

" O Pharaoh, why should you kill me ? It has pleased the gods to debase my House and to set up yours. Have I ever lifted up my heel against you because my forefathers were kings, or plotted with the discontented to overthrow you ! See, I am satisfied with my station, which is that of a noble and a soldier in your army. Therefore let me and my half-sister, the wise lady Asti whom I purpose to marry, dwell on in peace as your true and humble servants. Dip not your hands in our innocent blood, O Pharaoh, lest the gods send a curse upon you and your House and our ghosts come back from the grave to haunt you."

When Pharaoh heard these words, his heart was moved in him, and he stretched out his sceptre for Mermes to kiss, thereby granting to him life and protection.

" Mermes," he said, " you are an honourable man, and my equal in blood if not in place. For their own purposes the gods raise up one and cast down another that at last their ends may be fulfilled. I believe that you will work no harm against me and mine, and, therefore, I will work no harm against you and your sister Asti, Mistress of Magic. Rather shall you be my friend and counsellor."

Then Pharaoh offered high rank and office to him, but Mermes would not take them, answering that if he did, envy would be stirred up against him, and in this way or in that bring him to his death, since tall trees are the first to fall. So in the end Pharaoh made Mermes Captain of the Guard of Amen, and gave him land and houses enough to enable him to live as a noble of good estate, but no more. Also he became the friend of Pharaoh and one of his inner Council, to whose voice he always listened, for Mermes was a true-hearted man.

Afterwards Mermes married Asti, but like Pharaoh for a long while he remained childless, since he took no other wives. On the day of the birth of the Princess Tua, the Morning Star of Amen, however, Asti bore a son, a royal-looking child of great strength

and beauty and very fair in colour, as tradition said
that the kings of his race had been before him, but
with black and shining eyes.

" See," said the midwife, " here is a head shaped
to wear a crown."

Whereon Asti, his mother, forgetting her caution
in her joy, or perhaps inspired by the gods, for from
her childhood she was a prophetess, answered,

" Yes, and I think that this head and a crown
will come close together," and she kissed him and
named him Rames after her royal forefather, the
founder of their line.

As it chanced a spy overheard this saying and
repeated it to the Council, and the Council urged
Pharaoh to cause the boy to be put away, as they
had urged in the case of his father, Mermes, because
of the words of omen that Asti had spoken, and
because she had given her son a royal name, naming
him after the majesty of Ra, as though he were indeed
the child of a king. But Pharaoh would not, asking
with his soft smile whether they wished him to baptise
his daughter in the blood of another infant who drew
his first breath upon the same day, and adding :

" Ra sheds his glory upon all, and this high-born
boy may live to be a friend in need to her whom
Amen has given to Egypt. Let things befall as the
gods decree. Who am I that I should make myself a
god and destroy a life that they have fashioned ? "

So the boy Rames lived and throve, and Mermes
and Asti, when they came to hear of these things,
thanked Pharaoh and blessed him.

Now the house of Mermes, as Captain of the
Guard, was within the wall of the great temple of

Amen, near to the palace of the priestesses of Amen where the Princess Neter-Tua was nurtured. Thus it came about that when the Queen Ahura died, the lady Asti was named as nurse to the Princess, since Pharaoh said that she should drink no milk save that of one in whose veins ran royal blood. So Asti was Tua's foster mother, and night by night she slept in her arms together with her own son, Rames. Afterwards, too, when they were weaned the babes were taught to walk and speak together, and later, as children, they became playmates.

Thus from the first these two loved each other, as brother and sister love when they are twins. But although the boy was bold and brave, this little princess always had the mastery of him, not because she was a princess and heir to the throne of Egypt—for all the high titles they gave her fell idly on her ears, nor did she think anything of the bowings of courtiers and of priests—but from some strength within herself. She it was that set the games they played, and when she talked he was obliged to listen, for although she was so sound and healthy, this Tua differed from other children.

Thus she had what she called her " silent hours " when she would suffer no one to come near her, not her ladies or her foster-mother, Asti herself, nor even Rames. Then, followed by the women at a distance, she would wander among the great columns of the temple and study the sculptures on the walls; and, since all places were open to her, Pharaoh's child, enter the sanctuaries, and stare at the gods that sat in them fashioned in granite and in alabaster. This she would do even in the solemn moonlight when mortals were afraid to approach those sacred shrines, and come thence unconcerned and smiling.

" What do you see there, O Morning Star ? " asked little Rames of her once. " They are dull things, those stone gods that have never moved since the beginning of the world ; also they frighten me, especially when Ra is set."

" They are not dull, and they do not frighten me," answered Tua ; " they talk to me, and although I cannot understand all they say, I am happy with them."

" Talk ! " he said contemptuously, " how can stones talk ? "

" I do not know. I think it is their spirits that talk, telling me stories which happened before I was born and that shall happen after I am dead, yes, and after *they* seem to be dead. Now be silent—I say that they talk to me—it is enough."

" For me it would be more than enough," said the boy, " but then I am not called Child of Amen, who only worship Menthu, God of War."

When Rames was seven years of age, every morning he was taken to school in the temple, where the priests taught him to write with pens of reed upon tablets of wood, and told him more about the gods of Egypt than he ever wanted to hear again. During these hours, except when she was being instructed by great ladies of the Court, or by high-priestesses, Tua was left solitary, since by the command of Pharaoh no other children were allowed to play with her, perhaps because there were none in the temple of her age whose birth was noble.

Once when he came back from his school in the evening Rames asked her if she had not been lonely without him. She answered, No, as she had another companion.

" Who is it ? " he asked jealously. " Show me and I will fight him."

" No one that you can see, Rames," she replied. " Only my own Ka."

" Your Ka ! I have heard of Kas, but I never saw one. What is it like ? "

" Just like me, except that it throws no shadow, and only comes when I am quite by myself, and then, although I hear it often, I see it rarely, for it is mixed up with the light."

" I don't believe in Kas," exclaimed Rames scornfully, " you make them up out of your head."

A little while after this talk something happened that caused Rames to change his mind about Kas, or at any rate the Ka of Tua. In a hidden court of the temple was a deep pool of water with cemented sides, where, it was said, lived a sacred crocodile, an enormous beast that had dwelt there for hundreds of years. Rames and Tua having heard of this crocodile, often talked of it and longed to see it, but could not for there was a high wall round the tank, and in it a door of copper that was kept locked, except when once in every eight days the priests took in food to the crocodile—living goats and sheep, and sometimes a calf, none of which ever came back again.

Now one day Rames watching them return, saw the priest, who was called Guardian of the Door, put his hand behind him to thrust the key with which he had just locked the door, into his wallet, and

missing the mouth of the wallet, let it fall upon the
sand, then go upon his way knowing nothing of what
he had done.

When he had gone in a great hurry, for he was a
fat old priest and the dinner hour was at hand,
Rames pounced upon the key and hid it in his robe.
Then he sought out the princess and said,

" Morning Star, this evening, when I come back
from school and am allowed to play with you, we can
look at the wonderful beast in the tank, for look,
I have the key which that fat priest will not search
for till seven days are gone by, before which I can
take it to him, saying that I found it in the sand,
or perhaps put it back into his wallet."

When she heard this Tua's eyes shone, since above
all things she desired to see this holy monster. But
in the evening when the boy came running to her
eagerly—for he had thought of nothing but the
crocodile all day, and had bought a pigeon from a
school-fellow with which to feed the brute—he
found Tua in a different mood.

" I don't think that we will go to see the holy
crocodile, Rames," she said, looking at him thought-
fully.

" Why not ? " he asked amazed. " There is no
one about, and I have put fat upon the key so that
it will make no noise."

" Because my Ka has been with me, Rames,
and told me that it is a bad act and if we do trouble
will come to us."

" Oh ! may the fiend Set take your Ka," replied
the lad in a rage. " Show it to me and I will talk
with it."

"I cannot, Rames, for it is *me*. Mor over, if Set took it, he would take me also, and you are wicked to wish such a thing."

Now the boy began to cry with vexation, sobbing out that she was not to be trusted, and that he had paid away his bronze knife, which Pharaoh gave him when last he visited the temple, for a pigeon to tempt the beast to the top of the water, so that they might see it, although the knife was worth many pigeons, and Pharaoh would be angry if he heard that he had parted with it.

"Why should we take the life of a poor pigeon to please ourselves?" asked Tua, softening a little at the sight of his grief.

"It's taken already," he answered. "It fluttered so that I had to sit on it to hide it from the priest, and when he had gone it was dead. Look," and he opened the linen bag he held, and showed her the dove cold and stiff.

"As you did not mean to kill it, that makes a difference," said Tua judicially. "Well, perhaps my Ka did not mean that we should not have one peep, and it is a pity to waste the poor pigeon, which then will have died for nothing."

Rames agreed that it would be the greatest of pities, so the two children slipped away through the trees of the garden into the shadow of the wall, along which they crept till they came to the bronze door. Then guiltily enough Rames put the great key into the lock, and with the help of a piece of wood which he had also made ready, that he set in the ring of the key to act as a lever, the two of them turning together shot back the heavy bolts.

Taking out the key lest it should betray them,
they opened the door a little and squeezed themselves through into the forbidden place. No sooner
had they done so than almost they wished themselves back again, for there was something about
the spot that frightened them, to say nothing of
the horrible smell which made Tua feel ill. It
was a great tank, with a little artificial island in
its centre, full of slimy water that looked almost
black because of the shadow of the high walls,
and round it ran a narrow stone path. At one
spot in this path, however, where grew some dank-
looking trees and bushes, was a slope, also of stone,
and on the slope with its prow resting in the water
a little boat, and in the boat, oars. But of the
crocodile there was nothing to be seen.

"It is asleep somewhere," whispered Tua, "let
us go away, I do not like this stench."

"Stench," answered Rames. "I smell nothing
except the lilies on the water. Let us wake it up,
it would be silly to go now. Surely you are not
afraid, O Star."

"Oh, no! I am not afraid," answered Tua
proudly. "Only wake it up quickly, please."

What Rames did not add was that it would now
be impossible to retreat as the door had closed
behind them, and there was no keyhole on its inner
side.

So they walked round the tank, but wherever it
might lurk, the sleeping crocodile refused to wake.

"Let us get into the boat and look for it," suggested Rames. "Perhaps it is hiding on the island."

So he led her to the stone slope, where to her

horror Tua saw the remains of the crocodile's last meal, a sight that caused her to forget her doubts and jump into the boat very quickly. Then Rames gave it a push and sprang in after her, so that they found themselves floating on the water. Now, standing in the bow, the boy took an oar and paddled round the island, but still there were no signs of the crocodile.

"I don't believe it is here at all," he said, recovering his courage.

"You might try the pigeon," suggested Tua, who, now that there was less smell, felt her curiosity returning.

This was a good thought upon which Rames acted at once. Taking the dead bird from the bag he spread out its wings to make it look as though it were alive, and threw it into the water, exclaiming, "Arise, O Holy Crocodile!"

Then with fearful suddenness, whence they knew not, that crocodile arose. An awful scaly head appeared with dull eyes and countless flashing fangs, and behind the head cubit upon cubit of monstrous form. The fangs closed upon the pigeon and everything vanished.

"That was the Holy Crocodile," said Rames abstractedly as he stared at the boiling waters, "which has lived here during the reigns of eight Pharaohs, and perhaps longer. Now we have seen it."

"Yes," answered Tua, "and I never want to see it again. Get me away quick, or I will tell your father."

Thus adjured the boy, nothing loth, seized his oar, when suddenly the ancient crocodile, having swallowed the dove, thrust up its snout immediately beneath them and began to follow the boat. Now Tua screamed aloud and said something about her Ka.

" Tell it to keep off the crocodile," shouted Rames as he worked the oar furiously. " Nothing can hurt a Ka."

But the crocodile would not be kept off. On the contrary, it thrust its grey snout and one of its claws over the stern of the boat in such a fashion that Rames could no longer work the oar, dragging it almost under water, and snapped with its horrible jaws.

" Oh ! it is coming in ; we are going to be eaten," cried Tua.

At that moment the boat touched the landing-place and swung round, so that its bow, where Tua was, struck the head of the crocodile, which seemed to infuriate the beast. At least, it hurled itself upon the boat, causing the fore part to heel over, fill with water and begin to sink. Then the little lad, Rames, showed the courage that was in him. Shouting to Tua:

" Get on shore, get on shore ! " he plunged past her and smote the huge reptile upon the head with the blade of his oar. It opened its hideous mouth, and he thrust the oar into it and held on.

" Leave go," cried Tua, as she scrambled to land.

But Rames would not leave go, for in his brave little heart he thought that if he did the crocodile would follow Tua and eat her. So he clung to the handle till it was wrenched from him. Indeed he did more, for seeing that the crocodile had bitten the wooden blade in two and, having dropped it, was still advancing towards the slope where it was accustomed to be fed, he leapt into the water and struck it in the eye with his little fist. Feeling the pain of the blow the monster snapped at him, and catching him by the hand began to sink back into deep water, dragging the lad after it.

Rames said nothing, but Tua, who already was at the head of the stage, looked round and saw the agony on his face.

" Help me, Amen ! " she cried, and flying back, grasped Rames by his left arm just as he was falling over, then set her heels in a crack of the rock and held on. For one moment she was dragged forward till she thought that she must fall upon her face and be drowned or eaten with Rames, but the next something yielded, and she and the boy tumbled in a heap upon the stones. They rose and staggered together to the terrace. As they went Tua saw that Rames was looking at his right hand curiously ; also that it was covered with blood, and that the little finger was torn off it. Then she remembered nothing further, except a sound of shouts and of heavy hammering at the copper door.

When she recovered it was to find herself in the house of Mermes with the lady Asti bending over her and weeping.

" Why do you weep, Nurse ? " she asked, " seeing that I am safe ? "

" I weep for my son, Princess," she answered between her sobs.

" Is he dead of his wounds, then, Asti ? "

" No, O Morning Star, he lies sick in his chamber. But soon Pharaoh will kill him because he led her who will be Queen of Egypt into great danger of her life."

" Not so," said Tua, springing up, " for he saved my life."

As she spoke the door opened and in came Pharaoh himself, who had been summoned hastily from the palace. His face was white and he shook with fear, for it had been reported to him that his only child was drowned. When he saw that she lived and was not even hurt, he could not contain his joy, but casting his arms about her, sank to his knees giving thanks to the gods and the guardian spirits. She kissed him, and studying his face with her wise eyes, asked why he was so much afraid.

" Because I thought you had been killed, my daughter."

" Why did you think that, O my father, seeing that the great god, Amen, before I was born promised to protect me always, though it is true that had it not been for Rames——"

Now at the mention of this name Pharaoh was filled with rage.

" Speak not of that wicked lad," he exclaimed, " now or ever more, for he shall be scourged till he dies ! '

" My father," answered Tua, springing up, " forget those words, for if Rames dies I will die also. It is I who am to blame, not he, for my Ka warned me not to look upon the beast, but to Rames no Ka spoke. Moreover, when that evil god would have eaten me it was Rames who fought with it and offered himself to its jaws in my place. Listen, my father, while I tell you all the story."

So Pharaoh listened, and when it was done he sent for Rames. Presently the boy was carried in, for he had lost so much blood that he could not walk, and was placed upon a stool before him.

"Slay me now, O Pharaoh," he said in a weak voice, "for I have sinned. Moreover, I shall die happy since my spirit gave me strength to beat off the evil beast from the Princess whom I led into trouble."

"Truly you have done wickedly," said Pharaoh, shaking his head at him, "and, therefore, perhaps, you will lose your hand or even your life. Yet, child, you have a royal heart, who first saved your playmate and then, even in my presence, take all the blame upon yourself. Therefore I forgive you, son of Mermes; moreover, I see that I was wise not to listen to those who counselled that you should be put away at birth," and bending over the boy, Pharaoh kissed him on the brow.

Also he gave orders that the greatest physicians in the land should attend upon him and purge the poison of the crocodile's teeth from his body, and when he recovered—which save for the loss of the little finger of his right hand, he did completely—he sent him a sword with a handle of gold fashioned to the shape of a crocodile, in place of the knife which he had paid away for the pigeon, bidding him use it bravely all his life in defence of her who would be his queen. Further, although he was still so young, he gave to him the high title of Count in earnest of

his love and favour, and with it a name that meant
Defender of the Royal Lady.

After he had gone Asti the prophetess looked at
the sword which Pharaoh had given to her son.

" I see royal blood on it," she said, and handed
it back to Rames.

But Rames and Tua were no more allowed to
play together alone, for always after this the Princess
was accompanied by women of honour and an armed
guard. Also, within a year or two the boy was
placed in charge of a general to be brought up as a
soldier, a trade that he liked well enough, so that
from this time forward he and Neter-Tua met but
seldom. Still there was a bond between them which
could not be broken by absence, for already they
loved each other, and every night and morning when
Tua made her petitions to Amen, after praying for
Pharaoh her father, and for the spirit of her royal
mother, Ahura, she prayed for Rames, and that
they might meet soon. For the months when her
eyes did not fall upon his face were wearisome to
Tua.

CHAPTER IV

THE SUMMONING OF AMEN

THE years went by and the Princess Neter-Tua, who was called Morning Star of Amen, came at length to womanhood, and went through the ceremonies of Purification. In all Egypt there was no maiden so wise and spirited or so lovely. Tall and slender was her shape, blue as the sea were her eyes, rosy like the dawn were her cheeks, and when she did not wear it in a net of gold, her black and curling hair fell almost to her waist. Also she was very learned, for priests and priestesses taught her all things that she ought to know, together with the arts of playing on the harp and of singing and dancing, while her own excellent Spirit, that Ka which Amen had given her, instructed her in a deeper wisdom which she gathered unconsciously in sleep and waking dreams, as the slumbering earth gathers dew at night.

Moreover, her father, the wise old Pharaoh, opened to her the craft of statesmanship, by help of which she might govern men and overthrow her enemies. Indeed, he did more, for when her education was finished, he joined her with him in the government of Egypt, saying:

"I who always lacked bodily strength, grow aged and feeble. This mighty crown is too heavy for me to bear alone. Daughter, you must share its weight."

So the young Neter-Tua became a queen, and great
was the ceremony of her coronation.   The high priests
and priestesses, clothed in the robes and symbols
of their gods and goddesses, addressed speeches
to her and blessed her in their names, giving her
every good gift and promising to her eternal life.
Princes and nobles made her offerings ; foreign chiefs
and kings bowed before her by their ambassadors.
The Counts and headmen of the Two Lands swore
allegiance to her, and, finally, in the presence of
all the Court, Pharaoh himself set the double crown
upon her brow and gave her her throne-names of
" Glorious in Ra and Hathor Strong in Beauty."

So for a while Tua sat splendid on her golden
seat while the people adored her, but in that
triumphant hour her eyes searched for one face only,
that of the tall and gallant captain, Rames, her
foster-brother, and for a moment rested there content.
Yes, their eyes met, those of the new-crowned Empress
on her throne and of the youthful noble in the throng
below.   Short was the greeting, for next instant she
looked away, yet more full of meaning than whole
days of speech.

" The Queen does not forget what the child
remembered, the goddess is still a woman," it seemed
to say.   And so sweet was that message that Rames
staggered from the Court like one stricken by the
sun.

Night came at last, and having dismissed her
secretaries, scribes and tire-women the weary girl,
clad now in simple white, sat in her chamber alone.
She thought of all the splendours through which she

had passed ; she thought of the glories of her imperial state, of the power that she wielded, and of the proud future which stretched before her feet. But most of all she thought of the face of the young Count Rames, the playmate of her childhood, the man she loved, and wondered, ah ! how she wondered, if with all her power she could ever draw him to her side. If not, of what use was this rule over millions, this dominion of her world ? They called her a goddess, and in truth, at times, she believed that she was half-divine, but if so, why did her heart ache like that of any common maid ?

Moreover, was she really set above the misfortunes of her race ? Could a throne, however bright with gold, lift her above the sorrows of human kind ? She desired to learn the truth, the very truth. Her mind was urgent, it drove her on to search out things to come, to stand face to face with them, even if they were evil. Well, she believed she had the strength, although, as yet, she had never called it to her aid.

Also this thing could not be done alone. Tua thought a while, then going to the door of her chamber she bade a woman who waited without summon to her the Lady Asti, priestess of Amen, Interpreter of Heaven. Presently Asti came, for now, as always, she was in attendance upon the new-crowned queen, a tall and noble-looking woman with fine-cut features and black hair, that although she was fifty years of age, still showed no trace of grey.

" I was in the Sanctuary when your Majesty summoned me," she said, pointing to the sacred robe she wore. " Let your Majesty pardon me, therefore, if I have been long in coming," and she bowed low before her.

But the Queen lifted her up and kissed her, saying, " I weary of those high titles whereof I have heard more than enough to-day. Call me Tua, O my mother, for so you have ever been to me, from whose breast I drew the milk of life."

" What ails you, my child ? " asked Asti. " Was the crown too heavy for this young head of yours ? " she added, stretching out her delicate hand and stroking the black and curling hair.

"Aye, Mother, the weight of it seemed to crush me with its gems and gold. I am weary and yet I cannot sleep. Tell me, why did Pharaoh summon that Council after the feast ? Mermes was one of them, so you must know. And why was not I, who henceforth rule with Pharaoh, present with him ? "

" Would you learn ? " said Asti with a little smile. " Well, as Queen you have the right. It was because they discussed the matter of your marriage."

For a moment a light shone upon Tua's face. Then she asked anxiously :

" My marriage, and with whom ? "

" Oh ! many names were mentioned, Child, since she who rules Egypt does not lack for suitors."

" Tell me them quick, Asti."

So she told them, there were seven in all, the Prince of Kesh, the sons of foreign kings, great nobles, and a general of the army who claimed descent from a former Pharaoh.

As each name fell from Asti's lips Tua waved her hand, saying scornful words, such as " I know him

not," "Too old," "Fat and hideous," "A foreign
dog who spits upon our gods," and so forth, adding
at last:

"Go on."

"That is all, Lady, no other name was mentioned,
and the Council adjourned to consider these."

"No other name?"

"Do you then miss one, perchance, Tua?"

She made no answer, only her lips seemed to
shape themselves to a certain sound that they did not
utter. The two women looked each other in the
eyes, then Asti shook her head.

"It may not be," she whispered, "for many
reasons, and amongst them that by the solemn
decree of long ago whereof I have told you, our
blood is barred for ever from the throne. None
would dare to break it, not even Pharaoh himself.
You would not bring my son to his death, Tua, which
such another look as you gave him in yonder hall
would surely do."

"No," she answered slowly, "I would not bring
him to his death, but to life and honour and—love,
and one day *I* shall be Pharaoh. Only, Asti, if you
betray me to him I swear that I will bring you to
your death, although you are so dear."

"I shall not betray you," answered the priestess,
smiling again. "In truth, most Beautiful, I do not
think there is any need, even if I would. Say now,
why did a certain captain turn faint and leave the
hall to-day when your eyes chanced to fall on
him?"

"The heat," suggested Tua, colouring.

"Yes, it was hot, but he is stronger than most

men and had borne it long—like others. Still there
are fires——"

"Because he was afraid of my majesty," broke
in Tua hurriedly. "You know I looked very royal
there, Mother."

"Yes, doubtless fear moved him—or some other
passion. Yet, Beloved, put that thought from
your heart as I do. When you are Pharaoh you will
learn that a monarch is a slave to the people and to
the law. Breathe but his name in love, and never
will you see him more till you meet before
Osiris."

Tua hid her eyes in her hands for a moment, then
she glanced up and there was another look upon her
face, a strange, new look.

"When I am Pharaoh," she answered, "there
are certain matters in which I will be my own law,
and if the people do not like it, they may find another
Pharaoh."

Asti started at her words, and a light of joy shone
in her deep eyes.

"Truly your heart is high," she said ; "but, oh !
if you love me—and another—bury that thought,
bury it deep, or he will never live to see you
placed alone upon the golden seat. Know, Lady,
that already from hour to hour I fear for him—lest
he should drink a poisoned cup, lest at night he
should chance to stumble against a spear, lest an
arrow—shot in sport—should fall against his throat
and none know whence it came."

Tua clenched her hands.

"If so, there should be such vengeance as Egypt
has not heard of since Mena ruled."

" Of what use is vengeance, Child, when the heart is empty and the tomb is sealed ? "

Again Tua thought. Then she said:

" There are other gods besides Osiris. Now what do men call me, Mother ? Nay, not my royal names."

" They call you Morning Star of Amen ; they call you Daughter of Amen."

" Is that story true, Asti the Magician ? "

" Aye, at least your royal mother dreamed the dream, for she told it to me and I have read its record, who am a priestess of Amen."

" Then this high god should love me, should he not ? He should hear my prayers and give me power—he should protect those who are dear to me. Mother, they say that you, the Mistress of secret things, can open the ears of the gods and cause their mouths to speak. Mother, I command you as your Queen, call up my father Amen before me, so that I may talk with him, for I have words to which he must listen."

' Are you not afraid ? " asked Asti, looking at her curiously. " He is the greatest of all the gods, and to summon him lightly is a sacrilege."

" Should a daughter fear her father ? " answered Tua.

" When the divine Queen your mother and Pharaoh knelt before him in his shrine, praying that a child might be given to them, Amen did not deign to appear to them, save afterwards in a dream. Will you dare more than they ? Lie down and dream, O Star of the Morning."

" Nay, I trust no dreams which change like summer clouds and pass as soon," answered the girl boldly.

c

" If the god is my father, in the spirit or the flesh, I
know not which, let him appear before me face to
face. I ask his wisdom for myself and his favour
for another. Call him, if you have the power, Asti.
Call him even if he slay me. Better that I should
die than——"

" Hush ! " said Asti, laying her hand upon her
lips, " speak not that name. Well, I have some
skill, and for your sake—and another's—I will try,
but not here. Perchance he may listen, perchance
not, or, perchance, if he comes you and I must pay
the price. Put on your robes, now, O Queen, and
over them this veil, and follow me—if you dare."

Along narrow passages they crept and down
many a secret stair, till at length they came to a door
at the foot of a long slope of rock. This door Asti
unlocked and thrust open, then when they had
entered, re-locked it behind them.

" What is this place ? " whispered Tua.

" The burial crypt of the high priestesses of Amen,
where it is said that the god watches. None have
entered it for hard on thirty years. See here in
the dust run the footsteps of those who bore the last
priestess to her rest."

She held up her lamp, and by the light of it Tua
saw that they were in a great cave painted with
figures of the gods which had on either side of it recesses. In each of these was set a coffin with a
gilded face, and behind it an alabaster statue of her
who lay therein, and in front of it a table of offerings.
At the head of the crypt stood a small altar of black
stone, for the rest the place was empty.

Asti led Tua to a step in front of the altar and bidding her kneel, departed with the lamp which she hid away in some side chapel, so that now the darkness was intense. Presently, through the utter silence, Tua heard her creep back towards her, for although she walked so softly the dust seemed to cry beneath her feet, and her every footstep echoed round the vaulted walls. Moreover, a glow came from her, the glow of her life in that place of death. She passed Tua and knelt by the altar and the echo of her movements died away. Only it seemed to Tua that from each of the tombs to the right and to the left rose the Ka of her who was buried there, and drew near to watch and listen. She could not see them, she could not hear them, yet she knew that they were there and was able to count their number— thirty and two in all—while within herself rose a picture of them, each differing from the other, but all white, expectant, solemn.

Now Tua heard Asti murmuring secret invocations that she did not understand. In that place and silence they sounded weird and dreadful, and as she hearkened to them, for the first time fear crept over her. Kneeling there upon her knees she bent her head almost to the dust and put up prayers to Amen that he might be pleased to hear her and to satisfy the longings of her heart. She prayed and prayed till she grew faint and weary, while always Asti uttered her invocations. But no answer came, no deity appeared, no voice spoke. At length Asti rose, and coming to her, whispered in her ear :

" Let us depart ere the watching spirits, whose

rest we have broken, grow wrath with us. The god has shut his ears."

So Tua rose, clinging to Asti, for now, she knew not why, her fear grew and deepened. For a moment she stood upon her feet, then sank to her knees again, for there at the far end of the great tomb, near to the door by which they had entered, appeared a glow upon the darkness. Slowly it took form, the form of a woman clad in the royal robes of Egypt, and bearing in its hand a sceptre. The figure of light advanced towards them, so that presently they saw its face. Tua did not know the face, though it seemed to her to be like her own, but Asti knew it, and at the sight sank to the ground.

Now the figure stood in front of them, a thing of light framed in the thick darkness, and now in a sweet, low voice it spoke.

" Hail! Queen of Egypt," it said. " Hail! Neter-Tua, Daughter of Amen. Art thou afraid to look on the spirit of her who bore thee, thou that didst dare to summon the Father of the gods to do thy bidding ? "

" I am afraid," answered Tua, shaking in all her limbs.

" And thou, Asti the Magician, art thou afraid also, who but now wast bold enough to cry to Amen-Ra—' Come from thy high heaven and make answer ' ? "

" It is even so, O Queen Ahura," murmured Asti.

" Woman," went on the voice, " thy sin is great, and great is the sin of this royal one at thy side. Had Amen hearkened, how would the two of you have stood before his glory, who at the sight of this shape of mine that once was mortal like yourselves, crouch choking to the earth ? I tell you both that had the god arisen, as in your wickedness ye willed, there where ye knelt, there ye would have died. But he who knows all is merciful, and in his place has sent me his messenger that ye may live to look upon to-morrow's sun."

" Let Amen pardon us ! " gasped Tua, " it was my sin, O Mother, for I commanded Asti and she obeyed me. On me be the blame, not on her, for I am torn with doubts and fears, for myself and for another. I would know the future."

" Why, O Queen Neter-Tua, why wouldst thou know the future ? If hell yawns beneath thy feet, why wouldst thou see its torments ? If heaven awaits thee why wouldst thou peep through its golden doors before the time ? The future is hid from mortals because, could they pierce its veil, it would crush them with its terrors. If all the woes of life and death lay open the gaze, who would dare to live and who—oh ! who could dare to die ? "

" Then woes await me, O thou who wast my mother ? "

" How can it be otherwise ? Light and darkness make the day, joy and sorrow make the life. Thou art human, be content."

" Divine also, O Ahura, if all tales be true."

" Then pay for thy divinity in tears and be satisfied. Content is the guerdon of the beast, but gods are wafted upwards on the wings of pain. How can that gold be pure which has not known the fire ? "

" Thou tellest me nothing," wailed Tua, " and it is not for myself I ask. I am fair, I am Amen's daughter, and splendid is my heritage. Yet, O Dweller in Osiris, thou who once didst fill the place I hold to-day, I tell thee that I would pay away this pomp, could I but be sure that I shall not live loveless, that I shall not be given as a chattel to one I hate, that one—whom I do not hate—will live to call me—wife. Great dangers threaten him—and me, Amen is mighty; he is the potter that moulds the clay of men; if I be his child, if his spirit is breathed into me, oh! let him help me now."

"Let thine own faith help thee. Are not the words of Amen, which he spake concerning thee, written down? Study them and ask no more. Love is an arrow that does not miss its mark; it is the immortal fire from on high which winds and waters cannot quench. Therefore love on. Thou shalt not love in vain. Queen and Daughter, fare thee well awhile."

"Nay, nay, one word, Immortal. I thank thee, thou Messenger of the gods, but when these troubles come upon me—and another, when the sea of dangers closes o'er our heads, when shame is near and I am lonely, as well may chance, then to whom shall I turn for succour?"

"Then thou hast one within thee who is strong to aid. It was given to thee at thy birth, O Star of Amen, and Asti can call it forth. Come hither, thou Asti, and swiftly, for I must be gone, and first I would speak with thee."

Asti crept forward, and the glowing shape in the royal robe bent over her so that the light of it shone upon her face. It bent over her and seemed to whisper in her ear. Then it held out its hands

towards Tua as though in blessing, and instantly
was not.

Once more the two women stood in Tua's chamber.
Pale and shaken they looked into each other's
eyes.

" You have had your will, Queen," said Asti ;
" for if Amen did not come, he sent a messenger,
and a royal one."

" Interpret me this vision," answered Tua, " for
to me, at any rate, that Spirit said little."

" Nay, it said much. It said that love fails not
of its reward, and what more went you out to seek ? "

" Then I am glad," exclaimed Tua joyfully.

" Be not too glad, Queen, for to-night we have
sinned, both of us, who dared to summon Amen from
his throne, and sin also fails not of its reward. Blood
is the price of that oracle."

" Whose blood, Asti ? Ours ? "

" Nay, worse, that of those who are dear to us.
Troubles arise in Egypt, Queen."

" You will not leave me when they break, Asti ? "

" I may not if I would. The Fates have bound
us together till the end, and that I think is far away.
I am yours as once you were mine when you lay upon
my breast, but bid me no more to summon Amen
from his throne."

CHAPTER V

Now for a whole moon there were great festivals in Thebes, and in all of these Neter-Tua, " Glorious in Ra, Hathor Strong in Beauty, Morning Star of Amen," must take her part as new-crowned Queen of Egypt. Feast followed feast, and at each of them one of the suitors for her hand was the guest of honour.

Then after it was done, Pharaoh her father and his councillors would wait upon her and ask if this man was pleasing to her. Being wise, Tua would give no direct answer, only of most of them she was rid in this way.

She demanded that the writing of the dream of her mother, Ahura, should be brought and read before her, and when it had been read she pointed out that Amen promised to her a royal lover, and that these chiefs and generals were not royal, therefore it was not of them that Amen spoke, nor did she dare to turn her eyes on one whom the god had forbidden to her.

Of others who declared that they were kings, but who, being unable to leave their own countries, were represented by ambassadors, she said that not having seen them she could say nothing. When they appeared at the Court of Egypt, she would consider them.

So at length only one suitor was left, the man

whom she knew well Pharaoh and his councillors desired that she should take as husband. This was Amathel, the Prince of Kesh, whose father, an aged king, ruled at Napata, a great city far to the south, situated in a land that was called an island because the river Nile embraced it in its two arms. It was said that after Egypt this country was the richest in the whole world, for there gold was so plentiful that men thought it of less value than copper and iron ; also there were mines in which beautiful stones were found, and the soil grew corn in abundance.

Moreover, once in the far past, a race of Pharaohs sprung from this city of Napata, had sat on the throne of Egypt, until at length the people of Egypt, headed by the priests, had risen and overthrown them because they were foreigners and had introduced Nubian customs into the land. Therefore it was decreed by an unalterable law that none of their race should ever again wear the Double Crown. Of the descendants of these Pharaohs, Rames, Tua's playmate, was the last lawful child.

But although the Egyptians had cast them down, at heart they always grieved over the rich territory of Napata, which was lost to them, for when those Pharaohs fell Kesh declared itself independent and set up another dynasty to rule over it, of which dynasty Amathel Prince of Kesh was the heir.

Therefore they hoped that it might come back to them by marriage between Amathel and the young queen Neter-Tua. Ever since she was born the great lords and councillors of Egypt, yes, and Pharaoh himself, seeing that he had no son to whom

c*

he might marry her after the fashion of the country, had. been working to this end. It was by secret treaty that the Prince Amathel was present at the crowning of the queen, of whose hand he had been assured on the sole condition that he came to dwell with her at Thebes. It is true that there were other suitors, but these, as all of them knew well, were but pawns in a game played to amuse the people.

The king destined to take the great queen captive was Amathel and no other. Tua knew it, for had not Asti told her, and was it not because of her fear of this man and her love for Rames that she had dared to commit the sacrilege of attempting to summon Amen from the skies? Still, as yet, the Pharaoh had not spoken to her of Amathel, nor had she met him. It was said that he had been present at her crowning in disguise, for this proud prince gave it out that were she ten times Queen of Egypt, he would not pledge himself to wed as his royal wife, one who was displeasing to him, and that therefore he must see her before he pressed his suit.

Now that he had seen her in her loveliness and glory, he announced that he was well satisfied, which was but half the truth, for, in fact, she had set all his southern blood on fire, and there was nothing that he desired more than to call her wife.

On the night which had been appointed for Amathel to meet his destined bride, a feast had been prepared richer by far than any that went before. Tua, feigning ignorance, on entering the great unroofed hall lit with hundreds of torches down all its length, and seeing the multitudes at the tables, asked of the Pharaoh, her father, who was the guest that he would welcome with such magnificence which seemed worthy of a god rather than of a man.

" My daughter," answered the old monarch nervously, " it is none other than the Prince of Kesh, who in his own country they worship as divine, as we are worshipped here in Egypt, and who, in truth, is, or will be, one of the greatest of kings."

" Kesh ! " she answered, " I thought that we claimed sovereignty over that land."

" Once it was ours, Daughter," said her father with a sigh, " or rather the kings of Kesh were also kings of Egypt, but their dynasty fell before my great-great-grandfather was called to the throne, and now but three of their blood are left, Mermes, Captain of the Guard of Amen; Asti, the Seer and Priestess, his wife, your foster-mother and waiting lady, and the young Count Rames, a soldier in our army, who was your playmate, and as you may remember saved you from the sacred crocodile."

" Yes, I remember," said Tua. " But then why is not Mermes King of Kesh ? "

" Because the people of the city of Napata raised up another house to rule over them, of whom Amathel is the heir."

" A usurping heir, surely, my father, if there be anything in blood."

" Say not that, Tua," replied Pharaoh sharply, " for then Mermes should be Pharaoh in our place also."

Tua made no reply, only as they took their seats in the golden chairs at the head of the hall, she asked carelessly :

" Is this Prince of Kesh also a suitor for my hand, O Pharaoh ? "

" What else should he be, my daughter ? Did you not know it ? Be gracious to him now, since it is decreed that you shall take him as a husband. Hush ! answer not. He comes."

As he spoke a sound of wild music arose, and at the far end of the great hall appeared a band of players gorgeously attired, who blew horns made from small tusks of the elephant, clashed brazen cymbals and beat gilded drums. These advanced a little way up the hall and stood there playing, while after them marched a bodyguard of twenty gigantic Nubian soldiers who carried broad-bladed spears with shields of hippopotamus hide curiously worked, and were clothed in tunics and caps of leopard-skin.

Next appeared the Prince of Kesh himself, a short, stout, broad-shouldered young man, thick-featured, heavy-faced, and having large, rolling eyes. He was clad in festal garments, and hung about with heavy chains of gold fastened with clasps of glittering stones, while from his crisp, black hair rose a tall plume of nodding ostrich feathers. Fan bearers walked beside him, and the train of his long cloak was borne by two black and hideous dwarfs, full-grown men but no taller than a child of eight.

With one swift glance, while he was yet far away, Tua studied the man from head to foot, and hated him as she had never hated anyone before. Then she looked over his head, as from her raised seat upon the dais she was able to do, and saw that behind him came a second guard of picked Egyptian soldiers, and that in command of them, simply clad in his scaled armour of bronze, and wearing upon his thigh the golden-handled sword that Pharaoh had given him, was none other than the young Count Rames, her playmate and foster-brother, the man whom her heart loved. At the sight of his tall and noble form and fine-cut face rising above the coarse, squat figure of the Ethiopian prince, Tua blushed rosy red, but Pharaoh noting it, only thought, as others did, that it was because now for the first time her eyes fell upon him who would be her husband.

Why, Tua wondered, was Rames chosen to attend upon the Prince Amathel ? At once the answer rose in her mind. Doubtless it had been done to gratify the pride of Amathel, not by Pharaoh, who would know nothing of such matters, but by some bribed councillor, or steward of the household. Rames was of more ancient blood than Amathel, and by right should be the King of Kesh, as he should also be Pharaoh of Egypt ; therefore, to humble him he was set to wait upon Amathel.

Moreover, it was guessed that the young Queen looked kindly upon this Count Rames with whom she had been nursed, and who, like herself, was beautiful to behold. Therefore, to abase him in her eyes he had been commanded to appear walking in the train of Amathel and given charge over his sacred person at the feast.

In a moment Tua understood it all, and made a vow before her father Amen that soon or late those who had planned this outrage should pay its price, nor did she forget that promise in the after days.

Now the Prince had mounted the dais and was bowing low to Pharaoh and to her, and they must rise and bow in answer. Then Pharaoh welcomed him to Egypt in few, well-chosen words, giving him all his titles and speaking meaningly of the ancient ties which had linked their kingdoms, ties which, he prayed, might yet draw them close again.

He ceased and looked at Tua who, as Queen, had also a speech to deliver that had been given to her in writing. Although she remembered this well enough, for the roll lay beside her, never a word would she read, but turned round and bade one of her waiting-ladies bring her a fan.

So after a pause that seemed somewhat long Amathel delivered his answer that was learned by rote, for it replied to " gentle words from the lips of the divine Queen that made his heart to flower like the desert after rain," not one of which had she spoken. Thereon Tua, looking over the top of her fan, saw Rames smile grimly, while unable to restrain themselves, some of the great personages at the feast broke out laughing, and bowed down their heads to hide their merriment.

With an angry scowl the Prince turned and commanded that the gifts should be brought. Now slaves advanced bearing cups of worked gold, elephants and other beasts fashioned in gold, and golden vases full of incense, which he presented to Pharaoh on behalf of his father, the King of Kesh and himself, saying boastfully that in his country such things were common, and that he would have brought more of them had it not been for their weight.

When Pharaoh had thanked him, answering gently that Egypt too was not poor, as he hoped that he would find upon the morrow, the Prince, on his own behalf alone, offered to the Queen other presents, among them pectorals and necklaces without price fashioned of amethysts and sapphires. Also, because she was known to be the first of musicians and the sweetest-voiced lady in the land —for these were the greatest of the gifts that Tua had from Amen—he gave to her a wonderfully worked harp of ivory with golden strings, the frame of the harp being fashioned to the shape of a woman, and two black female slaves laden with ornaments, who were said to be the best singers in the Southern Land.

Now Pharaoh whispered to Tua to put on one of the necklaces, but she would not, saying that the colour of the stones did not match her white robe and the blue lotus flowers which she wore. Instead, she thanked Amathel coldly but courteously, and without looking at his gifts, told the royal Nurse, Asti, who stood behind her, to bear them away and to place them at a distance, as the perfumes that had been poured over them, oppressed her. Only, as though by an afterthought, she bade them leave the ivory harp.

Thus inauspiciously enough the feast began. At it Amathel drank much of the sweet wine of Asi or Cyprus, commanding Rames, who stood behind him, to fill his cup again and again, though whether he did this because he was nearest to him, or to lower him to the rank of a butler, Tua did not know. At least, having no choice, Rames obeyed, though cup-filling was no fitting task for a Count of Egypt and an officer of Pharaoh's guard.

When the waiting women, clad in net worked with spangles of gold, had borne away the meats, conjurers appeared who did wonderful feats, amongst other things causing a likeness of Queen Neter-Tua wearing her royal robes and having a star upon her brow, to arise out of a vase.

Then, as they had arranged, they strove to do the same for the Prince Amathel, but Asti who had more magic than all of them, watching behind Tua's chair, put out her strength and threw a spell upon them.

Behold! instead of the form of the Prince, which these conjurers summoned loudly and by name, there appeared out of the vase a monkey wearing a crown and feathers that yet resembled him somewhat, which black and hideous ape stood there for a while seeming to gibber at them, then fell down and vanished away.

Now some of the audience laughed and some were silent, but Pharaoh, not knowing whether this were a plot or an evil omen from the gods, frowned and looked anxiously at his guest. As it chanced, however, the Prince, fired with wine, was so engaged in staring at the loveliness of Tua, that he took no note of the thing, while the Queen looked upwards and seemed to see nothing. As for the conjurers, they fled from the hall, fearing for their lives, and wondering what strong spirit had entered into the vase and spoilt the trick which they had prepared.

As they went singers and dancing women hurriedly took their place, till Tua, wearying of the stare of Amathel, waved her hand and said that she wished to hear those two Nubian slaves whose voices were said to be so wonderful. So they were brought forward with their harps, and having prostrated themselves, began to play and sing very sweetly, Nubian songs melancholy and wild, whereof few could understand the meaning. So well did they sing, indeed, that when they had done, Neter-Tua said:

"You have pleased me much, and in payment I give you a royal gift. I give you your freedom, and appoint that henceforth you shall sing before the Court, if you think fit to stay here, not as slaves but for hire."

Then the two women prostrated themselves again before her Majesty and blessed her, for they knew that they could earn wealth by their gift, and the rich courtiers taking the Queen's cue, flung rings and ornaments to them, so that in a minute they got more gold than ever they had dreamed of, who were but kidnapped slaves. But Prince Amathel grew angry and said:

"Some might have been pleased to keep the priceless gift of the best singers in the world."

"Do you say that these sweet-voiced women are the best singers in the world, O Prince?" asked Tua, speaking to him for the first time. "Now if you will be pleased to listen, you provoke me to make trial of my own small skill that I may learn how far I fall short of 'the best singers in the world.'"

. Then she lifted up the ivory harp with the strings of gold and swept her fingers over it, trying its notes and adjusting them with the agate screws, looking at Amathel all the while with a challenge in her lovely eyes.

" Nay, nay, my daughter," said Pharaoh, " it
is scarcely fitting that a queen of Egypt should
sing before all this noble company."

" Why not, my father ? " she asked. " To-night
we all do honour to the heir of his Majesty of Kesh.
Pharaoh receives him, Pharaoh's daughter accepts
his gifts, the highest in the land surround him," then
she paused and added slowly, " one of blood more
ancient than his own waits on him as cup-bearer,
one whose race built up the throne his father
fills," and she pointed to Rames, who stood near by
holding the vase of wine. " Why, then, should not
Egypt's queen seek to please our royal guest as best
she may—since she has no other gift to give him ? "

Then in the dead silence that followed this bold
speech, whereof none could mistake the meaning,
Neter-Tua, Morning Star of Amen, rose from her seat.
Pressing the ivory harp against her young breast,
she bent over it, her head crowned with the crown
of Upper Egypt whereon glistened the royal *uræus*,
a snake about to strike, and swept the well-tuned
strings.

Such magic was in her touch that instantly all
else was forgotten, even the Pharaoh leaned back
in his golden chair to listen. Softly she struck at
first, then by slow degrees ever louder till the music
of the harp rang through the pillared hall. Now,
at length, she lifted up her heavenly voice and began
to sing in a strain so wild and sweet that it seemed
to pierce to the watching stars.

It was a sad and ancient love-tale that she sang,
which told how a priestess of Hathor of high degree
loved and was beloved by a simple scribe whom she

might not wed. It told how the scribe, maddened by
his passion, crept at night into the very sanctuary of
the temple hoping to find her there, and for his
sacrilege was slain by the angry goddess. It told how
the beautiful priestess, coming alone to make prayer in
the sanctuary for strength to resist her love, stumbled
over the lover's corpse and, knowing it, died of
grief. It told how Hathor, goddess of love, melted
by the piteous sight, breathed back life into their
nostrils, and since they might not remain upon earth,
wafted them to the Under-world, where they awoke
and embraced and dwell on for ever and for aye,
triumphant and rejoicing.

All had heard this old, old story, but none had
ever heard it so divinely sung. As Tua's pure and
lovely voice floated over them the listeners seemed
to see that lover, daring all in his desire, creep into
the solemn sanctuary of the temple. They saw
Hathor appear in her wrath and smite him cold in
death. They saw the beauteous priestess with her
lamp, and heard her wail her life away upon her
darling's corpse; saw, too, the dead borne by spirits
over the borders of the world.

Then came that last burst of music thrilling and
divine, and its rich, passionate notes seemed to open
the heavens to their sight. There in the deep
sky they perceived the awakening of the lovers and
their embrace of perfect joy, and when a glory
hid them, heard the victorious chant of the priestess
of love sighing itself away, faint and ever fainter,
till at length its last distant echoes died in the utter
silence of the place of souls.

Tua ceased her music. Resting her still quivering

harp upon the board, she sank back in her chair
of state, outworn, trembling, while in her pale face
the blue eyes shone like stars. There was stillness
in the hall; the spell of that magical voice lay on
the listeners; none applauded, it seemed even that
none dared to move, for men remembered that this
wonderful young Queen was said to be daughter of
Amen, Master of the world, and thought that it had
been given to them to hearken, not to a royal maiden,
but to a goddess of the skies.

Quiet they sat as though sleep had smitten them,
only every man of their number stared at the sweet
pale face and at those radiant eyes. Drunk with
passion and with wine, Amathel, Prince of Kesh,
leaned his heavy head upon his hand and stared like
the rest. But those eyes did not stay on him. Had
he been a stone they could not have noted him less;
they passed over him seeking something beyond.

Slowly he turned to see what it might be at which
the Morning Star of Amen gazed, and perceived that
the young captain who waited on him, he who was
said to be of a race more ancient and purer than his
own, he whose house had reigned in the Southern
Land when his ancestors were but traffickers in gold,
was also gazing at this royal singer. Yes, he bent
forward to gaze as though a spell drew him, a spell,
or the eyes of the Queen, and there was that upon
his face which even a drunken Nubian could not fail
to understand.

In the hands of Rames was the tall, golden vase
of wine, and as Amathel thrust back his chair its
topmost ivory bar struck the foot of the vase and
tilted it, so that the red wine poured in a torrent over

the Prince's head and gorgeous robes, staining him
from his crest of plumes to his feet as though with
blood. Up sprang the Prince of Kesh roaring with
fury.

" Dog-descended slave ! " he shouted. " Hog-
headed brother of swine, is it thus that you wait
upon my Royalty ? " and with the cup in his hand
he smote Rames on the face, then drew the sword
at his side to kill him.

But Rames also wore a sword, that sword hafted
with the golden crocodile which Pharaoh had given
him long ago—that sword which Asti the foresighted
had seen red with royal blood. With a wild, low
cry he snatched it from its sheath, and to avoid the
blow that Amathel struck at him before he could
guard himself, sprang backwards from the dais to
the open space in the hall that had been left clear for
the dancers. After him leapt Amathel calling him
" Coward," and next instant the pillars echoed,
not with Tua's music but with the stern ringing of
bronze upon bronze.

Now in their fear and amaze men looked up to
Pharaoh, waiting his word, but Pharaoh, overcome
by the horror of the scene, appeared to have swooned ;
at least, he lay back in his chair with his eyes shut
like one asleep. Then they looked to the Queen,
but Tua made no sign, only with parted lips and
heaving breast watched, watched and waited for the
end.

As for Rames he forgot everything save that he,
a soldier and a noble of royal race, had been struck
across the mouth by a black Nubian who called himself
a prince. His blood boiled up in him, and through

a red haze as it were, he saw Tua's glorious eyes beckoning him on to victory. He saw and sprang as springs the lion of the desert, sprang straight at the throat of Amathel. The blow went high, an ostrich plume floated to the ground—no more, and Amathel was a sturdy fighter and had the strength of madness. Moreover, his was the longer weapon ; it fell upon the scales of the armour of Rames and beat him back, it fell again on his shoulder and struck him to his knee. It fell a third time, and glancing from the mail wounded him in the thigh so that the blood flowed. Now a soldier of Pharaoh's guard shouted to encourage his captain, and the Nubians shouted back, crying to their prince to slit the hog's throat.

Then Rames seemed to awake. He leapt from his knees, he smote and the blow went home, though the iron which the Nubian wore beneath his robe stayed it. He smote again more fiercely, and now it was the blood of Amathel that flowed. Then bending almost to the ground below the answering stroke, he leapt and thrust with all the strength of young limbs trained to war. He thrust and behold ! between the broad shoulders of Amathel pierced from breast to back, appeared the point of the Egyptian's sword. For a moment the prince stood still, then he fell backwards heavily and lay dead.

Now, with a shout of rage the giants of the Nubian guard rushed at Rames to avenge their master's death, so that he must fly backwards before their spears, backwards into the ranks of Pharaoh's guard. In a flash the Nubians were on them also and, how none could tell, a fearful fray began, for these soldiers hated each other, as their fathers had done before them, and there were none who could come between them, since at this feast no man bore weapons save the guards. Fierce was the battle, but the Nubians lacked a captain while Rames led veterans of Thebes picked for their valour.

The giants began to give. Here and there they fell till at length but three of them were left upon their feet, who threw down their arms and cried for mercy. Then it was for the first time that Rames understood what he had done. With bent head, his red sword in his hand, he climbed the dais and knelt before the throne of Pharaoh, saying:

" I have avenged my honour and the honour of Egypt. Slay me, O Pharaoh ! "

But Pharaoh made no answer for his swoon still held him.

Then Rames turned to Tua and said:

" Pharaoh sleeps, but in your hand is the sceptre. Slay me, O Queen ! "

Now Tua, who all this while had watched like one frozen into stone, seemed to thaw to life again. Her danger was past. She could never be forced to wed that coarse, black-souled Nubian, for Rames had killed him. Yonder he lay dead in all his finery with his hideous giants about him like fallen trees, and oh ! in her rebellious human heart she blessed Rames for the deed.

But as she, who was trained in statecraft, knew well enough, if he had escaped the sword of Prince Amathel, it was but to fall into a peril from which there seemed to be no escape. This dead prince was the heir of a great king, of a king so great that for a century Egypt had dared to make no war upon his country, for it was far away, well-fortified and hard to come at across deserts and through savage tribes. Moreover, the man had been slain at a feast in Pharaoh's Court, and by an officer of Pharaoh's guard, which afterwards had killed his escort under the eyes of Egypt's monarchs, the hand of one of whom he sought in marriage. Such a deed must mean a bitter war for Egypt, and to those who struck the blow—death, as Rames himself knew well.

Tua looked at him kneeling before her, and her heart ached. Fiercely, despairingly she thought, throwing her soul afar to seek out wisdom and a way of escape for Rames. Presently in the blackness of her mind there arose a plan and, as ever was her fashion, she acted swiftly. Lifting her head she commanded that the doors should be locked and guarded so that none might go in or out, and that those physicians who were amongst the company should attend to the wounded, and to Pharaoh, who was ill. Then she called the High Council of the Kingdom, all of whom were gathered there about her, and spoke in a cold, calm voice, while the company flocked round to listen.

" Lords and people," she said, " the gods for their own purposes have suffered a fearful thing to come to pass. Egypt's guest and his guard have been slain before Egypt's kings, yes, at their feast and in their very presence, and it will be said far and wide that this has been done by treachery. Yet you know well, as I do, that it was no treachery, but a mischance. The divine prince who is dead, as all

of you saw, grew drunken after the fashion of his
people, and in his drunkenness he struck a high-
born man, a Count of Egypt and an officer of Pharaoh,
who to do him greater honour was set to wait upon
him, calling him by vile names, and drew his sword
upon him to kill him. Am I right ? Did you see and
hear these things ? "

" Aye," answered the Council and the audience.

" Then," went on Tua, " this officer, forgetting
all save his outraged honour, dared to fight for his
life even against the Prince of Kesh, and being the
better man, slew him. Afterwards the servants of
the Prince of Kesh attacked him and Pharaoh's guard,
and were conquered and the most of them killed,
since none here had arms wherewith to part them.
Have I spoken truth ? "

" Yea, O Queen," they answered again by their
spokesman. " Rames and the royal guard have
little blame in the matter," and from the rest of them
rose a murmur of assent.

" Now," went on Tua with gathering confidence,
for she felt that all saw with her eyes, " to add to
our woes Pharaoh, my father, has been smitten by
the gods. He sleeps ; he cannot speak ; I know not
whether he will live or die, and therefore it would
seem that I, the duly-crowned Queen of Egypt, must
act for him as was provided in such a case, since the
matter is very urgent and may not be delayed. Is it
your will," she added, addressing the Council, " that
I should so act as the gods may show me how to
do ? "

" It is right and fitting," answered the Vizier,
the King's companion, on behalf of all of them.

" Then, priests, lords and people," continued the Queen, " what course shall we take in this sore strait ? Speaking with the voice of all of you and on your behalf, I can command that the Count Rames and all those other chosen men whom Pharaoh loves, who fought with him, shall be slain forthwith. This, indeed," she added slowly, " I should wish to do, since although Rames had suffered intolerable insult such as no high-born man can be asked to bear even from a prince, and he and all of them were but fighting to save their lives and to show the Nubians that we are not cowards here in Egypt, without doubt they have conquered and slain the heir of Kesh and his black giants who were our guests, and for this deed their lives are forfeit."

She paused watching, while although here and there a voice answered " Yes " or " They must die," from the rest arose a murmur of dissent. For in their hearts the company were on the side of Rames and Pharaoh's guards. Moreover, they were proud of the young captain's skill and courage, and glad that the Nubians, whom they hated with an ancient hate, had been defeated by the lesser men of Egypt, some of whom were their friends or relatives.

Now, while they argued among themselves Tua rose from her chair and went to look at Pharaoh, whom the physicians were attending, chafing his hands and pouring water on his brow. Presently she returned with tears standing in her beautiful eyes, for she loved her father, and said in a heavy voice :

" Alas ! Pharaoh is very ill. Set the evil has smitten him, and it is hard, my people, that he per-

chance may be taken from us and we must bear such
woe, because of the ill behaviour of a royal
foreigner, for I cannot forget that it was he who
caused this tumult."

The audience agreed that it was very hard, and
looked angrily at the surviving Nubians, but Tua,
conquering herself, continued:

" We must bear the blows that the fates rain on
us, nor suffer our private grief to dull the sword of
justice. Now, as I have said, even though we love
them as our brothers or our husbands, yet the Count
Rames and his brave comrades should perish by a
death of shame, such a death as little befits the
flower of Pharaoh's guard."

Again she paused, then went on in the midst of
an intense silence, for even the physicians ceased
from their work to hearken to her decree, as supreme
judge of Egypt.

" And yet, and yet, my people, even as I was
about to pass sentence upon them, uttering the doom
that may not be recalled, some guardian spirit of our
land sent a thought into my heart, on which I think
it right to take your judgment. If we destroy these
men, as I desire to destroy them, will they not say
in the Southern Country and in all the nations around,
that first they had been told to murder the Prince of
Kesh and his escort, and then were themselves
executed to cover up our crime ? Will it not be
believed that there is blood upon the hands of Pharaoh
and of Egypt, the blood of a royal guest who, it is
well known, was welcomed here with love and joy,
that he might—oh ! forgive me, I am but a maiden,
I cannot say it. Nay, pity me not and answer not

till I have set out all the case as best I may, which
I fear me is but ill. It is certain that this will be
said—aye, and believed, and we of Egypt all
be called traitors, and that these men, who after all,
however evil has been their deed, are brave and
upright, will be written in all the books of all the
lands as common murderers, and go down to Osiris
with that ill name branded on their brows. Yes,
and their shame will cling to the pure hands of
Pharaoh and his councillors."

Now at this picture the people murmured, and
some of the noble women there began to weep outright.

"But," proceeded Tua with her pleading voice,
"how if we were to take another course ? How
if we commanded this Count Rames and his companions to journey, with an escort such as befits the
Majesty of Pharaoh, to the far city of Napata, and
there to lay before the great king of that land by
writings and the mouths of witnesses, all the sad
story of the death of his only son ? How if we sent
letters to his Majesty of Kesh, saying, ' Thou hast
heard our tale, thou knowest all our woe.   Now judge.
If thou art noble-hearted and it pleases thee to
acquit these men, acquit them and we will praise
thee.   But if thou art wroth and stern and it pleases
thee to condemn these men, condemn them, and
send them back to us for punishment, that punishment which thou dost decree.' Is that plan good,
my people ? Can his Majesty of Kesh complain if
he is made judge in his own cause ? Can the kings
and captains of other lands then declare that in Egypt
we work murder on our guests ? Tell me, who have

so little wisdom, if this plan is good, as I dare to say
to you, it seems to me."

Now with one voice the Council and all the guests,
and especially the guards themselves who were on
their trial, save Rames, who still knelt in silence
before the Queen, cried out that it was very good.
Yes; they clapped their hands and shouted, vowing
to each other that this young Queen of theirs was
the Spirit of Wisdom come to earth, and that her
excellent person was filled with the soul of a god.

But she frowned at their praises and, holding up
her sceptre, sternly commanded silence.

" Such is your decree, O my Council," she cried,
" and the decree of all you here present, who are the
noblest of my people, and I, as I am bound by my
oath of crowning, proclaim and ratify it, I, Neter-Tua,
who am named Star and Daughter of Amen, who
am named Glorious in Ra, who am named Hathor,
Strong in Beauty, who am crowned Queen of the
Upper and the Lower Land.   I proclaim—write it
down, O Scribes, and let it be registered this night
that the decree may stand while the world endures—
that two thousand of the choicest troops of Egypt
shall sail up Nile, forthwith, for Kesh, and that in
command of them, so that all may know his crime,
shall go the young Count Rames, and with him
those others who also did the deed of blood."

Now at this announcement, which sounded
more like promotion than disgrace, some started and
Rames looked up, quivering in all his limbs.

" I proclaim," went on Tua quickly. " that when
they are come to Napata they shall kneel before its
king and submit themselves to the judgment of his

Majesty, and having been judged, shall return and report to us the judgment of his Majesty, that it may be carried out as his Majesty of Kesh shall appoint. Let the troops and the ships be made ready this very night, and meanwhile, save when he appears before us to take his orders as general, in token of our wrath, we banish the Count Rames from our Court and Presence, and place his companions under guard."

So spoke Tua, and the royal decree having been written down swiftly and read aloud, she sealed and signed with her sign-manual as Queen, that it might not be changed or altered, and commanded that copies of it should be sent to all the Governors of the Nomes of Egypt, and a duplicate prepared and despatched with this royal embassy, for so she named it, to be delivered to the King of Kesh with the letters of condolence, and the presents of ceremony, and the body of Amathel, the Prince of Kesh, now divine in Osiris.

Then, at length, the doors were thrown open and the company dispersed, Rames and the guard being led away by the Council and placed in safe keeping. Also Pharaoh, still senseless but breathing quietly, was carried to his bed, and the dead were taken to the embalmers, whilst Tua, so weary that she could scarcely walk, departed to her chambers leaning on the shoulder of the royal Nurse, Asti, the mother of Rames.

CHAPTER VI

THE OATH OF RAMES AND OF TUA

STILL robed Tua lay upon a couch, for she would not seek her bed, while Asti stood near to her, a dark commanding figure.

" Your Majesty has done strange things to-night," said Asti in her quiet voice.

Tua turned her head and looked at her, then answered:

" Very strange, Nurse. You see, the gods and that troublesome son of yours and Pharaoh's sudden sickness threw the strings of Fate into my hand, and—I pulled them. I always had a fancy for the pulling of strings, but the chance never came my way before."

" It seems to me that for a beginner your Majesty pulled somewhat hard," said Asti drily.

" Yes, Nurse, so hard that I think I have pulled your son off the scaffold into a place of some honour, if he knows how to stay there, though it was the Council and the priests and the lords and the ladies, who thought that *they* pulled. You see one must commence as one means to go on."

" Your Majesty is very clever; you will make a great Queen—if you do not overpull yourself."

" Not half so clever as you were, Asti, when you made that monkey come out of the vase," answered Tua, laughing somewhat hysterically. " Oh! do not look innocent, I know it was your magic, for I could feel it passing over my head. How did you do it, Asti ? "

" If your Majesty will tell me how you made the lords of Egypt consent to the sending of an armed expedition to Napata under the command of a lad, a mere captain who had just killed its heir-apparent before their eyes, which decree, if I know anything of Rames, will mean a war between Kesh and Egypt, I will tell you how I made the monkey come out of the vase."

" Then I shall never learn, Nurse, for I can't because I don't know. It came into my mind, as music comes into my throat, that is all. Rames should have been beheaded at once, shouldn't he, for not letting that black boar tusk him ? Do you think he poured the wine over Amathel's head on purpose ? " and again she laughed.

" Yes, I suppose that he should have been killed, as he would have been if your Majesty had not chanced to be so fond——"

" Talking of wine," broke in Tua, " give me a cup of it. The divine Prince of Kesh who was to have been my husband—did you understand, Asti, that they really meant to make that black barbarian my husband ?—I say that the divine Prince, who now sups with Osiris, drank so much that I could not touch a drop, and I am tired and thirsty, and have still some things to do to-night."

Asti went to a table where stood a flagon of wine wreathed in vine leaves, and by it cups of glass, and filling one of them brought it to Tua.

" Here's to the memory of the divine prince, and

may he have left the table of Osiris before I come there. And here's to the hand that sent him thither," said Tua recklessly. Then she drained the wine, every drop of it, and threw the cup to the marble floor where it shattered into bits.

" What god has entered into your Majesty to-night ? " asked Asti quietly.

" One that knows his own mind, I think," replied Tua. " There, I feel strong again, I go to visit Pharaoh. Come with me, Asti."

When Tua arrived at the bedside of Pharaoh she found that the worst of the danger was over. Fearing for his life the physicians had bled him, and now the fit had passed away and his eyes were open, although he was unable to speak and did not know her or anyone. She asked whether he would live or die, and was told that he would live, or so his doctors believed, but that for a long while he must lie quite quiet, seeing as few people as possible, and above all being troubled with no business, since, if he were wearied or excited, the fit would certainly return and kill him. So, rejoicing at this news which was better than she had expected, Tua kissed her father and left him.

" Now will your Majesty go to bed ? " asked Asti when she had returned to her own apartments.

" By no means," answered Tua, " I wear Pharaoh's shoes and have much business left to do to-night. Summon Mermes, your husband."

So Mermes came and stood before her. He was still what he had been in the old days when Tua played as an infant in his house, stern, noble-looking and of few words, but now his hair had grown white and his face was drawn with grief, both for the sake of Rames, whose hot blood had brought him into so much danger, and because Pharaoh, who was his friend, lay between life and death.

Tua looked at him and loved him more than ever, for now that he was troubled some new likeness to Rames appeared upon his face which she had never seen before.

" Take heart, noble Mermes," she said gently, " they say that Pharaoh stays with us yet a while."

" I thank Amen," he answered, " for had he died, his blood would have been upon the hands of my House."

" Not so, Mermes ; it would have been upon the hands of the gods. You spring from a royal line ; say, what would you have thought of your son if, after being struck by that fat Nubian, he had cowered at his feet and prayed for his life like any slave ? "

Mermes flushed and smiled a little, then said:

" The question is rather—What would you have thought, O Queen ? "

" I ? " answered Tua. " Well, as a queen I should have praised him much, since then Egypt would have been spared great trouble, but as a woman and a friend I should never have spoken to him again. Honour is more than life, Mermes."

" Certainly honour is more than life," replied Mermes, staring at the ceiling, perhaps to hide the look upon his face, " and for a little while Rames seems to be in the way of it. But those who are set high have far to fall, O Queen, and — forgive me — he is my only child. Now when Pharaoh recovers——"

" Rames will be far away," broke in Tua. " Go, bring him here at once, and with him the Vizier and the chief scribe of the Council. Take this ring, it will open all doors," and she drew the signet from her finger and handed it to him.

" At this hour, your Majesty ? " said Mermes in a doubtful voice.

" Have I not spoken," she answered impatiently. " When the welfare of Egypt is at stake I do not sleep."

So Mermes bowed and went, and while he was gone Tua caused Asti to smooth her hair and change her robe and ornaments for others which, although she did not say so, she thought became her better. Then she sat her down in a chair of state in her chamber of audience, and waited, while Asti stood beside her asking no questions, but wondering.

At length the doors were opened, and through them appeared Mermes and the Vizier and the chief of the scribes, both of them trying to hide their yawns, for they had been summoned from their beds who were not wont to do state business at such hours. After them limped Rames, for his wound had grown stiff, who looked bewildered, but otherwise just as he had left the feast.

Now, without waiting for the greetings of ceremony, Tua began to question the Vizier as to what steps had been taken in furtherance of her decrees, and when he assured her that the business was on foot, went into its every detail with him, as to the ships and the officers and the provisioning of the men, and so forth. Next she set herself to dictate despatches to the captains and barons who held the fortresses on the Upper Nile, communicating to them Pharaoh's orders on this matter, and the commission of Rames, whereby he, whose hands had done the ill, was put in command of the great embassy that went to make amends.

These being finished, she sent away the scribe to spend the rest of the night in writing them in duplicate, bidding him bring them to her in the early morning to be sealed. Next addressing Rames, she commanded him to start on the morrow with those troops which were ready to Takensit above the first Cataract of the Nile, which was the frontier fortress of Egypt, and there wait until the remainder of the soldiers joined him, bearing with them her presents to the King of Kesh, and the embalmed body of the Prince Amathel.

Rames bowed and said that her orders should be obeyed, and the audience being finished, still bowing and supported by Mermes, began to walk backwards towards the door, his eyes fixed upon the face of Tua, who sat with bent head, clasping the arms of her chair like one in difficulty and doubt. When he had gone a few steps she seemed to come to some determination, for with an effort she raised herself and said :

" Return, Count Rames, I have a message to give you for the King of Kesh who, unhappy man, has lost his son and heir, and it is one that no other ears must hear. Leave me a while with this captain, O Mermes and Asti, and see that none listen to our talk. Presently I will summon you to conduct him away."

They hesitated, for this thing seemed strange,

then noting the look she gave them, departed through the doors behind the royal seat.

Now Rames and the Queen were left alone in that great, lighted chamber. With bent head and folded arms he stood before her while she looked at him intently, yet seemed to find no words to say. At length she spoke in a sweet, low voice.

" It is many years since we were playmates in the courts of the temple yonder, and since then we have never been alone together, have we, Rames ? "

" No, Great Lady," answered Rames, " for you were born to be a queen, and I am but a humble soldier who cannot hope to consort with queens."

" Who cannot hope ! Would you wish to then if you could ? "

" O Queen," answered Rames, biting his lips, " why does it please you to make a mock of me ? "

" It does not please me to do any such thing, for by my father Amen, Rames, I wish that we were children once more, for those were happy days before they separated us and set you to soldiering and me to statecraft."

" You have learnt your part well, Star of the Morning," said Rames, glancing at her quickly.

" Not better than you, playmate Rames, if I may judge from your sword-play this night. So it seems that we both of us are in the way of becoming masters of our trades."

" What am I to say to your Majesty ? You have saved my life when it was forfeit——"

" As once you saved mine when it was forfeit, and at greater risk. Look at your hand, it will remind you. It was but tit for tat. And, friend Rames, this day I came near to being eaten by a worse crocodile than that which dwells in the pool yonder."

" I guessed as much, Queen, and the thought made me mad. Had it not been for that I should only have thrown him down. Now that crocodile will eat no more maidens."

" No," answered Tua, rubbing her chin, " he has gone to be eaten by Set, Devourer of Souls, has he not ? But I think there may be trouble between Egypt and Kesh, and what Pharaoh will say when he recovers I am sure I do not know. May the gods protect me from his wrath."

" Tell me, if it pleases your Majesty, what is my fate ? I have been named General of this expedition over the heads of many, I who am but a captain and a young man and an evil-doer. Am I to be killed on the journey, or am I to be executed by the King of Kesh ? "

" If any kill you on the journey, Rames, they shall render me an account, be it the gods themselves, and as for the vengeance of the King of Kesh—well, you will have two thousand picked men with you and the means to gather more as you go. Listen now, for this is not in the decree or in the letters," she added, bending towards him and whispering. " Egypt has spies in Kesh, and, being industrious, I have read their reports. The people there hate the upstart race that rules them, and the king, who alone is left now that Amathel is dead, is old and half-witted, for all that family drink too much. So if the worst comes to the worst, do you think that you need be killed, you," she added meaningly,

" who, if the House of Amathel were not, would by descent be King of Kesh, as, if I and my House were not, you might be Pharaoh of Egypt ? "

Rames studied the floor for a little, then looked up and asked:

" What shall I do ? "

" It seems that is for you to find out," replied Tua, in her turn studying the ceiling. " Were I in your place, I think that, if driven to it, *I* should know what to do. One thing, however, I should *not* do. Whatever may be the judgment of the divine King of Kesh upon you, and that can easily be guessed, I should not return to Egypt with my escort, until I was quite sure of my welcome. No, I think that I should stop in Napata, which I am told is a rich and pleasant city, and try to put its affairs in order, trusting that Egypt, to which it once belonged, would in the end forgive me for so doing."

" I understand," said Rames, " that whatever happens, I alone am to blame."

" Good, and of course there are no witnesses to this talk of ours. Have you also been taking lessons in statecraft in your spare hours, Rames, much as I have tried to learn something of the art of war ? "

Rames made no answer, only these two strange conspirators looked at each other and smiled.

" Your Majesty is weary. I must leave your Majesty," he said presently.

" You must be wearier than I am, Rames, with that wound, which I think has not been dressed, although it is true that we have both fought to-night. Rames, you are going on a far journey. I wonder if we shall ever meet again."

"I do not know," he answered with a groan, "but for my sake it is better that we should not. O Morning Star, why did you save me this night, who would have been glad to die? Did not that Ka of yours tell you that I should have been glad to die, or my mother, who is a magician?"

"I have seen nothing of my Ka, Rames, since we played together in the temple—ah! those were happy days, were they not? And your mother is a discreet lady who does not talk to me about you, except to warn me not to show you any favour, lest others should be jealous and murder you. Shall you then be sorry if we do not meet again? Scarcely, I suppose, since you seem so anxious to die and be rid of me and all things that we know."

Now Rames pressed his hand upon his heart as though to still its beating, and looked round him in despair. For, indeed, that heart of his felt as though it must burst

"Tua," he gasped desperately, "can you for a minute forget that you are Queen of the Upper and the Lower Land, who perhaps will soon be Pharaoh, the mightiest monarch in the world, and remember only that you are a woman, and as a woman hear a secret and keep it close?"

"We have been talking secrets, Rames, as we used to do, you remember, long ago, and you will not tell mine which deal with the State. Why, then, should I tell yours? But be short, it grows late, or rather early, and as you know, we shall not meet again."

"Good," he answered. "Queen Neter-Tua, I, your subject, dare to love you."

" What of that, Rames ? I have millions of subjects who all profess to love me."

He waved his hand angrily, and went on :

" I dare to love you as a man loves a woman, not
as a subject loves a queen."

" Ah ! " she answered in a new and broken voice,
" that is different, is it not ? Well, all women love
to be loved, though some are queens and some are
peasants, so why should I be angry ? Rames, now,
as in past days, I thank you for your love."

" It is not enough," he said. " What is the
use of giving love ? Love should be lent. Love is
an usurer that asks high interest. Nay, not the
interest only, but the capital and the interest to
boot. Oh, Star ! what happens to the man who is
so mad as to love the Queen of Egypt ? "

Tua considered this problem as though it were
a riddle to which she was seeking an answer.

" Who knows ? " she replied at length in a low
voice. " Perhaps it costs him his life, or perhaps—
perhaps he marries her and becomes Pharaoh of
Egypt. Much might depend upon whether such a
queen chanced to care about such a man."

Now Rames shook like a reed in the evening wind,
and he looked at her with glowing eyes.

" Tua," he whispered, " can it be possible—do
you mean that I am welcome to you, or are you but
drawing me to shame and ruin ? "

She made no answer to him in words, only with
a certain grave deliberation, laid down the little
ivory sceptre that she held, and suffering her troubled
eyes to rest upon his eyes, bent forward and stretched
out her arms towards him.

D*

" Yes, Rames," she murmured into his ear a minute later, " I am drawing you to whatever may be found upon this breast of mine, love, or majesty, or shame, or ruin, or the death of one or both of us, or all of them together. Are you content to take the chances of this high game, Rames ? "

" Ask it not, Tua. You know, you know ! "

She kissed him on the lips, and all her heart and all her youth were in that kiss. Then, gently enough, she pushed him from her, saying:

" Stand there, I would speak with you, and as I have said, the time is short. Hearken to me, Rames, you are right ; I know, as I have always known, and as you would have known also had you been less foolish than you are. You love me and I love you, for so it was decreed where souls are made, and so it has been from the beginning and so it shall be to the end. You, a gentleman of Egypt, love the Queen of Egypt, and she is yours and no other man's. Such is the decree of him who caused us to be born upon the same day, and to be nursed upon the same kind breast. Well, after all, why not ? If love brings death upon us, as well may chance, at least the love will remain which is worth it all, and beyond death there is something."

" Only this, Tua, I seek the woman not a throne, and alas ! through me you may be torn from your high place."

" The throne goes with the woman, Rames, they cannot be separated. But say, something comes over me ; if that happened, if I were an outcast, a wanderer, with nothing save this shape and soul of mine, and it were you that sat upon a throne, would you still love me, Rames ? "

" Why ask such questions ? " he replied indignantly. " Moreover, your talk is childish. What throne can I ever sit on ? "

A change fell upon her at his words. She ceased to be the melting, passionate woman, and became once more the strong, far-seeing queen.

" Rames," she said, " you understand why, although it tears my heart, I am sending you so far away and into so many dangers, do you not ? It is to save your life, for after what has chanced to-night in this fashion or in that here you would certainly die, as, had it not have been for that plan of mine you must have died two hours ago. There are many who hate you, Rames, and Pharaoh may recover, as I pray the gods he will, and over-ride my will, for you have slain his guest who was brought here to marry me."

" I understand all these things, Queen."

" Then awake, Rames, look to the future and understand that also, if, as I think, you have the wit. I am sending you with a strong escort, am I not ? Well, that King of Kesh is old and feeble, and you have a claim upon his crown. Take it, man, and set it on your head, and as King of Kesh ask the hand of Egypt's Queen in marriage. Then who would say you nay—not Egypt's Queen, I think, or the people of Egypt who hunger for the rich Southern Land which they have lost."

So she spoke, and as these high words passed her lips she looked so splendid and so royal that, dazzled by the greatness of her majesty, Rames bowed himself before her as before the presence of a god. Then, aware that she was trying him in the balance of her judgment, he straightened himself and spoke to her as prince speaks to prince.

"Star of Amen," he said, " it is true that though here we are but your humble subjects, the blood of my father and of myself is as high as yours, and perhaps more ancient, and it is true that now yonder Amathel is dead, after my father, in virtue of those who went before us I have more right than any other to the inheritance of Kesh. Queen, I hear your words, I will take it if I can, not for its own sake, but to win you, and if I fail you will know that I died doing my best. Queen, we part and this is a far journey. Perhaps we may never meet again ; at the best we must be separated for long. Queen, you have honoured me with your love, and therefore I ask a promise of you, not as woman only, but as Queen. I ask that however strait may be the circumstances, whatever reasons of State may push you on, while I live you will take no other man to husband—no, not even if he offers you half the world in dower."

" I give it," she answered. " If you should learn that I am wed to any man upon the earth then spit upon my name as woman, and as Queen cast me off and overthrow me if you can. Deal with me, Rames, as in such a case I will deal with you. Only be sure of your tidings ere you believe them. Now there is nothing more to say. Farewell to you, Rames, till we meet again beneath or beyond the sun. Our royal pact is made. Come, seal it and begone."

She rose and stretched out her sceptre to him, which he kissed as her faithful subject. Next, with a swift movement, she lifted the golden *uræus* circlet from her brow and for a moment set it on his head, crowning him her king, and while it rested there she, the Queen of Egypt, bent the knee before him and did him homage. Then she cast down crown and sceptre, and as woman fell upon her lover's breast while the bright rays of morning, flowing suddenly through the eastern window-place of that splendid hall, struck upon them both, clothing them in a robe of glory and of flame.

Soon, very soon, it was done and Tua, seated there in light, watched Rames depart into the outer shadow, wondering when and how she would see him come again. For her heart was heavy within her, and even in this hour of triumphant love she greatly feared the future and its gifts.

CHAPTER VII

So that day Rames departed for Takensit with
what ships and men could be got together in such
haste. There, at the frontier post, he waited till
the rest of the soldiers joined him, bringing with
them the hastily embalmed body of Prince Amathel
whom he had slain, and the royal gifts to the King
of Kesh. Then, without a moment's delay, he
sailed southwards with his little army on the long
journey, fearing lest if he tarried, orders might come
to him to return to Thebes. Also he desired to
reach Napata before the heavy news of the death of
the King's son, and without warning of the approach
of Egypt's embassy.

With Tua he had no more speech, although as
his galley was rowed under the walls of the palace,
at a window of the royal apartments he saw a white
draped figure that watched them go by. It was
standing in the shadow so that he could not recognise the face, but his heart told him that this was
none other than the Queen herself, who appeared
there to bid him farewell.

So Rames rose from the chair in which he was
seated on account of the hurt to his leg and saluted
with his sword, and ordered the crew to do likewise
by lifting up their oars. Then the slender figure
bowed in answer, and he went on to fulfil his destiny,

leaving Neter-Tua, Morning Star of Amen, to fulfil hers.

Before he sailed, however, Mermes his father and Asti his mother visited him in a place apart.

" You were born under a strange star, my son," said Mermes, " and I know not whither it will lead you, who pray that it may not be a meteor which blazes suddenly in the heavens and disappears to return no more. All the people talk of the favour the Queen has shown you who, instead of ordering you to be executed for the deed you did which robbed her of a royal husband, has set you in command of an army, you, a mere youth, and received you in secret audience, an honour granted to very few. Fate that has passed me by gives the dice to your young hand, but how the cast will fall I know not, nor shall I live to see, or so I believe."

" Speak no such evil-omened words, my father," answered Rames tenderly, for these two loved each other. " To me it seems more likely that it is I who shall not live, for this is a strange and desperate venture upon which I go, to tell to a great king the news of the death of his only son at my own hand. Mother, you are versed in the books of wisdom and can see that which is hidden to our eyes. Have you no word of comfort for us ? "

" My son," answered Asti, " I have searched the future, but with all my skill it will open little of its secrets to my sight. Yet I have learned something. Great fortunes lie before you, and I believe that you and I shall meet again. But to your beloved father bid farewell."

At these words Rames turned his head aside

to hide his tears, but Mermes bade him not to grieve, saying :

"Great is the mystery of our fates, my son. Some there be who tell us that we are but bubbles born of the stream to be swallowed up by the stream, clouds born of the sky to be swallowed up by the sky, the offspring of chance like the beasts and the birds, gnats that dance for an hour in the sunlight and are gone. But I believe it not, who hold that the gods clothe us with this robe of flesh for their own purpose, and that the spirit within us has been from the beginning and eternally will be. Therefore I love not life and fear not death, knowing that these are but doors leading to the immortal house that is prepared for us. The royal blood you have came to you from your mother and myself, but that our lots should have been humble, while yours, mayhap, will be splendid, does not move me to envy who perchance have been that you may be. You go forth to fulfil your fortunes which I believe are great, I bide here to fulfil mine which lead me to the tomb. I shall never see you in your power, if power comes to you, nor will your triumphant footsteps stir my sleep.

"Yet, Rames, remember that though you tread on cloth of gold and the bowed necks of enemies, though love be your companion and diadems your crown, though flatteries float about you like incense in a shrine till, at length, you deem yourself a god, those footsteps of yours still lead to that same dark tomb and through it on to Judgment. Be great if you can, but be good as well as great. Take no man's life because you have the strength and hate

him; wrong no woman because she is defenceless
or can be bought. Remember that the beggar
child playing in the sand may have a destiny more
high than yours when all the earthly count is
reckoned. Remember that you share the air you
breathe with the cattle and the worm. Go your
road rejoicing in your beauty and your youth and
the good gifts that are given you, but know, Rames,
that at the end of it I, who wait in the shadow of
Osiris, I your father, shall ask an account thereof,
and that beyond me stand the gods of Justice to
test the web that you have woven. Now, Rames,
my son, my blessing and the blessing of him who
shaped us be with you, and farewell."

Then Mermes kissed him on the brow and, turning, left the room, nor did they ever meet again.

But Asti stayed awhile, and coming to him
presently, looked Rames in the eyes, and said:

"Mourn not. Separations are no new thing,
death is no new thing; all these sorrows have been
on the earth for millions of years, and for millions
of years yet shall be. Live out your life, rejoicing
if the days be good, content if they be but ill, regret-
ting nothing save your sins, fearing nothing, expect-
ing nothing, since all things are appointed and cannot
be changed."

"I hear," he answered humbly, "and I will not
forget. Whether I succeed or fail you shall not be
ashamed for me."

Now his mother turned to go also, but paused
and said:

"I have a gift for you, Rames, from one whose
name may not be spoken."

" Give it to me," he said eagerly, " I feared that it was all but a dream."

" Oh ! " replied Asti scanning his face, " so there was a dream, was there ? Did it fall upon you last night when the daughter of Amen, my foster-child, instructed you in secret ? "

" The gift," said Rames, stretching out his hand.

Then, smiling in her quiet fashion, his mother drew from the bosom of her robe some object that was wrapped in linen and, touching her forehead with the royal seal that fastened it, gave it to Rames. With trembling fingers he broke the seal and there within the linen lay a ring which for some years, as Rames knew, Tua had worn upon the first finger of her right hand. It was massive and of plain gold, and upon the bezel of it was cut the symbol of the sun, on either side of which knelt a man and a woman crowned with the double crown of Egypt, and holding in their right hands the looped Sign of Life which they stretched up towards the glory of the sun.

" Do you know who wore that ring in long past days ? " asked Asti of Rames who pressed it to his lips.

He shook his head who remembered only that Tua had worn it.

" It was your forefather and mine, Rames, the last of the royal rulers of our line, who reigned over Egypt and also over the Land of Kesh. A while ago the embalmers re-clothed his divine body in the tomb, and the Princess, who was present there with your father and myself, drew this ring off his dead hand and offered it to Mermes, who would not take it, seeing that it is a royal signet. So she wore it herself, and now for her own reasons she sends it to you, perhaps to give you authority in Kesh where that mighty seal is known."

" I thank the Queen," he murmured. " I shall wear it always."

" Then let it be on your breast till you have passed the frontier, lest some should ask questions that you find it hard to answer. My son," she went on quickly, " you dare to love this queen of ours."

" In truth I do, Mother. Did not you, who know everything, know that ? Also it is your fault who brought us up together."

" Nay, my son, the fault of the gods who have so decreed. But—does she love you ? "

" You are always with her, Mother, ask her yourself, if you need to ask. At least, she has sent me her own ring. Oh ! Mother, Mother, guard her night and day, for if harm comes to her, then I die. Mother, queens cannot give themselves where they will as other women can ; it is policy that thrusts their husbands on them. Keep her unwed, Mother. Though it should cost her her throne, still I say let her not be cast into the arms of one she hates. Protect her in her trial, if such should come ; and if strength fails and the gods desert her, then hide her in the web of the magic that you have, and preserve her undefiled, for so shall I bless your name for ever."

" You fly at a rare bird, Rames, and there are many stronger hawks about besides that one you slew ; yes, royal eagles who may strike down the pair of you. Yet I will do my best, who have long foreseen this hour, and who pray that before my eyes shut in death, they may yet behold you seated on the throne of your forefathers, crowned with power and with such love and beauty as have never yet been given to man. Now hide that ring upon your heart and your secret in it, as I shall, lest you should return no more to Egypt. Moreover, follow your royal Star and no other. Whatever counsel she may have given you, follow it also, stirring not to right or left, for I say that in that maiden breast of hers there dwells the wisdom of the gods."

Then holding up her hands over his head as though in blessing, Asti, too, turned and left him.

So Rames went and was no more seen, and by degrees the talk as to the matter of his victory over the Prince of Kesh, and as to his appointment by the whim of the maiden Queen to command the splendid embassy of atonement which she had despatched to the old King, the dead man's father, died away for lack of anything to feed on.

Tua kept her counsel well, nor was aught known of that midnight interview with the young Count her general. Moreover, Napata was far away, so far that starting at the season when it did, the embassy could scarce return till two years had gone by, if ever it did return. Also few believed that whoever came back, Rames would be one of them, since it was said openly that so soon as he was beyond the frontiers of Egypt, the soldiers had orders to kill him and take on his body as a peace-offering.

Indeed, all praised the wit and wisdom of the Queen, who by this politic device, had rid herself of a troublesome business with as little scandal as possible, and avoided staining her own hands in the blood of a foster-brother. Had she ordered his death forthwith, they said, it would have been supposed also that she had put him away because he was of a royal race, one who, in the future, might prove a rival, or at least cause some rebellion.

Meanwhile greater questions filled the mouths of men. Would Pharaoh die and leave Neter-Tua, the young and lovely, to hold his throne, and if so, what would happen ? It was a thousand years since a woman had reigned in Egypt, and none had reigned who were not wed. Therefore it seemed necessary that a husband should be found for her as soon as might be.

But Pharaoh did not die. On the contrary, though very slowly, he recovered and was stronger than he had been for years, for the fit that struck him down seemed to have cleared his blood. For some three months he lay helpless as a child, amusing himself as a child does with little things, and talking of children whom he had known in his youth, or when some of these chanced to visit him as old men, asking them to play with him with tops or balls.

Then one day came a change, and rising from his bed he commanded the presence of his Councillors, and when they came, inquired of them what had happened, and why he could remember nothing since the feast.

They put him off with soft words, and soon he grew weary and dismissed them. But after they had gone and he had eaten he sent for Mermes, the Captain of the Guard of Amen and his friend, and questioned him.

" The last thing I remember," he said, " was seeing the drunken Prince of Kesh fighting with your son, that handsome, fiery-eyed Count Rames whom some fool, or enemy, had set to wait upon him at table. It was a dog's trick, Mermes, for after all your blood is purer and more ancient than that of the present kings of Kesh. Well, the horror of the sight of my royal guest, the suitor for my daughter's hand, fighting with an officer of my own guard at my own board, struck me as a butcher strikes an ox, and after it all was blackness. What chanced, Mermes ? "

" This, Pharaoh : My son killed Amathel in fair fight, then those black Nubian giants in their fury attacked your guard, but led by Rames the Egyptians, though they were the lesser men, overcame them and slew the most of them. I am an old soldier, but never have I seen a finer fray——"

" A finer fray ! A finer fray," gasped Pharaoh. " Why this will mean a war between Kesh and Egypt. And then ? Did the Council order Rames to be executed, as you must admit he deserved, although you are his father ? "

" Not so, O Pharaoh ; moreover, I admit nothing, though had he played a coward's part before all the lords of Egypt, gladly would I have slain him with my own hand."

" Ah ! " said Pharaoh, " there speaks the soldier and the parent. Well, I understand. He was affronted, was he not, by that bedizened black man ?

Were I in your place I should say as much. But— what happened ? "

" Your Majesty having become unconscious," explained Mermes, " her Majesty the Queen Neter-Tua, Glorious in Ra, took command of affairs according to her Oath of Crowning. She has sent an embassy of atonement of two thousand picked soldiers to the King of Kesh, bearing with them the embalmed body of the divine Amathel and many royal gifts."

" That is good enough in its way," said Pharaoh. " But why two thousand men, whereof the cost will be very great, when a score would have sufficed ? It is an army, not an embassy, and when my royal brother of Kesh sees it advancing, bearing with it the ill-omened gift of his only son's body, he may take alarm."

Mermes respectfully agreed that he might do so.

" What general is in command of this embassy, as it pleases you to call it ? "

" The Count Rames, my son, is in command, your Majesty."

Now weak as he was still, Pharaoh nearly leapt from his chair :

" Rames ! That young cut-throat who killed the Prince ! Rames who is the last of the old rightful dynasty of Kesh ! Rames, a mere captain, in command of two thousand of my veterans ! Oh, I must still be mad ! Who gave him the command ? "

" The Queen Neter-Tua, Star of Amen, she gave him the command, O Pharaoh. Immediately after the fray in the hall she uttered her decree and caused it to be recorded in the usual fashion."

" Send for the Queen," said Pharaoh with a groan.

So Tua was summoned, and presently swept in gloriously arrayed, and on seeing her father sitting up and well, ran to him and embraced him and for a long time refused to listen to his talk of matters of State. At length, however, he made her sit by him still holding his hand, and asked her why in the name of Amen she had sent that handsome young firebrand, Rames, in command of the expedition to Kesh. Then she answered very sweetly that she would tell him. And tell him she did, at such length that before she had finished, Pharaoh, whose strength as yet was small, had fallen into a doze.

" Now, you understand," she said as he woke up with a start. " The responsibility was thrust upon me, and I had to act as I thought best. To have slain this young Rames would have been impossible, for all hearts were with him."

" But surely, Daughter, you might have got him ᷤot of the way."

" My father, that is what I have done. I have sent him to Napata, which is very much out of the way—many months journey, I am told."

" But what will happen, Tua ? Either the King of Kesh will kill him and my two thousand soldiers, or perhaps he will kill the King of Kesh as he killed his son, and seize the throne which his own fore-fathers held for generations. Have you thought of that ? "

" Yes, my father, I thought of it, and if this last should happen through no fault of ours, would Egypt weep, think you ? "

Now Pharaoh stared at Tua, and Tua looked back at Pharaoh and smiled.

" I perceive, Daughter," he said slowly, " that in you are the makings of a great queen, for within the silken scabbard of a woman's folly I see the statesman's sword of bronze. Only run not too fast lest you should fall upon that sword and it should pierce you."

Now Tua, who had heard such words before from Asti, smiled again but made no answer.

" You need a husband to hold you back," went on Pharaoh ; " some great man whom you can love and respect."

" Find me such a man, my father, and I will wed him gladly," answered Tua in a sweet voice. " Only," she added, " I know not where he may be sought now that the divine Amathel is dead at the hand of the Count Rames, our general and ambassador to Kesh."

So when he grew stronger Pharaoh renewed his search for a husband meet to marry the Queen of Egypt. Now, as before, suitors were not lacking, indeed, his ambassadors and councillors sent in their names by twos and threes, but always when they were submitted to her, Tua found something against everyone of them, till at last it was said that she must be destined for a god since no mere mortal would serve her turn. But when this was reported to her, Tua only answered with a smile that she was destined to that royal lover of whom Amen had spoken to her mother in a dream ; not to a god, but to the Chosen of the god, and that when she saw him, she felt sure she would know him at once and love him much.

After some months had gone by Pharaoh, quite weary of this play, asked the advice of his Council. They suggested to him that he should journey through the great cities of Egypt, both because the change might completely re-establish his divine health, and in the hope that on her travels the Queen Neter-Tua would meet someone of royal blood with whom she could fall in love. For by now it was evident to all of them that unless she did fall in love, she would not marry.

So that very night Pharaoh asked his daughter if she would undertake such a journey.

She answered that nothing would please her better as she wearied of Thebes, and desired to see the other great cities of the land, to make herself known to those who dwelt in them, and in each to be proclaimed as its future ruler. Also she wished to look upon the ocean whereof she had heard that it was so big that all the waters of the Nile flowing into it day and night made no difference to its volume.

Thus then began that pilgrimage which afterwards Tua recorded in the history of her reign on the walls of the wonderful temples that she built. Her own wish was that first they should sail south to the frontiers of Egypt, since there she hoped that she might hear some tidings of Rames and his expedition, whereof latterly no certain word had come. This project, however, was over-ruled because in the south there were no great towns, also the inhabitants of the bordering desert were turbulent, and might choose that moment to attack.

So in the end they went down and not up the Nile, tarrying for a while at every great city, and

especially at Abtu, the holy place where the head
of Osiris is buried, and tens of thousands of the great
men of Egypt have their tombs.   Here Tua was
crowned afresh in the very shrine of Osiris amidst
the rejoicings of the people.

Then they sailed away to On, the City of the
Sun, and thence to make offerings at the Great
Pyramids which were built by some of the early kings
who had ruled Egypt, to serve them as their tombs.

Neter-Tua entered the Pyramids to look upon
the bodies of these Pharaohs who had been dead for
thousands of years, and whose deeds were all forgotten, though her father would not accompany her
there because the ways were so steep that he did not
dare to tread them.   Afterwards, with Asti and a
small guard of the Arab chiefs of the desert, she
mounted a dromedary and rode round them in the
moonlight, hoping that she would meet the ghosts
of those kings, and that they would talk with her
as the ghost of her mother had done.   But she saw
no ghosts, nor would Asti try to summon them from
their sleep, although Tua prayed her to do so.

" Leave them alone," said Asti, as they paused
in the shadow of the greatest of the pyramids and
stared at its shining face engraved from base to
summit with many a mystic writing.

" Leave them alone lest they should be angry as
Amen was, and tell your Majesty things which you do
not wish to hear.   Contemplate their mighty works,
such as no monarch can build to-day, and suffer
them to rest therein undisturbed by weaker folk."

" Do you call these mighty works ? " asked Tua
contemptuously, for she was angry because Asti

would not try to raise the dead. " What are they
after all, but so many stones put together by the
labour of men to satisfy their own vanity ?   And
of those who built them what story remains ?
There is none at all save some vain legends.   Now
if *I* live I will rear a greater monument, for history
shall tell of me till time be dead."

" Perhaps, Neter-Tua, if you live and the gods
will it, though for my part I think that these old
stones will survive the story of most deeds."

On the morrow of this visit to the Pyramids
Pharaoh and the Queen his daughter made their
state entry into the great white-walled city of
Memphis, where they were royally received by
Pharaoh's brother, the Prince Abi, who was still the
ruler of all this town and district.   As it chanced
these two had not met since Abi, many years before,
came to Thebes, asking a share in the government
of Egypt and to be nominated as successor to the
throne.

Like every other lord and ruler, he had been
invited to be present at the great ceremony of
the Crowning of Neter-Tua, but at the last moment
sent his excuses, saying that he was ill, which seemed
to be true.   At any rate, the spies reported that he
was confined to his bed, though whether sickness or
his own will took him thither at this moment, there
was nothing to show.   At the time Pharaoh and
his Council wondered a little that he had made no
proposal for the marriage of one of his sons, of whom
he had four, to their royal cousin, Neter-Tua, but
decided that he had not done so because he was sure

that it would not be accepted. For the rest, during
all this period Abi had kept quiet in his own Government, which he ruled well and strongly, remitting
his taxes to Thebes at the proper time with a cere-
monial letter of homage, and even increasing the
amount of them.

So it came about that Pharaoh, who by nature
was kindly and unsuspicious, had long ago put away
all mistrust of his brother, whose ambitions, he was
sure, had come to an end with the birth of an heiress
to the throne.

Yet, when escorted only by five hundred of his
guard, for this was a peaceful visit, Pharaoh rode
into the mighty city and saw how impregnable
were its walls and how strong its gates; saw also that
the streets were lined with thousands of well-armed
troops, doubts which he dismissed as unworthy, did
creep into his heart.   But if he said nothing of them,
Tua, who rode in the chariot with him, was not so silent.

" My father," she said in a low voice while the
crowds shouted their welcome, for they were alone
in the chariot, the horses of which were led, " this
uncle of mine keeps a great state in Memphis."

" Yes, Daughter, why should he not ? He is
its governor."

" A stranger who did not know the truth might
think he was its king, my father, and to be plain,
if I were Pharaoh, and had chosen to enter here, it
would have been with a larger force."

" We can go away when we like, Tua," said
Pharaoh uneasily.

" You mean, my father, that we can go away
when it pleases the Prince your brother to open

those great bronze gates that I heard clash to behind us—then and not before."

At this moment their talk came to an end, for the chariot was stayed at the steps of the great hall where Abi waited to receive his royal guests. He stood at the head of the steps, a huge, coarse, vigorous man of about sixty years of age, on whose fat, swarthy face there was still, oddly enough, some resemblance to the delicate, refined-featured Pharaoh.

Tua summed him up in a single glance, and instantly hated him even more than she had hated Amathel, Prince of Kesh. Also she who had not feared the empty-headed, drunken Amathel, was penetrated with a strange terror of this man whom she felt to be strong and intelligent, and whose great, greedy eyes rested on her beauty as though they could not tear themselves away.

Now they were ascending the steps, and now Prince Abi was welcoming them to his " humble house," giving them their throne names, and saying how rejoiced he was to see them, his sovereigns, within the walls of Memphis, while all the time he stared at Tua.

Pharaoh, who was tired, made no reply, but the young Queen, staring back at him, answered:

" We thank you for your greeting, but then, my uncle Abi, why did you not meet us outside the gates of Memphis where we expected to find its governor waiting to deliver up the keys of Pharaoh's city to the officers of Pharaoh ?"

Now Abi, who had thought to see some shrinking child clothed in the emblems of a queen, looked astonished at this tall and royal maiden who had so sharp a tongue, and found no words to answer her.

So she swept past him and commanded to be shown where she should lodge in Memphis.

They led her to its greatest palace that had been prepared for Pharaoh and herself, a place surrounded by palm groves in the midst of the city, but having studied it with her quick eyes, she said that it did not please her. So search was made elsewhere, and in the end she chose another smaller palace that once had been a temple of Sekhet, the tiger-headed goddess of vengeance and of chastity, whereof the pylon towers fronted on the Nile which at its flood washed against them. Indeed, they were now part of the wall of Memphis, for the great unused gateway between them had been built up with huge blocks of stone.

Surrounding this palace and outside its courts, lay the old gardens of the temple where the priests of Sekhet used to wander, enclosed within a lofty limestone wall. Here, saying that the air from the river would be more healthy for him, Tua persuaded Pharaoh to establish himself and his Court, and to encamp the guards under the command of his friend Mermes, in the outer colonnades and gardens.

When it was pointed out to the Queen that, owing to the lack of dwelling-rooms, none which were fitting were left for her to occupy, she replied that this mattered nothing, since in the old pylon tower were two small chambers hollowed in the thickness of its walls, which were very pleasing to her, because of the prospect of the Nile and the wide flat lands and the distant Pyramids commanded from the lofty roof and window-places. So these chambers, in which none had dwelt for generations, were hastily cleaned out and furnished, and in them Tua and Asti her foster-mother, took up their abode.

CHAPTER VIII

THE MAGIC IMAGE

THAT night Pharaoh and Tua rested in privacy with
those members of the Court whom they had brought
with them, but on the morrow began a round of
festivals such as history scarcely told of in Egypt.
Indeed, the feast with which it opened was more
splendid than any Tua had seen at Thebes even at
the time of her crowning, or on that day of blood
and happiness when Amathel and his Nubian guards
were slain and she and Rames declared their love.
At this feast Pharaoh and the young Queen sat in
chairs of gold, while the Prince Abi was placed on
her right hand, and not on that of Pharaoh as he
should have been as host and subject.

"I am too much honoured," said Tua, looking
at him sideways. "Why do you not sit by Pharaoh,
my uncle?"

"Who am I that I should take the seat of honour
when my sovereigns come to visit me?" answered
Abi, bowing his great head. "Let it be reserved for
the high-priest of Osiris, that Holy One whom, after
Ptah, we worship here above all other deities, for
he is clothed with the majesty of the god of death."

"Of death," said Tua. "Is that why you put
him by my father?"

"Indeed not," replied Abi, spreading out his hands,
"though if a choice must be made, I would rather

that he sat near one who is old and must soon be called the 'ever-living,' than at the side of the loveliest queen that Egypt has ever seen, to whom it is said that Amen himself has sworn a long life," and again he bowed.

"You mean that you think Pharaoh will soon die. Nay, deny it not, Prince Abi, I can read your thoughts, and they are ill-omened," said Tua sharply and, turning her head away, began to watch those about her.

Soon she noticed that behind Abi amongst his other officers stood a tall, grizzled man clad in the robes and cap of an astrologer, who appeared to be studying everything, and especially Pharaoh and herself, for whenever she looked round it was to find his quick, black eyes fixed upon her.

"Who is that man?" she whispered presently to Asti, who waited on her.

"The famous astrologer, Kaku, Queen. I have seen him before when he visited Thebes with the Prince before your birth. I will tell you of him afterwards. Watch him well."

So Tua watched and discovered several things, among them that Kaku observed everything that she and Pharaoh did, what they ate, to whom they spoke, and any words which fell from their lips, such as those that she had uttered about the god Osiris. All of these he noted down from time to time on his waxen tablets, doubtless that he might make use of them afterwards in his interpretation of the omens of the future.

Now, among the ladies of the Court who fanned Pharaoh and waited on him was that dancing girl

F

of Abi's who many years before had betrayed him at
Thebes, Merytra, Lady of the Footstool, now a woman
of middle age, but still beautiful, of whom, although
Tua disliked her, Pharaoh was fond because she was
clever and witty of speech and amused him.   For
this reason, in spite of her history, he had advanced
her to wealth and honour, and kept her about his
person as a companion of his lighter hours.   Something in this woman's manner attracted Tua's atten-
tion, for continually she looked at the astrologer,
Kaku, who suddenly awoke to her presence and
smiled as though he recognised an old friend.   Then,
when it was the turn of another to take her place
behind Pharaoh, Merytra drew alongside of Kaku,
and under shelter of her broad fan, spoke to him
quickly, as though she were making some arrangement
with him, and he nodded in assent, after which they
separated again.

   The feast wore on its weary course till, at length,
the doors opened and slaves appeared bearing the
mummy of a dead man, which they set upon its feet
in the centre of the hall, whereon a toast-master
cried :

   " Drink and be merry, all ye great ones of the
earth, who know not how soon ye shall come to this
last lowly state."

   Now this bringing in of the mummy was a very
ancient rite, but one that had fallen into general
disuse, so that as it chanced Tua, who had never seen
it practised before, looked on it with curiosity not un-
mingled with disgust.

   " Why is a dead king dragged from his sepulchre
back into the world of life, my Uncle ? " she asked,

pointing to the royal emblems with which the corpse was clothed.

" It is no king, your Majesty," answered Abi, " but only the bones of some humble person, or perhaps a block of wood that wears the *urœus* and carries the sceptre in honour of Pharaoh, our chief guest."

Now Tua frowned, and Pharaoh, who had over-heard the talk, said, smiling sadly :

" A somewhat poor compliment, my brother, to one who, like myself, is old and sickly and not far from his eternal habitation. Yet why should I grumble at it who need no such reminder of that which awaits me and all of us ? " and he leaned back in his chair and sighed, while Tua looked at him anxiously.

Then Abi ordered the mummy to be removed, declaring, with many apologies, that it had been brought there only because such was the ancient custom of Memphis, which, unlike Thebes, did not change its fashions. He added that this same body or figure, for he knew not which it was, having never troubled to inquire, had been looked upon by at least thirty Pharaohs, all as dead as it to-day, since it was the same that was used at the royal feasts before, long ago, the seat of government was moved to Thebes.

" If so," broke in Tua, who was angry, " it is time that it should be buried, if flesh and bone, or burned if wood. But Pharaoh is wearied. Have we your leave to depart, my Uncle ? "

Without answering Abi rose, as she thought to dismiss the company. But it was not so, for he raised a great, golden cup of wine and said :

" Before we part, my guests, let Memphis drink
a welcome to the mighty Lord of the Two Lands
who, for the first time in his long and glorious reign,
honours it with his presence here to-day. As he said
to me but now, my royal brother is weak and aged
with sickness, nor can we hope that once his visit is
ended, he will return again to the White-walled City.
But as it chances the gods have given him a boon
which they denied for long, the lovely daughter who
shares his throne, and who, as we believe and pray,
will reign after him when it pleases him to ascend
into the kingdom of Osiris. Yet, my friends, it is
evil that the safe and lawful government of Egypt
should hang on one frail life. Therefore this is the
toast to which I drink—that the Queen Neter-Tua,
Morning Star of Amen, Hathor Strong in Beauty,
who has rejected so many suitors, may before she
departs from among us, find one to her liking, some
husband of royal blood, skilled in the art of rule,
whose strength and knowledge may serve to support
her woman's weakness and inexperience in that sad
hour when she finds herself alone."

Now, the audience, who well understood the
inner meaning and objects of this speech, rose
and cheered furiously, as they had been schooled to
do, emptying their cups to Pharaoh and to Tua and
shouting :

" We know the man. Take him, glorious Queen,
take him, Daughter of Amen, and reign for ever."

" What do they mean ? " muttered Pharaoh,
" I do not understand. Thank them, my daughter,
my voice is weak, and let us begone."

So Tua rose when at length there was silence

and, looking round her with flashing eyes, said in her
clear voice that reached the furthest recesses of the
hall :

" The Pharaoh, my father, and I, the Queen of
the Upper and the Lower Lands, return thanks to you,
our people of this city, for your loyal greetings.
But as for the words that the Prince Abi has spoken,
we understand them not. My prayer is that Pharaoh
may still reign in glory for many years, but if he
departs and I remain, learn, O people, that you have
naught to fear from the weakness and inexperience
of your Queen. Learn also that she seeks no husband,
nor when she seeks will she ever find one within the
walls of Memphis. Rest you well, O people and
you, my Uncle Abi, as now with your good leave we
will do also."

Then, turning, she took her father by the hand
and went without more words, leaving Abi staring
at his guests while his guests stared back at him.

When Tua had reached the pylon tower, where
she lodged, and her ladies had unrobed her and gone,
she called Asti to her from the adjoining chamber
and said :

" You are wise, my nurse, tell me, what did Abi
mean ? "

" If your Majesty cannot guess, then you are
duller than I thought," answered Asti in her quick,
dry fashion, adding ; " however, I will try to translate.
The Prince Abi, your noble uncle, means that he
has trapped you here, and that you shall not leave
these walls save as his wife."

Now fury took hold of Tua.

" How dare he speak such words ? " she gasped,

springing to her feet. "I, the wife of that old river-hog, my father's brother who might be my grand-father, that hideous, ancient lump of wickedness who boasts that he has a hundred sons and daughters; I, the Queen of Egypt, whose birth was decreed by Amen, I—how dare you?" and she ceased, choking in her wrath.

"The question is—how he dares, Queen. Still, that is his plot which he will carry through if he is able. I suspected it from the first, and that is why I always opposed this visit to Memphis, but you will remember you bade me be silent, saying that you had determined to see the most ancient city in Egypt."

"You should not have been silent. You should have said what was in your mind, even if I ordered you from my presence. Neither Abi nor any of his sons proposed for my hand when the others did, therefore *I* suspected nothing——"

"After the fashion of women who have already given their hearts, Queen, and forget that they have other things to give—a kingdom for instance. The snake does not roar like the lion, yet it is more to be feared."

"Once I am out of this place it is the snake that shall have cause to fear, Asti, for I will break its back and throw it writhing to the kites. Nurse, we must leave Memphis."

"That is not easy, Queen, since some ceremony is planned for each of the next eight days. If Pharaoh were to go away without attending them, he would anger all the people of the North which he has not visited since he was crowned."

" Then let them be angered ; Pharaoh can do as he wills."

" Yes, Queen, at least, that is the saying. But do you think that Pharaoh wishes to bring about a civil war and risk his crown and yours ? Listen : Abi is very strong, and under his command he has a greater army than Pharaoh can muster in these times of peace, for in addition to his trained troops, all the thousands of the Bedouin tribes of the desert look on him as lord, and at his word will fall on the wealth of Egypt like famished vultures on a fatted ox. Moreover, here you have but a guard of five hundred men, whereas Abi's regiments, summoned to do you honour, and his ships of war block the river and the southern road. How then will you leave Memphis without his good leave ; how will you even send messengers to summon aid which could not reach you under fifty days ? "

Now when she saw the greatness of the danger, Tua grew quite calm and answered :

" You have done wrong, Asti ; if you foresaw all these things of which I never thought, you should have warned Pharaoh and his Council."

" Queen, I did warn them, and Mermes warned them also, but they would not listen, saying that they were but the idle dreams of one who strives to peep into the future and sees false pictures there. More, Pharaoh sent for me himself, and whilst thanking me and Mermes my husband, told me that he had inquired into the matter. and found no cause to distrust Abi or those under his command. Moreover, he forbade me to speak to your Majesty about it, lest, being but young and a woman, you might be frightened and your pleasure spoilt."

" Who was his counsellor ? " asked Tua.

" A strange one, I think, Queen. You know his waiting-woman, Merytra, she of whom he is so fond, and who stood behind him with a fan this night."

" Aye, I know her," replied Tua, with emphasis. " She was ever whispering with that tall astrologer at the feast. But does Pharaoh take counsel with waiting-ladies of his private household ? "

" With this waiting-lady, it seems, Queen. Perhaps you have not heard all her story. In the year before your birth Merytra came up the Nile with Abi. She was then quite young and very pretty; one of Abi's women. It seems that the Prince struck her for some fault, and being clever she determined to be revenged upon him. Soon she got her chance, for she heard Abi disclose to the astrologer Kaku, that same man whom you saw to-night talking with her, a plan that he had made to murder Pharaoh and declare himself king, from which Kaku dissuaded him. Having this secret and being bold, she fled at once from the ship of Abi, and that night told Pharaoh everything. But he forgave Abi, and sent him home again with honour who should have slain him for his treason. Only Merytra remained in the Court, and from that time forward Pharaoh, who trusted her and was caught by her wit and beauty, made it a habit to send for her when he wished to have news of Memphis where she was born, because she seemed always to know even the most secret things that were passing in that city. Moreover, often her information proved true."

" That is not to be wondered at, Nurse, seeing that doubtless it came from this Kaku, Abi's astrologer and magician."

" No, Queen, it is not to be wondered at, especially as she paid back secret for secret. Well, I believe that after I had warned Pharaoh of what I knew, never mind how, he sent for Merytra, who laughed the tale to scorn, and told him that Abi his brother had long ago abandoned all ambitions, being well content with his great place and power which one of his sons would inherit after him. She told him also that the troops were but assembled to do the greater honour to your Majesties who had no more loyal or loving subject than the Prince Abi, whom for her part she hated with good cause, as she loved Pharaoh and his House—with good cause. If there were any danger, she asked would she dare to put herself within the reach of Abi, the man that she had once betrayed because her heart was pure and true, and she was faithful to her king. So Pharaoh believed her, and I obeyed the orders of Pharaoh, knowing that if I did not do so he would grow angry and perhaps separate me from you, my beloved Queen and fosterling, which, now that Rames has gone, would, I think, have meant my death. Yet I fear that I have erred."

" Yes, I fear also that you have erred, Asti, but everything is forgiven to those who err through love," answered Tua kindly and kissing her. " Oh, my father, Pharaoh! What god fashioned you so weak that an evil spirit in a woman's shape can play the rudder to your policy! Leave me now, Asti, for I must sleep and call on Amen to aid his daughter.

E*

The snare is strong and cunning, but, perchance, in my dreams he will show me how it may be broke."

That night when the feast was ended Merytra, Pharaoh's favoured waiting-maid, did not return with the rest of the royal retinue to the temple where he lodged. As they went from the hall in state she whispered a few words into the ear of the chief Butler of the Household who, knowing that she had the royal pass to come in and out as she would, answered that the gate should be opened to her, and let her go.

So covering her head with a dark cloak Merytra slipped behind a certain statue in the ante-hall and waited till presently a tall figure, also wrapped in a dark cloak, appeared and beckoned to her. She followed it down sundry passages and up a narrow stair that seemed almost endless, until, at length, the figure unlocked a massive door, and when they had passed it, locked it again behind them.

Now Merytra found herself in a very richly furnished room lit by hanging-lamps, that evidently was the abode of one who watched the stars and practised magic, for all about were strange-looking brazen instruments and rolls of papyrus covered with mysterious signs, and suspended above the table a splendid divining ball of crystal. Merytra sank into a chair, throwing off her dark cloak.

" Of a truth, friend Kaku," she said, so soon as she had got her breath, " you dwell very near the gods."

" Yes, dear Merytra," he answered with a dry chuckle, " I keep a kind of half-way house to heaven. Perched here in my solitude I see and make note of what goes on above," and he pointed to the skies, " and retail the information, or as much of it as I think fit, to the groundlings below."

" At a price, I suppose, Kaku."

" Most certainly, at a price, and I may add, a good price. No one thinks much of the physician who charges low fees. Well, you have managed to get here, and after all these years I am glad to see you again, looking almost as young and pretty as ever. Tell me your secret of eternal youth, dear Merytra."

Merytra, who was vain, smiled at this artful flattery, although, in truth, it was well deserved, for at an age when many Egyptians are old, she remained fresh and fair.

" An excellent conscience," she answered, " a good appetite and the virtuous, quiet life, which is the lot of the ladies of Pharaoh's Court—there you have the secret, Kaku. I fear that you keep too late hours, and that is why you grow white and withered like a mummy—not but that you look handsome enough in those long robes of yours," she added to gild the pill.

" It is my labours," he replied, making a wry face, for he too was vain. " My labours for the good of others, also indigestion and the draughts in this accursed tower where I sit staring at the stars, which give me rheumatism. I have got both of them now, and must take some medicine," and filling two goblets from a flask, he handed her one of them, saying, " drink it, you don't get wine like that in Thebes."

" It is very good," said Merytra when she had drunk, " but heavy. If I took much of that I think

I should have ' rheumatism,' too. Now tell me, old friend, am I safe, in this place ? No, not from Pharaoh, he trusts me and lets me go where I will upon his business—but from his royal brother. He used to have a long memory, and from the look of him I do not think that his temper has improved. You may remember a certain slap in the face and how I paid him back for it."

" He never knew it was you, Merytra. Being a mass of self-conceit, he thought that you ran away because he had banished you from his royal presence and presented you—to me."

" Oh, he thought that, did he ! What a vain fool ! "

" It was a very dirty trick you played me, Merytra," went on Kaku with indignation, for the rich wine coursing through his blood revived the sting of his loss. " You know how fond I always was of you, and indeed am still," he added, gazing at her admiringly.

" I felt that I was not worthy of so learned and distinguished a man," she replied, looking at him with her dark eyes. " I should only have hampered your life, dear Kaku, so I went into the household of that poor creature, Pharaoh, instead—Pharaoh's Nunnery we call it. But you will not explain the facts to Abi, will you ? "

" No, I think not, Merytra, if we continue to get on as well as we do at present. But now you are rested, so let us come to business, for otherwise you will have to stop here all night and Pharaoh would be angry."

" Oh, to Set with Pharaoh ! Though it is true

that he is a good paymaster, and knows the value of a clever woman. Now, what is this business ? "

The old astrologer's face grew hard and cunning. Going to the door he made sure that it was locked and drew a curtain over it. Then he took a stool and sat himself down in front of Merytra, in such a position that the light fell on her face while his own remained in shadow.

" A big business, Merytra, and by the gods I do not know that I should trust you with it. You tricked me once, you have tricked Pharaoh for years ; how do I know that you will not play the same game once more and earn me an order to cut my own throat, and so lose life and soul together ? "

" If you think that, Kaku, perhaps you will unlock the door and give me an escort home, for we are only wasting time."

" I don't know what to think, for you are as cunning as you are beautiful. Listen, woman," he continued in a savage whisper, and clasping her by the wrist. " If you are false, I tell you that you shall die horribly, for if the knife and poison fail, I am no charlatan, I have arts. I can make you turn loathsome to the sight and waste away, I can haunt you at nights so that you may never sleep a wink, save in full sunshine, and I will do it all and more. If I die, Merytra, we go together. Now will you swear to be true, will you swear it by the oath of oaths ? "

The spy looked about her. She knew Kaku's power which was famous throughout Egypt, and that it was said to be of the most evil sort, and she feared him.

" It seems that this is a dangerous affair," she replied uneasily, " and I think that I can guess your aim. Now if I help you, Kaku, what am *I* to get ? "

" Me," he answered.

" I am flattered, but what else ? "

" After Pharaoh the greatest place and the most power in Egypt, as the wife of Pharaoh's Vizier."

" The wife ? Doubtless from what I have heard of you, Kaku, there would be other wives to share these honours."

" No other wife—upon the oath, none, Merytra."

She thought a moment, looking at the wizened but powerful-faced old magician, then answered:

" I will take the oath and keep my share of it. See that you keep yours, Kaku, or it will be the worse for you, for women have their own evil power."

" I know it, Merytra, and from the beginning the wise have held that its spirit dwells, not in the heart or brain or liver, but in the female tongue. Now stand up."

She obeyed, and from some hidden place in the wall Kaku produced a book, or rather a roll of magical writings, that was encased in iron, the metal of the evil god, Typhon.

" There is no other such book as this," he said, " for it was written by the greatest of wizards who lived before Mena, when the god-kings ruled in Egypt, and I, myself, took it from among his bones, a terrible task for his Ka rose up in the grave and threatened me. He who can read in that book, as I can, has much strength, and let him beware who breaks an oath taken on that book. Now press it to your heart, Merytra, and swear after me."

Then he repeated a very terrible oath, for should it be violated it consigned the swearer to shame, sickness and misfortune in this world, and to ever-lasting torments in the next at the claws and fangs of beast-headed demons who dwell in the darkness beyond the sun, appointing, by name, those beings who should work the torments, and summoning them as witnesses to the bond.

Merytra listened, then said,

" You have left out your part of the oath, Friend, namely, that you promise that I shall be the only wife of Pharaoh's Vizier and hold equal power with him."

" I forgot," said Kaku, and added the words.

Then they both swore, touching their brows with the book, and as she looked up again, Merytra saw a strange, flame-like light pulse in the crystal globe that hung above her head, which became presently infiltrated with crimson flowing through it as blood might flow from a wound, till it glowed dull red, out of which redness a great eye watched her. Then the eye vanished and the blood vanished, and in place of them Queen Neter-Tua sat in glory on her throne, while the nations worshipped her, and by her side sat a man in royal robes whose face was hidden in a cloud.

"What do you see ? " asked Kaku, following her gaze to the crystal.

She told him, and he pondered a while, then answered doubtfully:

" I think it is a good omen ; the royal consort sits beside her. Only why was his face hidden ? "

" I am sure I do not know," answered Merytra.

" I think that strong, red wine of yours was doctored and has got into my head. But, come, we have sworn this oath, which I dare say will work in more ways than we guess, for such accursed swords have two edges to them. Now out with the plot, and throw a cloth over that crystal for I want to see no more pictures."

" It seems a pity since you have such a gift of vision," replied Kaku in the same dubious voice. Yet he obeyed, tying up the shining ball in a piece of mummy wrapping which he used in his spells.

" Now," he said, " I will be brief. My fat master, Abi, means to be Pharaoh of Egypt, and it seems that the best way to do so is by climbing into his niece's throne, where most men would like to sit."

" You mean by marrying her, Kaku."

" Of course. What else ? He who marries the Queen, rules in right of the Queen."

" Indeed. Do you know anything of Neter-Tua ? "

" As much as any other man knows; but what do you mean ? "

" I mean that I shall be sorry for the husband who marries her against her will, however beautiful and high-placed she may be. I tell you that woman is a flame. She has more strength in her than all the magicians in Egypt, yourself among them. They say she is a daughter of Amen, and I believe it. I believe that the god dwells in her, and woe be to him whom she may chance to hate, if he comes to her as husband."

" That is Abi's business, is it not ? Our business,

Merytra, is to get him there. Now we may take it this will not be with her consent."

" Certainly not, Kaku," she answered. " The gossip goes that she is in love with young Count Rames, who fought and killed the Prince of Kesh before her eyes, and now has gone to make amends to the king his father at the head of an army."

" That may be true, Merytra. Why not ? He is her foster-brother and of royal blood, bold, too, and handsome, they say. Well, queens have no business to be in love. That is the privilege of humbler folk like you and me, Merytra. Say, is she suspicious—about Prince Abi, I mean ? "

" I do not know, but Asti, her nurse and favourite lady, the wife of Mermes and mother of Rames, is suspicious enough. She is a greater magician than you are, Kaku, and if she could have had her way Pharaoh would never have set foot in Memphis. But I got your letter and over-persuaded him, the poor fool. You see he thinks me faithful to his House, and that is why I am allowed to be here to-night, to collect information."

"Ah ! Well, what Asti knows the Queen will know, and she is stronger than Pharaoh, and not-withstanding all Abi's ships and soldiers, may break away from Memphis and make war upon him. So it comes to this—Pharaoh must stay here, for his daughter will not desert him."

" How will you make him stay here, Kaku ? Not by——" and she glanced towards the shrouded crystal.

" Nay, no blood if it can be helped. He must

not even seem to be a prisoner, it is too dangerous.
But there are other ways."

" What ways ? Poison ? "

" Too dangerous again. Now, if he fell sick as
he has been sick before, and could not stir, it would
give us time to bring about the marriage, would it
not ? Oh ! I know that he is well at present—for
him, but look here, Merytra, I have something to
show you."

Then going to a chest Kaku took from it a plain
box of cedar wood which was shaped like a mummy
case, and, lifting off its lid, revealed within it a waxen
figure of the length of a hand. This figure was
beautifully fashioned to the living likeness of Pharaoh,
and crowned with the double crown of Egypt.

" What is it ? " asked Merytra, shrinking back.
" An *ushapti* to be placed in his tomb ? "

" No, woman, a magic Ka fashioned with many
a spell out of yonder ancient roll, that can bring *him*
to the tomb if it be rightly used, as you shall use it."

" I ! " she exclaimed, starting. " How ? "

" Thus : You, as one of Pharaoh's favourite
ladies, have charge of the chamber where he sleeps.
Now you must make shift to enter there alone and
lay this figure in his bed, that the breath of Pharaoh
may enter into it. Then take it from the bed and
say these words, ' Figure, figure, I command thee
by the power within thee and in the name of the
Lord of Ill, that as thy limbs waste, so shall the
limbs of him in whose likeness thou art fashioned
waste also.' Having spoken thus, hold the legs
of the image over the flame of a lamp until it be half
melted, and convey the rest of it away to your

own sleeping-place and hide it there. So it shall come about that during that night the nerves and muscles in the legs of Pharaoh will wither and grow useless to him, and he be paralysed and unable to stir. Afterwards, if it be needful, I will tell you more."

Now, bold though she was, Merytra grew afraid.

" I cannot do it," she said, " it is black sorcery against one who is a god, and will bring my soul to hell. Find some other instrument, or place the waxen imp in the bed of Pharaoh yourself, Kaku."

The face of the magician grew fierce and cruel.

" Come with me, Merytra," he said, and taking her by the wrist he led her to the open window-place whence he observed the stars.

So giddy was the height at the top of this lofty tower that the houses beneath looked small and far away, and the sky quite near.

" Behold Memphis and the Nile, and the wide lands of Egypt gleaming in the moonlight, and the Pyramids of the ancient kings. You wish to rule over all these, like myself—do you not, Merytra ?— and if you obey me you shall do so."

" And if I do not obey ? "

" Then I will throw my spell upon you, and your senses shall leave you and you shall fall head-long to that white line, which is a street, and before to-morrow morning the dogs will have picked your broken bones, so that none can know you, for you have heard too much to go hence alive unless it be to do my bidding. Oh, no ! Think not to say ' I will ' and afterwards deceive me, for that image which you take with you is my servant, and will keep watch on you and make report to me and to the god, its master. Now choose."

"I will obey," said Merytra faintly, and as she spoke she thought that she heard a laugh in the air outside the window.

"Good. Now hide the box beneath your cloak and drop it not, for if so that which is within will call aloud after you, and they will kill you for a sorceress. Unless my word come to you, lay the figure in Pharaoh's bed to-morrow evening, and at the hour of moonrise hold its limbs in the flame in your own chamber, and hide it away, and afterwards bring it back to me that I may enchant it afresh, if there be any need. Now come, and I will guard you to the gates of the old temple of Sekhet, where Pharaoh dwells."

CHAPTER IX

THE DOOM OF PHARAOH

On the morrow when the lady Asti came to dress the Queen for that day's ceremony, she asked her if Amen had given her the wisdom that she sought.

" Not so," answered the young Queen, " all he gave me was very bad dreams, and in every one of them was mixed up that waiting woman of my father, Merytra, of whom you spoke to me. If I believed in omens I should say that she was about to bring some evil upon our House."

" It may well be so, Queen," answered Asti, " and in that case I think that she is at the work. At any rate, watching from the little window of my room, by the light of the moon I saw her return across the temple court at midnight. Moreover, it seemed to me that she was carrying something beneath her robe."

" Whence did she return ? "

" From the city, I suppose. She has Pharaoh's pass, and can go in and out when she will. I have caused Mermes to question the officer of the guard, and he says that she came to the gate accompanied by a tall man wrapped in a dark cloak, who spoke with her earnestly, and left her. From his description I think it must have been the astrologer, Kaku, with whom she was talking at the feast."

" That is bad news, Nurse. What else have you to tell ? "

" Only this, Queen. The gates are guarded more closely even than we thought. I tried to send out a man to Thebes this morning with a message on my own account—never mind what it was—and the sentries turned him back."

" By the gods ! " exclaimed Tua, " before I have reigned a year every gate in Memphis shall be melted down for cooking vessels, and I will set their captains to work in the desert mines. Nay, such threats are foolishness, I'll not threaten, I'll strike when the time comes, but that is not yet. Can I speak with Pharaoh ? "

" No, Queen. He is up already giving audience to the nobles of Memphis, and trying cases from the Lower Land with his Counsellors; until it is time to start for this ceremony of the laying of the foundation-stone of the temple, whither you accompany him in state. Also it is as well—by to-night we may learn more. Come, let me set the crown upon your head that these dogs of Memphis may know their mistress."

The ceremony proved very wearisome. First there was the long chariot ride through the crowded, shouting streets, Pharaoh and Abi going in the first chariot, and Tua, attended by Abi's eldest daughter, a round-eyed lady much older than herself, in the second. Next came the office of the priests of Amen, over which Neter-Tua as daughter of Amen and high-priestess, must preside, to dedicate the temple to the glory of the god. Then the foundation deposit of little vases of offerings and models of workmen's tools, and a ring drawn from Pharaoh's hand engraved with his royal name, were blessed and set by the masons in hollows prepared for them, and the two great corner-stones let down, hiding them for ever, and declared respectively by Pharaoh and by Neter-Tua, Morning Star of Amen, Joint Sovereign of Egypt, to be well and truly laid.

Afterwards architects, those who " drew the line," exhibited plans of the temple, and received gifts from Pharaoh, and when these things were done came the mid-day feast and speeches.

At length all was over, and the great procession returned by another route to the temple of Sekhet, where Pharaoh lodged, a very tedious journey in the hot sun, since it involved a circuit of the endless walls of Memphis, with stoppages before all the temples of the gods, at each of which Pharaoh must make offerings. Nor, weary as he was, might he rest, for in the outer court of the old shrine thrones had been set up and seated on them he and Tua must hear petitions till sunset and give judgment, or postpone them for further consideration.

At last these came to an end, but, as Pharaoh, tired out, rose from his throne, Abi, his brother, who all this time had not left them, said that he also had a private petition to prefer. So they went into an inner court that had been a sanctuary, and sat down again, there being present besides the scribes only Pharaoh, the Queen, some councillors, Mermes, captain of the guard, and certain women of the royal household, among them Asti, the Queen's nurse, and Merytra, Pharaoh's favourite attendant. With Abi were his astrologer, Kaku, his two eldest sons, and a few of the great officers of his government, also the high-priests of the temples of Memphis, and three powerful chiefs of the Desert tribes.

" What is your prayer, my brother ? " asked Pharaoh, as soon as the doors were closed.

" A great one, your Majesties," answered the Prince, prostrating himself, " which for the good of Egypt, and for your own good, and for my good, who reverence you as a loyal subject, I pray that you will be pleased to grant." Then he drew himself up and said slowly, " I am here to ask the hand of the glorious Queen Neter-Tua, daughter of Amen, in marriage."

Now Pharaoh stared at him, while Tua, who knew well what was coming, turned her head aside, and asked a councillor who stood near, if in the history of the land any Queen of Egypt had ever married her uncle.

The councillor who was noted for his historical studies, answered that at the moment he could recall no such case.

" Then," said Tua coolly, and still addressing him, " it seems that it would be scarcely wise to create a precedent which other poor young women of the royal race might be called upon to follow."

Pharaoh caught something of the words, though Abi did not for they were spoken in a low voice, and bethought him of a way out of his difficulty.

" The Queen Neter-Tua sits at my side, and is co-regent with me of this kingdom, her mind is my mind, and what she approves it is probable I shall approve. Prefer your request to her," he said.

So Abi turned to the Queen, and laying his hands upon his heart, bowed, ogled, and began :

" A burning love of your most excellent Majesty moves me——"

" I pray you, my Uncle," interrupted Tua, " correct your words, which should begin ' A burning love of your most excellent Majesty's throne and power move me,' and so on."

Now Abi frowned while everyone else smiled, not excepting Pharaoh and the astrologer, Kaku. Again he began his speech, but so confusedly that presently Tua stopped him for the second time, saying :

" I am not deaf, most noble prince, my Uncle. I heard the words you used to Pharaoh, and even understood their import. In fact, I have already consulted our councillor here, a learned master of the law, as to the legality of such an alliance as you propose, and he gives his judgment against it."

Now Abi glared at the Councillor, a humble, dusty old man who spent all his life among rolls and chronicles.

" May it please your Majesty," this lawyer exclaimed in a thin, agitated voice, " I only said there was no record of such a marriage that I can remember, though once I think a queen adopted a nephew, who afterwards became Pharaoh."

" It is the same thing, Friend," replied Tua sweetly, " for that of which there is no record in the long history of Egypt must of necessity be illegal. Still, if my uncle here wishes to adopt me, I thank him, though his lawful heirs may not, and the matter is one that can be considered."

Now, guessing that he was being played with, Abi grew angry.

"I have put a plain question to your Majesty," he said, "and perhaps I am worthy of a plain answer. As all men know, O Queen, it is time that you should be wed, and I offer myself as your husband. It is true that I am somewhat older than you are——"

"In what year was the Prince Abi born, the same as yourself, did you say?" asked Tua in an audible aside of the aged and learned Councillor, who thereon vanished behind the throne, and was seen no more.

"But," went on Abi, taking no notice of this interruption, "on the other hand I have much to offer. I rule here, your Majesties, who am also of the royal blood, and there is some disaffection in the North, especially among the great Bedouin tribes of the Desert who watch the frontier of the Kingdom. Now if this alliance comes about, and in days to be I sit upon the double throne as King-Consort of Egypt, they will be loyal, and north and south will be united more closely than they ever were before. Whereas if it does not come about——" Here Kaku, pretending to brush a fly from his face, caught his hand in Abi's robe, a signal at which his master paused.

"Go on, my Uncle, I pray you," said Tua. "If it does not come about, what then?"

"Then, Queen, there may be trouble. Nay, leave me alone, Magician, I will speak the truth, chance what may. Pharaoh, you have reigned for many years; yes, forty times has the Nile overflowed its banks since we laid our divine father in the tomb.

Now, during all those years but one child has been born to you, and that after I came to Thebes to pray you to name me as your heir. Know, Pharaoh, that there are many who find this strange, and wonder whether this beautiful queen, who is called Daughter of Amen, and resembles you so little in body or in mind, sits rightfully on the throne of Egypt. If I marry her these questionings will cease. If I do not marry her the whisperings of men may grow to a wind that will blow the crown from off her head."

Now a gasp of fear and wonder rose from all who heard this bold and treasonable speech, and Tua, reddening to the eyes, bent forward as though to answer. But before ever a word had passed her lips Pharaoh sprang from his seat transformed with rage. All his patient gentleness was gone, and he looked so fierce and royal that everyone present there, even Abi himself, quailed before him.

" Is it for this that I have borne with you for so long, my brother ? " he cried, rending at his robes. " Is it for this that I spared you years ago in Thebes, when your life was forfeit for your treachery ? Is it for this that I have suffered you to rise to great honour, and to rule here almost as a king in my city of Memphis ? Was it not enough that I should sit quiet, while you, an old man, the son of our father's barbarian slave, the loose-living despot, dare to ask for the pure hand of Egypt's Queen in marriage, you, her uncle, who might well be her grandfather also ? Must I also hear your foul mouth beslime her royal birth, and the honour of her divine mother, and spit sneers at Amen, Father of the gods ? Well, Amen shall deal with you when you come to the

doors of his Eternal House, but here on earth I
am his son and servant. Mermes, call my guards,
and arrest this man and hold him safe. At Thebes,
whither we depart to-morrow, he shall be judged
according to our law."

Now Mermes blew a shrill call on the silver
whistle that hung about his neck, and, springing
forward, seized the Prince by the arm. Abi drew
his sword to cut him down, and at the sight of the
blade, all who were with him rushed to the door to
escape, sweeping before them certain of Pharaoh's
ladies, among them the waiting-woman, Merytra.
But before ever they could pass it, the guards who
had heard the signal of Mermes, ran in with lifted
spears, driving them back again. Leaping upon
Abi, they tore the sword from his hand, and threw
him to the ground, huddling the rest together like
frightened sheep.

"Bind this traitor and keep him safe, for to-
morrow he accompanies us to Thebes," said Pharaoh.

"What of his sons, and those with him, your
Majesty?" asked the officer of the guard.

"Let them go," answered Pharaoh wearily,
"for they have not sinned against us. Let them
go, and take warning from their master's fate."

Now, as it chanced in the confusion, Merytra had
been pushed against Kaku.

"Hearken," whispered the astrologer into the
woman's ear. "Do as I bid you last night, and
all will yet be well. Do it or die. Do you hear
me?"

"I hear, and I will obey," answered Merytra in
the same low voice.

Then they were separated, for the guards took Kaku by the arm and thrust him out of the temple together with the sons of Abi.

An hour later Mermes and Asti stood before Pharaoh, and prayed him that he would depart from Memphis that very night, saying that such was the counsel also of the Queen and of his officers. But Pharaoh was tired out, and would not listen.

"To-morrow, when I have slept, will be time enough," he answered. "Moreover, shall I fly from my own city like a thief when naught is ready for our journey? Why do you press me to such a coward's act?" he added peevishly.

"For this reason, your Majesty," answered Mermes. "We are sure there is a plot to keep you here. This afternoon you could not have gone, had you tried, but to-night, Abi being a prisoner, his people are dismayed, and having no leader will open the gates. By to-morrow one may be found, and they will be double-barred and guarded."

"What!" asked the King scornfully, "do you mean that I am a prisoner also, and here in Egypt, which I rule? Nay, good friends, at Pharaoh's word those gates will open. Or if they do not, I will pull down Memphis stone by stone, and drive out its people to share their caves with jackals. Do they think because I am kind and gentle, that I cannot lift the sword if there be need? Have they forgotten how I smote those rebels in my youth, and gave their cities to the flames, and set my yoke on Syria, that aided them. We march to-morrow, and not before. I have spoken."

Now Mermes bowed and turned to go, since

when those words had passed Pharaoh's lips it was not lawful to answer them. Yet Asti dared to do so.

"O Pharaoh," she said, "be not wrath with your servant. Pharaoh, as you know, I have skill in divination, the spirits of the dead whisper at times in my ears of things that are to be. It seemed to me just now when having left the presence of the Queen, my foster-child, I stood a while alone in the darkness, that the divine Majesty of the great lady, the royal wife, Ahurá, who was my friend and mistress, stood beside me and said :

" ' Go, Asti, to Pharaoh, and say to Pharaoh that great danger threatens him and our royal daughter. Say to him—Fly from Memphis, lest there he should be prepared for burial, and the Star of Amen hidden by a cloud of shame. Bid him beware of one about his throne, and of that evil magician with whom she made a pact last night.' "

Now Pharaoh looked at Asti and said :

"O dreamer of dreams, interpret your own dream. Who is she about my throne of whom I should beware, and who is the magician with whom she made a pact ? "

"The divine Queen did not tell me, Pharaoh," answered Asti stubbornly, "but my own skill tells me. She is Merytra, your favourite, and the magician is Kaku, whom she visited last night."

"What !" exclaimed Pharaoh, laughing. "That long-legged old astrologer with the painted cap who ran so fast when his master was taken ? Why ! he is nothing but a spy who has been in my pay for years ; a charlatan who pretends to knowledge that he may win the secrets of his Prince. And Merytra, too, Merytra, who in bygone times warned me of this Abi's foolish plot. Asti, you are high-born and wise, one whom I love and honour much, as does the Queen, my daughter, but you can still be jealous, as I have noted long. Asti, be not deceived, it was jealousy of Merytra that whispered in your ears, not the spirit of the divine Ahura. Now go and take your terrors with you, for this dark conspirator, Merytra, waits in my chamber to unrobe me, and talk me to sleep with her pleasant jests and gossip."

" Pharaoh has spoken, I go," said Asti in her quiet voice. " May Pharaoh's rest be sweet, and his awaking happy."

That night Tua could not sleep. Whenever she shut her eyes visions rose before her mind, terrifying, fantastic visions in all of which the fat and hideous Abi played a part. Thus she saw again the scene at her father's fatal feast to the Prince of Kesh, when Asti by her magic had caused the likeness of a monkey to come from the juggler's vase. Only now it was Abi who emerged from the vase, a terrible Abi, with a red sword in his hand, and Pharaoh's crown upon his head. He leapt from the mouth of the vase, he devoured her with his greedy eyes, with stealthy steps he came to seize her, and she could not stir an inch, something held her fast upon her throne.

She could bear it no more—she opened her eyes, staring at the darkness, and out of the darkness came voices, telling of death and war.

She thrust her fingers into her ears, and tried to
fix her thoughts on Rames, that bright-eyed, light-
footed lover of hers, whom she so longed to see again,
without whom she was so lonely and undefended.

Where was Rames? she wondered. What fate
had overtaken him? Something in her seemed
to answer—Death. Oh! if Rames were dead,
what should she do? Of what use was it to be
Queen of Egypt, the first woman in the world, if
Rames were dead?

Loneliness, insufferable loneliness seemed to get
a hold of her. She slipped from her bed, and through
the doorway of her little pylon chamber. Now she
was upon the narrow stair, and in face of her was
that other chamber where Asti slept. Someone
was talking with her! Perhaps Mermes was with
his wife, and if so she could not enter. No, it was
Asti's voice, and, listening, she could hear her murmuring prayers or invocations in solemn tones.
She pushed open the door and entered. A little
lamp burned in the room, and by its feeble light
she saw the white-robed Asti, whose long hair fell
about her, standing with upturned eyes and arms
outstretched to Heaven. Suddenly Asti saw her
also, though but dimly for she stood in the dense
shadow, and knew her not.

"Advance, O thou Ghost, and declare thyself,
for never was thy help more needed," she said.

"It is no ghost, but I," said Tua. "What dealings are these that you have with ghosts at this
deadest hour of the night, Asti? Do not enough
terrors encompass us that you must needs call on
your familiar spirits to add to them?"

" I call on the spirits to save us from them,
Queen, for, like you, I think that we are set in the
midst of perils. This night is full of sorcery ; I
scent it in the air, and strive to match spell with
spell. But why do you not sleep ? "

" I cannot, Asti, I cannot. Fear has got hold
of me. Oh ! I would that we had never come to
this hateful Memphis, or set eyes upon its ill-omened
lord, that foul brute who seeks to make a wife of
me."

" Be not afraid, Lady," said Asti, throwing her
arms about Tua's slight and quivering form. " To-
morrow morning we march ; I have it from Pharaoh,
and already the guard make preparation, while as
for the accursed Abi, he is in prison."

" There is no prison that will hold him, Asti,
save the grave. Oh ! why did not my Father
command him to be slain, as I would have done ?
Then, at least, we should be free of him, and he could
never marry me."

" Because it was otherwise decreed, O Neter-Tua,
and Pharaoh must fulfil his fate and ours, for though
he is so gentle, none can turn him."

As she spoke the words, somewhere, far beneath
them, arose a cry, a voice of one in dread or woe,
and with it the sound of feet upon the stairs.

" What passes ? " said Asti, leaping to the
door.

" Pharaoh is dead or dying," answered the
terrified voice without. " Let her Majesty come to
Pharaoh."

They threw on their garments, they ran down
the narrow stair and across the halls till they came
F

to the chamber of Pharaoh. There upon his bed he lay and about him were the physicians of his Court. He was speechless, but his eyes were open, and he knew his daughter, for, raising his hand feebly, he beckoned to her, and pointed at his feet.

" What is it, man ? " she asked of the head physician, who, by way of answer, lifted the linen on the bed, and showed her Pharaoh's legs and feet, white and withered as though with fire.

" What sickness is this ? " asked Tua again.

" We know not, O Queen," answered the physician, " for in all our lives we have never seen its like. The flesh is suddenly wasted, and the limbs are paralysed."

" But I know," broke in Asti. " This is not sickness, it is sorcery. Pharaoh has been smitten by some foul spell of the Prince Abi, or of his wizards. Say, who was with him last ? "

" It seems that the Lady of the Footstool, Merytra, sang him to sleep, as was her custom," answered the physician, " and left him about two hours ago, so say the guard. When I came in to see how his Majesty rested but now, I found him thus."

Now Tua lifted up her head and spoke, saying :

" My divine Father is helpless, and therefore again I rule alone in Egypt. Hear me and obey. Let the Prince Abi be brought from his prison to the inner hall, for I would question him at once. Let the waiting-woman, Merytra, be brought also under guard with drawn swords."

The officer of the watch bowed and departed to

do the bidding of her Majesty, while others went to light the hall.

Soon he returned to an outer chamber whither Tua had withdrawn herself while the physicians examined Pharaoh.

" O Queen," he said, with a frightened face, " be not wrath, but the Prince Abi has gone. He has escaped out of his prison, and the waiting-woman, Merytra, is gone also."

" How came this about ? " asked Tua in a cold voice.

" O Queen, the small gate was open, for people passed in and out of it continually, making preparation for to-morrow's march. It seems that about an hour ago the lady Merytra came to the gate and showed Pharaoh's signet to the officer, saying that she was on Pharaoh's business. With her went a fat man dressed in the robe of a master of camels that in the darkness the officer thought was a certain Arab of the Desert who has been to and fro about the camels. It is believed that this man was none other than the Prince Abi, dressed in the Arab's robe, and that he escaped from his cell by some secret passage which was known to him, a passage of the old priests. The Arab, whose robes he wore, cannot be found, but perhaps he is asleep in some corner."

" Bar the gates," said Tua, " and let none pass in or out. Asti, take men with you, and go search the room where Merytra slept. Perchance she has returned again."

So Asti went, and a while after re-appeared carrying something enveloped in a cloth.

"Merytra has gone, O Queen," she said in an ominous voice, "leaving this behind hidden beneath her bed," and she placed the object on a table.

"What is it ? The mummy of a child ?" asked Tua, shrinking back.

"Nay, Queen, the image of a man."

Then throwing aside the cloth Asti revealed the waxen figure shaped to the exact likeness of Pharaoh, or rather what remained of it, for the legs were molten and twisted, and in them could be seen the bones of ivory and the sinews of thin wire, about which they had been moulded. Also beneath the chin where the tongue would be, sharp thorns had been thrust up to the roof of the mouth. The thing was life-like and horrible, and as it was, so was the dumb and stricken Pharaoh on his bed.

Neter-Tua hid her eyes for a little, and leaned against the wall, then she drew herself up and said :

"Call the physicians and the members of the Council, and those who can be spared of the officers of the guard, that everyone of them may see and bear witness to the hideous crime which has been worked against Pharaoh by his brother, the Prince Abi, and the wizard Kaku, and their accomplice, the woman Merytra."

So they were called, and came, and when they saw the dreadful thing lying in its waxen whiteness before them, they wailed and cursed those who had wrought this abominable sorcery.

"Curse them not," said Neter-Tua, "who are already accursed, and given over to the Devourer of Souls when their time shall come. Make a record of this deed, O Scribes, and do it swiftly."

So the scribes wrote the matter down, and the Queen and others who were present signed the writings as witnesses. Then Neter-Tua commanded that they should take the image and destroy it before it worked more evil, and a priest of Osiris who was present seized it and departed.

But Neter-Tua went to Pharaoh's room and knelt by his bed, watching him, for he seemed to be asleep. Presently he awoke, and looked round him wildly, moving his lips. For a while he could not speak, then of a sudden his voice burst from him in a hoarse, unnatural cry.

"They have bewitched me! I burn, I burn!" he screamed, rolling himself to and fro upon the bed. "Avenge me, my daughter, and fear nothing, for the gods are about you. I see their awful eyes. Oh! I burn, I burn!"

Then his head fell back, and the peace of death descended on his tortured face.

Tua kissed his dead brow, and knelt at his side in prayer. After a little while she rose and said:

"It has pleased Pharaoh, the just and perfect, to depart to his everlasting habitation in Osiris. Make it known that this god is dead, and that I rule alone in Egypt. Send hither the priest of Osiris, that he may repeat the Ritual of Departing, and you, physicians, do your office."

So the priest came, but at the door Asti caught him by the hand and asked:

"How did you destroy the image of wax?"

" I burned it upon the altar in the old sanctuary of this temple," he answered.

" O, Fool ! " said Asti, " you should have buried it. Know that with the enchanted thing you have burned away the life of Pharaoh also."

Then that priest fell swooning to the ground, and another had to be summoned to utter the Ritual of Departing.

CHAPTER X

THE COMING OF THE KA

Now it was morning, and while the physicians embalmed the body of Pharaoh as best they could, Tua consulted with her officers. Long and earnest was that council, for all of them felt that their danger was very great. Abi had escaped, and if he were re-taken, none knew better than he that his death and that of all his House would be the reward of his crimes and sorceries which could only be covered up in one way—by marriage with the Queen of Egypt. Moreover, he had thousands of soldiers in the city and around it, all of them sworn to his service, whereas the royal guard was but five companies, each of a hundred men, trapped in a snare of streets and stone.

One of them suggested that they should break a way through the wall of the temple, and escape to the royal barges that lay moored on the Nile beneath them, and this plan was approved. But when they went to set about the work it was seen that these barges had been seized and were already sailing away up the river. So but two alternatives remained—to bide within the fortifications of the old temple, and send out messengers for help, or to march through the city boldly, break down the gates if these were shut against them, seize boats, and sail up the Nile for some loyal town, or if that could not be done, to take their chance in the open lands.

Now some favoured one scheme, and some the other, so that at last the decision was left with her Majesty. She thought awhile, then said:

"Here I will not stay, to be starved out as we must ere ever an army could be gathered to rescue us, and be given into the power of that vile and wicked man, the murderer of the good god, my father. Better that I should die fighting in the streets, for then at least I shall pass undefiled to join him in his eternal habitation beyond the sun. We march at midnight."

So they bowed beneath her word, and made ready while the women of his household raised a death-wail for Pharaoh, and criers standing on the high towers proclaimed the accession of Neter-Tua, Morning-Star of Amen, Glorious in Ra, Hathor, Strong in Beauty, as sole Lord and Sovereign of the North and South, and of Egypt's subject lands. Again and again they proclaimed it, and of the multitudes who listened beneath, some cheered, but the most remained silent, fearing the vengeance of their Prince, whom the heralds summoned to do homage, but who made no sign.

Night came at last. At a signal the gates were opened, and through them, borne upon the shoulders of his Councillors, preceded by a small body of guards, and followed by his women and household, went the remains of Pharaoh, in a coffin roughly fashioned from the sycamore timbers of the temple. With solemn step and slow, they went as though they feared no harm, the priests and singers chanting

some ancient, funeral hymn. Next followed the
baggage bearers, and after these the royal bodyguard in the midst of whom the Queen, clad in mail,
as a man, rode in a chariot, and with her the waiting-
lady, Asti, wife of Mermes.

At first all went well, for the great square in
front of the temple was empty. The procession
of the body of Pharaoh passed it, and vanished down
the street that led to the main gate, a mile away.
Now the guard formed into line to enter this street
also, when suddenly, barring the mouth of it, appeared
great companies of men who had been hidden in
other streets.

A voice cried " Halt ! " and while the guards
re-shaped themselves into a square about the person
of the Queen, an embassy of officers, among whom
were recognised the four lawful sons of Abi, advanced
and demanded in the Prince's name that her Majesty
should be given over to them, saying that she would
be treated with all honour, and that those who
accompanied her might go free.

" Answer that the Queen of Egypt does not
yield herself into the hands of rebels, and of murderers ; then fall on them, and slay them all," cried
Neter-Tua when Mermes, her captain, had given
her this message.

So he went forward and returned the answer,
and next moment a flight of arrows from the
Queen's guard laid low the four sons of Abi, and
most of those who were with them.

Then the fight began, one of the fiercest that
had been known in Egypt for many a generation.
The royal regiment, it is true, was but small, but they

F*

were picked men, and mad with despair and rage. Moreover, Tua the Queen played no woman's part that night, for when these charged, striving to cut a path through the opposing hosts, she charged with them, and by the moonlight was seen standing like an angry goddess in her chariot, and loosing arrows from her bow. Also no hurt came to her or those with her, or even to the horses that drew her. It was as though she were protected by some unseen strength, that caught the sword cuts and turned aside the points of spears.

Yet it availed not, for the men of Abi were a multitude, and the royal guard but very few. Slowly, an ever-lessening band, they were pressed back, first to the walls of the old temple of Sekhet, and then within its outer court. Now all who were left of them, not fifty men under the command of Mermes, strove to hold the gate. Desperately they fought, and one by one went down to death beneath the rain of spears.

Tua had dismounted from her chariot, and leaning on her bow, for all her arrows were spent, watched the fray with Asti at her side. With a yell the troops of Abi rushed through the gate, killing as they came. Now, surrounded by all who remained to her, not a dozen men, they were driven back through the inner courts, through the halls, to the pylon stairs.

Here the last stand was made. Step by step they held the stairs, till at length there were left upon their feet only Tua, Asti and Mermes, her husband, who was sorely wounded in many places. At the little landing between the rooms of the Queen and Asti while the assailants paused a moment, the Captain Mermes, mad with grief and pain, turned and kissed his wife. Next he bowed before the Queen, saying :

" What a man may do, I have done to save your Majesty. Now I go to make report to Pharaoh, leaving you in charge of Amen, who shall protect you, and to Rames, my son, the heritage of vengeance. Farewell, O Daughter of Amen, till I see your star rise in the darkness of the Under-World, and to you, beloved wife, farewell."

Then, uttering the war-cry of his fathers, those Pharaohs who once had ruled in Egypt, the tall and noble Mermes grasped his sword in both his hands, and rushed upon the advancing foe, slaying and slaying until he himself was slain.

" Come with me, O Wife of a royal hero," said Tua to Asti, who had covered her eyes with her hand, and was leaning against the wall.

" Widow, not wife, Queen. Did you not see his spirit pass ? "

Then Tua led her up more steps to the top of the pylon tower, where Asti sank down moaning in her misery. Tua walked to the outermost edge of the tower and stood there waiting the end. It was the moment of dawn. On the eastern horizon the red rim of the sun arose out of the desert in a clear sky. There upon that lofty pinnacle, clad in shining mail, and wearing a helm shaped like the crown of Lower Egypt, Tua stood in its glorious rays that turned her to a figure of fire set above a world of shadow. The thousands of the people watching from the streets below, and from boats

upon the Nile, saw her, and raised a shout of wonder
and of adoration.

"The Daughter of Amen-Ra!" they cried.
"Behold her clad in the glory of the god!"

Soldiers crept up the stairs to the pylon roof
and saw her also, while, now that the fray was
ended, with them came the Prince Abi.

"Seize her," he panted, for the stairs were steep
and robbed him of his breath.

But the soldiers looked and shrank back before
the Majesty of Egypt, wrapped in her robe of light.

"We fear," they answered, "the ghost of Pharaoh
stands before her."

Then Neter-Tua spoke, saying:

"Abi, once a Prince of Egypt and Hereditary
Lord of Memphis, but now an outcast murderer,
black with the blood of your King, and of many
a loyal man, hear me, the anointed Queen of Egypt,
hear me, O man upon whom I decree the judgment
of the first and second death. Come but one step
nearer to my Majesty, and before your eyes, and the
eyes of all the multitude who watch, I hurl myself
from this hideous place into the waters of the
Nile. Yet ere I go to join dead Pharaoh, and side
by side with him to lay our plaint against you before
the eternal gods, listen to our curse upon you. From
this day forward a snake shall prey upon your
vitals, gnawing upwards to your heart. The spirits
of Pharaoh and of all his servants whom you have
slain shall haunt your sleep; never shall you know
one more hour of happy rest. Through life henceforth you shall fly from a shadow, and if you climb
a throne, it shall be such a one as that on which

I stand encircled with the perilous depths of darkness. Thence you shall fall at last, dying by a death of shame, and the evil gods shall seize upon you, O Traitor, and drag you to the maw of the Eater-up of Souls, and therein you shall vanish for ever and for aye, you and all your House, and all those who cling to you. Thus saith Neter-Tua, speaking with the voice of Amen who created her, her father and the god of gods."

Now when the soldiers heard these dreadful words, one by one they turned and crept down the stairs, till at last there were left upon the pylon roof only the Queen, Asti crouching at her feet, and the monstrous Abi, her uncle.

He looked at her, and thrice he tried to speak but failed, for the words choked in his throat. A fourth time he tried, and they came hoarsely:

" Take off your curse, O mighty Queen," he said. " and I will let you go. I am old, to-night all my lawful sons are dead; take off your curse, leave me in my Government, and though I desire you more than the throne of Egypt, O Beautiful, still I will let you go."

" Nay," answered the Queen, " I cannot if I would. It is not I who spoke, but a Spirit in my mouth. Do your worst, O son of Set. The curse remains upon you."

Now Abi shook in the fury of his fear, and answered:

" So be it, Star of Amen, having nothing more to dread I will do my worst. Pharaoh my enemy is dead, and you, his daughter, shall be my wife of your own free will, or since no man will lay a finger upon you, here in this tower you shall starve.   Death is not yet ; I shall have my day, it is sworn to me. Reign with me if you will, or starve without me if you will—I tell you, Daughter of Amen, that I shall have my day."

"And I tell you, Son of Set, that after the day comes the long terror of that night which knows no morrow."

Then finding no answer, he too turned and went.

When he was gone Neter-Tua stood a while looking down upon the thousands of people gathered in the great square where the battle had been fought, who stared up at her in a deadly silence.   Then she descended from the coping-stone, and, taking Asti by the arm, led her from the roof to the little chamber where she had slept.

Six days had gone by, and Queen Neter-Tua starved in the pylon tower.   Till now the water had held out for there was a good supply of it in jars, but at last it was done, while, as for food, they had eaten nothing except a store of honey which Asti took at night from the bees that hived among the topmost pylon stones.   That day the honey was done also, and if it had not been, without water to wash it down they could have swallowed no more of the sickly stuff.   Indeed, although in after years in memory of its help, Neter-Tua chose the bee as her royal symbol, never again could she bring herself to eat of the fruit of its labours.

"Come, Nurse," said Tua, "let us go to the roof, and watch the setting of Ra, perhaps for the last time, since I think that we follow him through the Western Gates."

So they went, supporting each other up the steps, for they grew weak. From this lofty place they saw that save on the Nile side of it which was patrolled by the warships of Abi, all the temple was surrounded by a double ring of soldiers, while beyond the soldiers, on the square where the great fight had been, were gathered thousands of the people who knew that the starving Queen was wont to appear thus upon the pylon at sunset.

At the sight of her, clad in the mail which she still wore, a murmur rose from them like the murmur of the sea, followed by a deep silence since they dared not declare the pity which moved them all. In the midst of this silence, whilst the sun sank behind the Pyramids of the ancient kings, Neter-Tua lifted up her glorious voice and sang the evening hymn to Amen-Ra. As the last notes died away in the still air, again the murmur rose while the darkness gathered about the pylon, hiding her from the gaze of men.

Hand in hand as they had come, the two deserted women descended the stair to their sleeping-place.

"They dare not help us, Asti," said Tua, "let us lie down and die."

"Nay, Queen," answered Asti, "let us turn to one that giveth help to the helpless. Do you remember the words spoken by the shining spirit of Ahura the Divine?"

"I remember them, Asti."

"Queen, I have waited long, since the spell she

whispered to me may be used once only, but now I am sure that the moment is at hand when that which dwells within you must be called forth to save you."

"Then call it forth, Asti," answered Tua wearily, "if you have the power. If not, oh! let us die. But say, whom would you summon? The glory of Amen or the ghost of Pharaoh, or Ahura, my mother, or one of the guardian gods?"

"None of these," answered Asti, "for I have been bidden otherwise. Lie you down and sleep, my fosterling, for I have much to do in the hours of darkness. When you awake you shall learn all."

"Aye," said Tua, "when I awake, if ever I do awake. Is it in your mind to kill me in my sleep, Asti? Is that your command? Well, if so, I shall not blame you, for then I will break this long fast of mine with Pharaoh and the divine mother, Ahura, who bore me, and together in the pleasant Fields of Peace we will wait for Rames, my lover and your son. Being a queen, they will give me burial in my father's tomb, and that is all I crave of them, and of this weary world. Sing me to rest, Nurse, as you were wont to do when I was little, and, if it be your will, tarry not long behind me."

So she laid herself down upon the bed, and, taking her hand that had grown so thin, the tall and noble Asti bent over her in the darkness, and began to sing a gentle chant or lullaby.

Tua's eyes closed, her breath came slow and deep. Then Asti the magician ceased her song and, gathering up her secret strength, put out her prayers, prayer after prayer, till at length all her soul was pure, and she dared to utter the awful spell that Ahura had whispered in her ear. At the muttered, holy words wild voices cried through the night, the solid pylon rocked, and in the city the crystal globe into which Kaku and Merytra gazed was suddenly shattered between them, and, white with terror at he knew not what, Abi sprang from his couch.

Then Asti also sank into sleep or swoon, and all was silent in that chamber, silent as the grave.

Neter-Tua awoke. Through the pylon window-place crept the first grey light of dawn. Her eyes searching the gloom fell first upon the dark-robed figure of Asti sleeping in a chair, her head resting upon her hand. Then a brightness drew them to the foot of her bed, and there, clothed in a faint, white light, that seemed as though it were drawn from the stars and the moon, wearing the Double Crown, and arrayed in all the royal robes of Egypt, she saw—*herself.*

Now Tua knew that she dreamed, and for a long while lay still, for it pleased her, starved and wretched as she was, a prisoner in the hands of her foes, a netted bird, to let her fancy dwell upon this splendid image of what she had been before an evil fate, speaking with the voice of Merytra, Lady of the Foot-stool, had beguiled dead Pharaoh to Memphis. If things had gone well with her, she should be as that image was to-day, that image which wore her crown and robes of state, yes, and her very jewels. Such were the changes of fortune even in the lives of princes whose throne seemed to be set upon a rock, princes whom the god of gods had fathered. Never before in her young life had the thing come so home to her, for until now, even through the hunger and the fear, her pride had borne her up. But in this chilly hour that precedes the dawn, the hour when, as they say, men are wont to die, it was otherwise with her. Her end was near—she knew it and understood that between the mightiest monarch in the world and the humblest peasant maid at the last there is no difference, save perchance a difference of the soul within.

Here she lay, a shadow, who must choose between a miserable end by thirst and hunger, or a loathsome marriage. And what availed it that she was called Morning-Star of Amen, she the only child of Pharaoh and of his royal wife, and that when she was dead they would grant her a state funeral, and inscribe her name among the lists of kings, while Abi, the foul usurper, sat upon her throne. Here on the bed lay what she was, there at the foot of it stood what she should be if the gods had not deserted her.

Her poor heart was filled with bitterness like a cup with vinegar, bitterness flowed through her in the place of blood. It seemed hard to die so young, she whom men named a god ; to die robbed of her crown, robbed of her vengeance, and taking with her her deep, unfruitful love. Would she and Rames meet beyond the grave, she wondered ? Would they wed· and bear children there, who should rule as Pharaohs in the Under-world ? Would Osiris redeem her mortal flesh, and Amen the Father, receive her ; or would she rush down into everlasting blackness where sleep is all in all ?

Oh! for one hour of strength and freedom, one short hour while at the head of her armies she rolled down upon rebellious Memphis in her might, and trod its high walls flat, and gave its palaces to the flames, and cast its accursed prince to the jaws of crocodiles. Her sunk eyes flashed at the thought of it, and her wasted bosom heaved, and lo! the eyes of that royal queen of her dreams flashed also as though in answer, and on its breast the jewels rose as though pride or anger lifted them.

Then this marvel came to pass, for the beautiful face—could her own ever have been so beautiful?—the imperial face, bent forward a little, and from the red lips came a soft voice, her own rich voice, that said:

"Speak your will, Queen, and it shall be done. I, who stand here, am your servant to command, O Morning-Star, O Amen's royal child."

Tua sat up in her bed and laughed at the vision.

"My will!" she said. "O Dream, why do you mock me? Let me think. What is my will? Well, Dream, it is that of the beggar at the gate—I desire a drink of water, and a crust of bread."

"They are there," answered the figure, pointing with the crystal sceptre in her hand to the table beside the couch.

Idly enough Tua looked, and so it was! On the table stood pure water in a silver cup, and by it cakes of bread upon a golden platter. She stretched out her hand, for surely this fantasy was pleasant, and took that ghost of a silver cup, her own cup that Pharaoh had given her as a child, and brought it to her lips and drank, and lo! water pure and

cold flowed down her throat, until at length even
her raging thirst was satisfied. Then she stretched
out her hand again, and took the loaves of bread,
and ate them hungrily till all were gone, and as
she swallowed the last of them, exclaimed in bitter
shame :

"Oh ! what a selfish wretch am I who have
drunk and eaten all, leaving nothing for my foster-
mother, Asti, who lies asleep, and dies of want as
I did."

"Fear not," answered the Dream. "Look,
there are more for Asti." And it was true, for the
silver cup brimmed once more with cold water, and
on the golden platter were other cakes.

Now the Dream spoke again :

"Surely," it said, "there were other wishes in
your heart, O Morning-Star, than that for human
sustenance ? "

"Aye, O Dream, I wished for vengeance upon
Abi, the traitor, Abi the murderer of my father,
who would bring me to the last shame of womanhood. I wished for vengeance upon Abi, and all
who cling to him."

The bright figure bowed, stretching out its jewelled
hands, and answered :

"I am your servant to obey. It shall be worked,
O Queen, such vengeance as you cannot dream of,
vengeance poured drop by drop like poison in his
veins, the torment of disappointed love, the torment
of horrible fear, the torment of power given and
snatched away, the torment of a death of shame,
and the everlasting torment of the Eater-up of
Souls—this vengeance shall be worked upon Abi

and all who cling to him. Was there not another wish in your heart, O Morning-Star, O Queen divine ? "

" Aye," answered Tua, " but I may not speak it all even to myself in sleep."

" It shall be given to you, O Morning-Star. You shall find your love though far away beyond the horizon, and he shall return with you, and you twain shall rule in the Upper and the Lower Land, and in all the lands beyond with glory such as has not been known in Egypt."

Now, at length, Tua seemed to awake. She rubbed her eyes and looked. There was the sleeping Asti ; there on the table beside her were the water and the bread ; there at the foot of the couch, glimmering in the low lights of dawn, was the glorious figure of herself draped in the splendid robes.

" Who, and what are you ? " she cried. " Are you a god or a spirit, or are you but a mocking vision caught in the web of my madness ? "

" I am none of these things, O Morning-Star, I am yourself. I am that Ka whom our father Amen gave to you at birth to dwell with you and protect you. Do you not remember me when as a child we played together ? "

" I remember," answered Tua. " You warned me of the danger of the sacred crocodile in the Temple tank, but since then I have never seen you. What gives you strength to appear in the flesh before me, O Double ? "

" The magic of Asti with which she has been endowed from on high to save you, Neter-Tua, that gives me strength. Know that although you cannot always see me, I am your eternal companion.

Through life I go with you, and when you die I watch in your tomb, perfect, incorruptible, preserving your wisdom, your loveliness, and all that is yours, until the day of resurrection. I have power, I have the secret knowledge which dwells in you, although you cannot grasp it; I remember the Past, the infinite, infinite Past that you forget, I foresee the Future, the endless, endless Future that is hidden from you, to which the life you know is but as a single leaf upon the tree, but as one grain of sand in the billions of the Desert. I look upon the faces of the gods, and hear their whisperings; Fate gives me his book to read; I sleep secure in the presence of the Eternal who sent me forth, and to whom at last I return again, my journey ended, my work fulfilled, bearing you in my holy arms. O Morning-Star, the spells of Asti have clothed me in this magic flesh, the might of Amen has set me on my feet. I am here, your servant to obey."

Now, amazed, bewildered, Tua called out:

"Awake, Nurse, awake, for I am mad. It seems to me that a messenger from on high, robed in my own flesh, stands before me and speaks with me."

Asti opened her eyes, and, perceiving the beautiful figure, rose and did obeisance to it, but said no word.

"Be seated," said the Ka, "and hear me, time is short. I awoke at the summons, I came forth, I am present, I endure until the spell is taken off me, and I return whence I came, O Interpreter, speak the will of her of whom I am, that I may do it in my own fashion. There is food—eat and drink, then speak."

So Asti ate and drank as Tua had done, and
when she had finished and was satisfied, behold !
the cup and the platter vanished away. Next in
a slow, quiet voice she spoke, saying :

"O Shadow of this royal Star, by my spells
incorporate, this is our case : Here we starve in
misery, and without the gate Abi waits the end.
If the Queen lives, he will take her who hates him
to be his wife ; if she dies he will seize her throne.
Our wisdom is finished. What must we do to save
this Star that it may shine serene until its appointed
hour of setting ?"

"Is that all you seek ?" asked the Double,
when she had finished.

"Nay," broke in Tua hurriedly, "I would not
shine alone, I seek another Star to share my sky
with me."

"Have you faith and will you obey ?" asked the
Double again. "For without faith I can do
nothing."

Now Asti looked at Tua who bowed her head in
assent to an unspoken question, then she answered :

"We have faith, we will obey."

"So be it," said the Shadow. "Presently Abi
will come to ask whether the Queen consents to be
his wife, or whether she will bide here until she
dies. I who wear the fashion of the Queen will
go forth and be his wife, oh ! such a wife as man never
had before," and as she spoke the words an awful
look swept across her face, and her deep eyes flamed.
"Ill goes it with the mortal man who weds a wraith
that hates him and is commanded to work his woe,"
she added.

Now Asti and Tua understood and smiled, then the Queen said:

"So you will sit in my seat, O Shadow, and as your lord, Abi will sit on Pharaoh's throne and find it hard. But what of Egypt and my people?"

"Fear not for Egypt and your people, O Morning Star. With these it shall go well enough until you come back to claim them."

"And what of my companion and myself?" asked Tua.

The Double raised her sceptre, and pointed to the open window-place between them, beneath which, hundreds of feet beneath, ran the milky waters of the river.

"You shall trust yourselves to the bosom of Father Nile," she answered solemnly.

Now the Queen and Asti stared at each other.

"That means," said Tua, "that we must trust ourselves to Osiris, for none can fall so far and live."

"Think you so, O Star? Where, then, is that faith you promised, without which I can do nothing? Nay, I may tell no more. Do my bidding, or let me go, and deal with Abi as it pleases you. Choose now, he draws near," and as she spoke the words they heard the bronze gates of the temple clash upon their hinges.

Tua shivered at the sound, then sprang from the couch, and drew herself to her full height, exclaiming:

"For my part I have chosen. Never shall it be said that Pharaoh's daughter was a coward. Better the breast of Osiris than the arms of Abi, or slow death in a dungeon. In Amen and in thee, O Double, I put my trust."

The Shadow looked from her to Asti, who answered briefly:

"Where my Lady goes there I follow, knowing that Mermes always waits. What shall we do?"

The Ka motioned to them to stand together in the narrow window-place, and this they did, their arms about each other. Next she lifted her sceptre and spoke some word.

Then fire flashed before their eyes, a rush of wind beat upon their brows, and they knew no more.

CHAPTER XI

THE DREAM OF ABI

On the night of the drawing-forth of the Ka of Neter-Tua, Kaku the wizard, and Merytra the spy, she who had been Lady of the Footstool to Pharaoh, sat together in that high chamber where Merytra had vowed her vow, and received the magic image.

"Why do you look so disturbed ? " asked the astrologer of his accomplice who glanced continually over her shoulder, and seemed very ill at ease. "All has gone well. If Set himself had fashioned that image, it could not have done its work more thoroughly."

"Thoroughly, indeed," broke in Merytra in an angry voice. "You have tricked me, Wizard, I promised to help you to lame Pharaoh, not to murder him."

"Hush ! Beloved," said Kaku nervously, "murder is an ugly word, and murderers come to ugly ends—sometimes. Is it your fault if an accursed fool of a priest chose to burn the mannikin upon an altar, and thus bring this god to his lamented end ? "

"No," answered Merytra, "not mine, or the priest's, but yours, and that hog, Abi's ; and Set's the master of both of you. But I shall get the blame of it, for the Queen and Asti know the truth, and soon or late it will come out, and they will

burn me as a sorceress, sending me to the Under-
world with the blood of Pharaoh upon my hands,
Pharaoh who never did me aught but good. And
then, what will happen to me ? "

Evidently Kaku did not know, for he rose and
stood opposite to her, scratching his lean chin and
smiling in a sickly, indeterminate fashion that
enraged Merytra.

" Cease grinning at me like an ape of the rocks,"
she said, " and tell me, what is to be the end of this
evil business ? "

" Why trouble about ends, Fair One ? " he asked.
" They are always a long way off ; indeed, the best
philosophers hold that there is no such thing as an
end. You know the sacred symbol of a snake
with its tail in its mouth that surrounds the whole
world, but begins where it ends, and ends where it
begins. It may be seen in any tomb——"

" Cease your talk of snakes and tombs," burst
in Merytra. " The thought of them makes me
shudder."

" By all means, Beloved. I have always held
that we Egyptians dwell too much on tombs, and
—whatever it may be that lies beyond them, which
after all remains a matter of doubt—fortunately.
So let us turn from tombs and corpses to palaces
and life. As I said just now, although we grieve
over the accident of Pharaoh's death, and that of
all his guard—and I may add, of Abi's four legitimate
sons, things have gone well for us. To-day I have
received from the Prince, in writing, my appointment as Vizier, and first King's companion, to come
into force when he mounts the throne as he must

do, and to-day you have received from me, with
all the usual public rites and ceremonies, the name
of wife, as I promised that you should. Merytra,
you are the wife of the great Vizier, the pre-eminent
lord, the sole Companion of the King of Egypt,
a high position for one who after all during the late
reign was but Pharaoh's favourite, and Lady of
the Footstool."

" A footstool of silk is more comfortable to sit
on than a state chair fashioned of blood-stained
swords. Hearken you, Kaku ! I am afraid. You
say that you are the greatest of seers, and can read
the future. Well, I desire to know the future, so
if you are not a charlatan, show it to me."

" A charlatan ! How can you suggest it, Merytra,
remembering the adventure of the image ? "

" That may have been an accident. Pharaoh
was sickly for years, and had a stroke before. If
you are not a cheat show me the future in that magic
crystal. I would learn the worst, so that I may
know how to meet it when it comes."

" Well, Wife, we will try, though to see such
high visions the spirit should be calm, which I fear
yours is not—nay, be not angry. We will try, we
will try. Sit here now, and gaze, and above all
be silent while I say the appropriate spells."

So the ball of crystal having been set upon the
table, the pair stared into it as Kaku muttered
his charms and invocations. For a long while
Merytra saw nothing, till suddenly a shadow gathered
in the ball, which slowly cleared away, revealing
the image of dead Pharaoh clothed in his mummy
wrappings. As she started back to scream the

image seemed to loose its hands from the cloths that bound them, and strike outwards, whereon the crystal suddenly shattered, so that the pieces of it flew about the room, one of which struck her on the mouth, knocking out two of her front teeth, and gashing her lips.

Merytra uttered a cry, and fell backwards to the floor, while Kaku sprang from his chair as though to run away, then thought better of it, and stood still, shivering with fear.

" What was that ? " said Merytra, rising from the ground, and wiping the blood from her cut mouth.

" I do not know," answered Kaku, in a quavering voice. " It would seem that the gods deny to us that knowledge of the future which you sought. Be content with the present, Merytra."

" Content with the present," she screamed, infuriated. " Look at what the present has given me—a mouthful of blood and teeth. I, who was beautiful, am spoiled for ever ; I am become an old hag. Pharaoh burst the ball with his hand, and threw the pieces at me. I saw him do it, and you set him there. Wretch, I will pay you back for this evil trick," and springing at Kaku, she tore off his astrologer's cap, and the wig beneath it, and beat his bald head with them till he cried for mercy.

It was at this moment that the door opened, and through it, breathless, white with terror, half-clothed, appeared none other than the Prince Abi.

" What passes here ? " he gasped, sinking into a chair. " Is this the way you conduct your midnight studies, Kaku ? "

" Certainly not, most high Lord," replied the astrologer, trying to bow with his eye fixed on Merytra, who stood by him, the torn wig in her hand, in the act of striking. " Certainly not, exalted Prince. A domestic difference, that is all. This wild cat of a woman whom I have married having met with an accident, gave way to her devilish temper."

" Repeat that," exclaimed Merytra, " and I will throw you from the window-place to find out whether your sorceries can make paving-stones as soft as air. See, Lord, what he has done to me by his accursed wizardry," and she exhibited her two front teeth in her shaking hand. " I say that he set the spirit of Pharaoh whom he beguiled me to do to death, in the crystal, for I saw him there wrapped in his mummy clothes, and caused dead Pharaoh to burst the crystal and stone me with its fragments."

" Be silent, Woman," shouted Abi, " or I will have you beaten with rods, till your feet hurt more than your mouth. What is this about the spirit of Pharaoh, Kaku ? Is he everywhere, for know, it is of Pharaoh, the dweller in Osiris, that I came to speak to you."

" Most exalted Ruler of the North, Son of Royal Blood, Hereditary Count who shall be King——"

" Cease your titles, Knave," exclaimed Abi, " and listen, for I need counsel, and if you cannot give it I will find one who can. Just now I lay on my bed asleep, and a dreadful vision came to me. I dreamed that I woke up, and feeling a weight on the bed beside me turned to learn what it was, and saw there the body of my brother, Pharaoh, in his death-wrappings——"

" As I saw him in the ball," broke in Merytra.
" Did he pelt you also, O Abi ? "

" Nay, Woman, he did worse, he spoke to me.
He said—' You, my brother, to whom I forgave
all your sins, you and the woman-snake that I
cherished in my bosom, and your servant, the black-
souled magician, her accomplice, have done me
miserably to death, and set the Queen of both the
Lands, Amen's royal child, to starve in yonder
tower with the noble lady Asti, until she dies or
takes you to be her husband—you, her uncle, who
seek her beauty and my throne. Now I have a
message for you from the gods, who write down
these things in their eternal books against the day
of judgment, when we all shall meet and plead our
cause before them, Osiris the Redeemer standing on
the right hand, and the Eater-up of Souls standing
on the left.

" ' This is the message, O Abi—Go to the Temple
of Sekhet at the dawn. There you shall find that
Royal Loveliness which you desire. Take it to be
your wife as you desire, for it shall not say you nay.
Be wedded to that Loveliness with pomp before all
the eyes of Egypt, and reign by right of that Royalty,
until you meet one Rames, son of Mermes, whom you
also murdered, and with him a certain Beggar-man
who is charged with another message for you, O Abi.
Ascend the Nile to Thebes, and lay this body of
mine in the splendid tomb which I have made ready
and sit in my seat, and do those things which that
Royal Loveliness you have wed, commands to you,
for It you shall obey. But hasten, hasten, Abi,
to hollow for yourself a grave, and let it be near

to mine, for when you are dead this my Ka would come to visit you, as it does to-night.'

" Then the Ka or the body of Pharaoh—I know not which it was—ceased from speaking, and lay there a while staring at me with its cold eyes, till at length the spirits of my four sons who are dead entered the chamber and, lifting up the shape, carried it away. I awoke, shaking like a reed in the wind, and ran hither up a thousand steps to find you brawling with this low-born slut, dead Pharaoh's worn-out shoe that in bygone years I kicked from off my foot."

Now Merytra would have answered, for she loved not such names, but the two men looked at her so fiercely that her rage died, and she was silent.

" Read me this vision, Man, and be swift, for the torment of it haunts me," went on Abi. " If you cannot I strip you of your offices, and give your carcase to the rods until you find wisdom. It was you who set me on this path, and by the gods you shall keep me safe in it or die by inches."

Now, seeing his great danger, Kaku grew cold and cunning.

" It is true, O Prince," he said, " that I set you on this path, this high and splendid path, and it is true also that from the beginning I have kept you safe in it. Had it not been for me and my counsel, long ago you would have become but a forgotten traitor. Remember that night at Thebes, when in your pride you desired to smite at the heart of Pharaoh, and how I held your hand, and remember how, many a time, my wisdom has been your guide, when left to your own rash folly you must have

failed or perished. It is true also, Prince, that in
the future as in the past, with me and by me you
stand or fall. Yet if you think otherwise, find some
wiser man to lead you, and wait the end. All the
rods in Egypt cannot be broken on my back, O Abi.
Now shall I speak who alone have knowledge, or
will you seek another counsellor ? "

" Speak on," answered Abi sullenly, " we are
fish in the same net, and share each other's fortune
to the end, whether it be Set's gridiron or fat
Egypt's pleasure pond. Fear not, what I have
promised you shall have while it is mine to give."

" Just now you promised rods," remarked Kaku,
making a wry face and replacing the remains of
his wig upon his bald head, " but let that pass.
Now as to this dream of yours, I find its meaning
good. How did Pharaoh come to you ? Not as a
living spirit, but in the fashion of a dead man, and
who cares for dead men ? "

" I do, for one, when they cut my mouth with
broken crystals," interrupted Merytra, who was
bathing her wounds in a basin of water.

" Would that they had cut your tongue instead of
your lips, Woman," snarled Abi. " Continue, Kaku,
and heed her not."

" And what was his message ? " went on the
magician. " Why, that you shall marry the Majesty
of Egypt, and rule in her right and sit in the seat of
kings. Are not these the very things that you desire,
and have worked for years to win ? "

" Yes, Kaku, but you forget all that about one
Rames, and the tomb that I must hollow, and the rest."

" Rames ? Merytra here can tell you of him,

G

Prince. He is the madcap young Count who killed the Prince of Kesh, and was sent by Neter-Tua far to the South-lands, that the barbarians there might make an end of him without scandal. If ever he should come back with the Beggar-man and his message, which is not likely, you can answer him with the halter he deserves."

"Aye, Kaku, but how will the Queen answer him ? There are stories afloat——"

"Lies, every one of them, Prince. She would have executed him at once had it not been for the influence of Mermes, and her foster-mother, Asti. This Rames has in him the royal blood of the last dynasty, and the Star of Amen is not one who will share her sky with a rival star, unless he be her lawful Lord, which is your part. If Rames or the foul Beggar brings you any message it will be that you are King of Kesh as well as of Egypt, and then you can kill him and take the heritage. A fig for Rames and its stalk for the Beggar!"

"Perhaps," replied Abi more cheerfully, "at any rate I do not fear that risk ; but how about all Pharaoh's talk of tombs ? "

"Being dead, Prince, it is natural that the mind of his Ka should run on tombs, and his own royal burial, which as a matter of policy we must give to him. Besides there the prophecy was safe, since to these same tombs all must come, especially those of us who have seen the Nile rise over sixty times— as I have," he added hastily. "When we reach the tomb it will be time to deal with its affairs ; till then let us be content with life, and the good things it offers, such as thrones, and the love of

the most beautiful woman in the world, and the rest.
Harvest your corn when it is ripe, Prince, and do
not trouble about next year's crop or whether in
his grave Pharaoh's Double eats white bread or
brown. Pharaoh's daughter—or Amen's—is your
business, not his ghost."

"Yes, good soothsayer," said Abi, "she is my
business. But one more question. Why did that
accursed mummy speak of her as ' It '—in my dream
I mean—as though she were no woman, but something
beyond woman ? "

For a moment Kaku hesitated, for the point
was hard to answer, then he replied boldly :

"Because as I believe, Prince, this Queen with
whom the gods are rewarding your deserts is in
truth more than woman, being Amen's very daughter,
and therefore in those realms whence the dream came,
she is known not as woman, but by her title of Royal
Loveliness. Oh ! " went on Kaku, simulating an
enthusiasm that in truth did not glow within his
breast, "great and glorious is your lot, King of the
world, and splendid the path which I have opened
to your triumphant feet. It was I who showed
you how Pharaoh might be trapped in Memphis,
being but a poor fool easy to deceive, and it was
I—or rather Merytra yonder—who rid you of him.
And now it is I, the Master whom you threatened
with rods, that alone can interpret to you the happy
omen of a dream which you thought fearsome.
Think of the end of it, Prince, and banish every
doubt. Who bore away the shape of Pharaoh ?
Why the spirits of your sons, thus symbolising the
triumph of your House."

" At least they will have no share in it, Kaku, for they are dead," said Abi with a groan, for he had loved his sons.

" What of that, Prince ? They died bravely, and we mourn them, but here again Fortune is with you, for had they lived trouble might have arisen between them and those other sons which the Queen of Egypt shall bear to you."

" Mayhap, mayhap," replied Abi, waving his hand, for the subject was painful to him, " but this Queen is not yet my wife. She is starving in yonder tower, and what am I to do ? If I try to force my presence upon her, she will destroy herself as she swore, and if I leave her there any longer, being mortal, she must die. Moreover, I dare not, for even these folk of Memphis, who love me, begin to murmur. Egypt's Queen is Egypt's Queen, and they will not suffer that she should perish miserably, being beautiful and young, and one who takes all hearts. This night at sunset they gathered in tens of thousands round the tower to hear her sing that evening hymn to Ra, and afterwards marched past my palace, shouting in the darkness, ' Give food to Her Majesty, and free her, or we will.' Moreover, by now the news must have come to Thebes, and there a great army will gather to liberate or avenge her. What am I to do, Prophet ? "

" Do what dead Pharaoh bade you in your dream, Prince. At the hour of dawn go to the Temple of Sekhet, where you will find the Queen become obedient to your wishes, for did not the dream declare that she will not say you nay ? Then lead her to your palace, and marry her in the face of all men, and rule by right of her Majesty and of your own conquering arm."

" It can be tried," said Abi, " for then, at least, we shall learn what truth there is in dreams. But what of this Asti her companion ? "

" Asti has been an ill guide to her Majesty, Prince," replied Kaku, rubbing his chin as he always did when there was mischief in his mind. " Moreover, she is advanced in years, and must be weak with grief and hunger. If she still lives Merytra here will take her in charge and care for her. You are old friends, are you not, Merytra ? "

" Very," answered that lady with emphasis, " like the cat and the bird which were pets of the same master. Well, we shall have much to say to each other. Only, beware, Husband, Asti is no weakling. Your magic may be strong, but hers is stronger, for she is a great priestess and draws it from gods—not devils."

So it came about that at dawn Prince Abi, clad in magnificent robes, and accompanied by Councillors, among them Kaku, and by a small guard, was carried in a litter to the gates of the old temple of Sekhet, being too heavy to walk so far, and there descended. As there were none to defend them these gates were opened easily enough, and they passed through, leaving the guard without. When they came to the inner court, Abi stopped and asked where they should search.

" In one place only, your Highness," answered Kaku, " that pylon tower which overlooks the Nile, for there her Majesty starves with Asti."

" Pylon tower," grumbled Abi. " Have I not climbed enough steps this night ? Still, lead on."

So they went to the narrow stair, up which the thin Kaku ran like a cat, while the officers pushed and led the huge Abi behind him. On the third landing they all halted at Abi's command.

" Hurry not," he said in a thick whisper. " Her Majesty dwells on the next floor of this hateful tower, and since Asti is with her she cannot be surprised. Beware, then, of frightening her by your sudden appearance, lest she should run to the top of the pylon, and hurl herself into the Nile, as she has sworn that she will do. Halt now, and I will call to her when I have got my breath."

So after a while he called, saying :

" O Queen, cease to starve yourself in this miserable abode, and come down to dwell in plenty with your faithful subject."

He called it once, and twice, and thrice, but there was no answer. Now Abi grew afraid.

" She must have perished," he said, " and Egypt will demand her blood at my hands. Kaku, go up and see what has happened. You are a magician, and have nothing to fear."

But the astrologer thought otherwise, and hesitated, till Abi in a rage lifted his cedar wand to strike him on the back. Then he went, step by step, slowly, pausing at each step to address prayers and praises to her Majesty of Egypt. At length he came to the door of the Queen's chamber, and kneeling down, peeped round it, to see that it was quite empty. Next he crawled across the landing to the chamber opposite, that which had been Asti's, and found it empty also. Then, made bold by fear, he ascended to the pylon roof. But here, too, there was no one to be seen. So he returned, and told Abi, who shouted:

"By Ptah, great Lord of Memphis! either she has escaped to raise Egypt on me, or she has sought death in the Nile to raise the gods upon me, which is worse. So much for your interpretation of dreams, O Cheat."

"Wait till you are sure before you call me such names, Prince," replied Kaku indignantly. "Let us search the temple, she may be elsewhere."

So they searched it court by court, and chamber by chamber, till they came to that inner hall in front of the Sanctuary where Pharaoh had set up his throne while he sojourned at Memphis. This hall was a dark place, into which light flowed only through the gratings in the clerestory, being roofed in with blocks of granite laid upon its lotus-shaped columns. Now, at the hour of sunrise, the gloom in it was still deep, so deep that the searchers felt their way from pillar to pillar, seeing nothing. Presently, however, a ray of light from the rising sun sped through the opening shaped like the eye of Osiris in the eastern wall, and as it had done for thousands of years, struck upon the shrine of the goddess, and the throne that was set in front of it, revealing the throne, and seated thereon Neter-Tua, her Majesty of Egypt.

Glorious she looked indeed, a figure of flame set in the midst of darkness. The royal robe she wore glittered in the sunlight, glittered her sceptre, her jewels, and the *uræi* on her Double Crown, but more than all of them glittered her fierce and splendid eyes. Indeed, there was something so terrible in those eyes that the beholders who discovered them thus suddenly, shrank back, whispering to each other that here sat a goddess, not a woman. For in her calmness, her proud beauty and her silence, she seemed like an immortal, one victorious who had triumphed over death, not a woman who for seven days had starved within a tower.

They shrank back, they huddled themselves together in the doorway, and there remained whispering till the growing light fell on them also. But the figure on the throne took no heed, only stared over their heads as though it were lost in mystery and thought.

At length Kaku, gathering courage, said to Abi :

" O Prince, there is your bride, such a bride as never man had before. Go now and take her," and all the others echoed :

" Go now, O Prince, and take her."

Thus adjured for very shame's sake Abi advanced, looking often behind him, till he came to the foot of the throne, and stood there bowing.

For a long while he stood bowing thus, till he grew weary indeed, for he knew not what to say. Then suddenly a clear and silvery voice spoke above him, asking :

" What do you here, Lord of Memphis ? Why are you not in the cell where Pharaoh bound you ? Oh ! I remember—the footstool-bearer, Merytra, your paid spy, let you out, did she not ? Why is she not here with Kaku the Sorcerer, who fashioned the enchanted image that did Pharaoh to death ? Is it because she stays to doctor those false lips of hers that were cut last night before you went to ask yonder Kaku to interpret a certain dream which came to you ? "

" How did you learn these things ? Have you spies in my palace, O Queen ? "

" Yes, my uncle, I have spies in your palace and everywhere. What Amen sees his daughter knows. Now you have come to lead me away to be your wife, have you not ? Well, I await you, I am ready. Do it if you dare ! "

" If I dare ? Why should I not dare, O Queen ? " asked Abi in a doubtful voice.

" Surely that question is one for you to answer, Count of Memphis and its subject nomes. Yet tell me this—why did the magic crystal burst asunder without cause in the chamber of Kaku last night, and why do you suppose that Kaku interpreted to you all the meaning of your dream—he who will never tell the truth unless it be beneath the rods ? "

" I do not know, Queen," answered Abi, " but with Kaku I can speak later, if need be after the fashion you suggest," and he glanced at the magician wrathfully.

" No, Prince Abi, you know nothing, and Kaku knows nothing, save that rods break the backs of snakes, unless they can find a wall to hide in," and she pointed to the astrologer slinking back into the shadow. " No one knows anything save me, to whom Amen gives wisdom with sight of the future, and what I know I keep. Were it otherwise, O Abi, I could tell you things that would turn your grey hair white, and to Kaku and to Merytra the spy,

G*

promise rewards that would make the torture-chamber seem a bed of down. But it is not lawful, nor would they sound pleasant in this bridal hour."

Now while Kaku between his chattering teeth muttered the words of Protection in the shadow, Abi and his courtiers stared at this terrible queen as boys seeking wild fowls' eggs in the reeds, and stumbling on a lion, stare ere they fly. Twice, indeed, the Prince turned looking towards the door and the pleasant light without, for it seemed to him that he was entering on a dark and doubtful road. Then he said :

" Your words, O Queen, cut like a two-edged sword, and methinks they leave a poison in the wound. Say now, if you are human, how it comes about that after seven days of want your flesh is not minished nor has your beauty waned. Say also who brought to you those glorious robes you wear here in this empty temple, and where is your foster-mother, Asti ? "

" The gods fed me," answered the Queen gently, " and brought me these robes that I might seem the more worthy of you, O Prince. And as for Asti, I sent her to Cyprus to fetch a scent they make there and nowhere else. No, I forgot, it was yesterday she went to bring the scent from Cyprus that now is on my hair ; to-day she is in Thebes, seeing to a business of mine. That is no secret, I will tell it you—it is as to the carving of all the history of his murder and betrayal in the first chamber of Pharaoh's tomb."

Now at these magical and ill-omened words the courage of the company left them, so that they began

to walk backwards towards the door, Abi going with
them.

" What ! " cried the Queen in a voice of sorrow
that yet seemed laden with mockery. " Would you
leave me here alone ? Do my power and my wisdom
frighten you ? Alas ! I cannot help them, for when
the full vase is tilted the wine will run out, and when
light is set behind alabaster, then the white stone
must shine. Yet am I one meet to adorn the palace
of the King, even such a king as you shall be, O Abi,
whom Osiris loves. See, now, I will dance and sing
to you as once I sang to the Prince of Kesh
before the sword of Rames took away his life, so
that you may judge of me, Abi, you, who have
looked upon so many lovely women."

As she spoke, very slowly, so slowly that they
could scarcely see her move, she glided from the
throne, and standing before them, began to move
her feet and body, and to chant a song.

What were the words of that song none could
ever remember, but to every man there present
it opened a door in his heart, and brought back the
knowledge of youth. She whom he had loved best
danced before him, her tender hands caressed him ;
the words she sang were sighs which the dead had
whispered in his ears. Even to Abi, old, unwieldy
and steeped in cunning, these soft visions came,
although it is true that it seemed to him that this
lovely singer led him to a precipice, and that when
she ceased her song and appeared to vanish, to
seek her he leapt into the clouds that rushed
beneath.

Now the dance was done, and the last echoes

of the music died away against the ancient walls whence the images of Sekhet the cat-headed watched them with her cruel smile of vengeance. The dance was done, and the beautiful dancer stood before them unflushed, unheated, but laughing gently.

"Now go, divine Prince," she said, "and you his followers, go, all of you, and leave me to my lonely house, until Pharaoh sends for me to share that new realm which he inherits beyond the West."

But they would not go and could not if they would, for some power bound them to her, while, as for Abi he scarce could take his eyes from her, but heedless of who heard them, babbled out his passion at her feet, while the rest glowered on him jealously. She listened always smiling that same smile that was so sweet, yet so inhuman. Then when he stopped exhausted, at last she spoke, saying :

"What! do you love now more greatly than you fear, as the divine Prince of Kesh loved after Amen's Star had sung to him. May your fate be happier, O noble Abi, but that, since it is not lawful that I should tell it to you, you shall discover. Abi, there shall be a royal marriage in Memphis of such joy and feasting as has not been known in the history of the Northern or the Southern Land, and for your allotted span you shall sit by the side of Egypt's Queen and shine in her light. Have you not earned the place by right of blood, O conqueror of Pharaoh, and did not Pharaoh promise it to you in your sleep ? Come, the sun of this new day shines, let us walk in it, and bid farewell to shadows."

CHAPTER XII

THE ROYAL MARRIAGE

A STRANGE rumour ran through Memphis. It was
said that the Queen had yielded ; it was said that
she would marry the Prince Abi, that she was already
at the great White House waiting to be made a
bride. Men wrangled about it in the streets. They
swore that it could not be true, for would this high
lady, the anointed Pharaoh of Egypt, take her
father's murderer, and her own uncle to husband ?
Would she not rather die in her prison tower on
which night by night they had seen her stand and
sing ? In their hearts they thought that she should
die, for thus they had summed her up, this pure,
high-hearted daughter of Amen, whom Fate had
caught in an evil net. Yes, being men they held
that she ought to die, and leave a story in the world,
whereof Egypt could be proud for ever.

But their wives and daughters mocked at them.
After all she was but a woman, they argued, and was
it likely that she would throw aside the pomp of rule
and the prospect of long years in order to steal away
into the shadows of a forgotten tomb ? Henceforth,
it was true, she must take a second place, for Abi
would be a stern master to her. Still, any place
was better than a funeral barge. She had felt the
pinch of hunger yonder in that old temple ; her
fierce spirit had been tamed ; she had kissed the

rod, and after long years of waiting, Abi would be Pharaoh in Egypt.

The dispute grew hot, for even those men who rebelled against her, in their hearts had set her high, and grieved to think of her, the divine Lady, bowing her neck to the common yoke of circumstance, and selling herself for safety, and a seat on the steps of her own throne. But the women mocked on, and showed them that as they had always said, she was no better than others of her sex.

Presently the matter was settled, for heralds appeared crying through the city that the marriage would take place in the great hall of the White House one hour before sundown. Then the women laughed in triumph, and the men were silent.

It was the appointed hour, and that hall was filled to overflowing by all who could gain entrance there. Between the towering obelisks that stood on either side the open cedar doors, folk hung upon its steps like hiving bees; the vast square without and all the streets that led to it were black with them. Here, it is true, they could see nothing, still they fought for the merest foothold, and some of those who fell never rose again. At the head of the hall were set two thrones, the greater and the richer throne for Abi the Prince, the lesser throne for Neter-Tua the Queen. He had arranged it thus since Kaku the cunning pointed out to him that from the first he should show the people that it was he who ruled, and not Pharaoh's daughter.

It was the appointed hour, and at some signal from every temple top rang out the blare of trumpets. Thrice they sounded, and echoed into silence in

that hot, still air, thus announcing that in the temple
of Hathor, and the presence of the priests of all
the gods, the hands of Abi and Neter-Tua had been
joined in marriage.

Another rumour began to run among the crowd ;
like the ring set circling by a stone in water it spread
from mouth to mouth, ever widening as it went.

Marvels had happened in the temple of Hathor,
that was the rumour. Moreover it gave details :
that the High-Priest had handed to the bride the
accustomed lotus-bud, the flower of the goddess,
and lo ! it opened in her hand. Also, it was said,
that presently the stem of it turned to a sceptre
of gold, and the cup of the bloom to sapphire stones
more perfect far than any from the desert mines.

Nor was this all, so went the tale, for when, as he
must, Abi the bridegroom offered the white dove to
Hathor in her shrine, a hawk swept through the
doorway and smote it in his very hand. Yes, there
in the gloom of the shrine smote it and left it dead,
blood running from its beak and breast, dead upon
the knees of the goddess ; left it and was gone again !

Now what hawk, asked the people of each other,
dare such a deed as this, unless in truth it was sent
by the hawk-headed Horus, the son of Amen-Ra.

Soon these matters were forgotten for the moment,
since now it was known that the royal pair were
entering the great White Hall, there to show themselves to the people, and receive the homage of the
nobles, chiefs, and captains. First, advancing by
the covered way which led from the temple of Hathor,
appeared the priests in their robes, chanting as they
walked, followed by the masters of ceremonies,

butlers, and heralds. Next, surrounded by his officers
and guard, came the Prince Abi himself, accompanied by his vizier, Kaku, he whose magic was
said to have brought Pharaoh to his end.

Not all his pomp nor the splendour of his apparel,
whereof the whiteness, as many noted, was spotted
with ill-omened blood, nor even the royal crown which
now, for the first time, was set upon his huge, round
head, could hide from those who watched that this
bridegroom was ill at ease. Even as he stood there,
bowing in answer to the obsequious shouts of the
multitude, the sceptre in his fat hand shook, and
his red lips blanched and trembled. Still he smiled
and bowed on, till at length the shouting died away,
and quiet fell upon the place.

Abi was forgotten, they waited the coming of
the Queen, and though no herald called her advent,
yet every heart of all those thousands felt that she
drew near to them. Look! Yonder she stood.
They had watched closely enough, yet none saw
her come, doubtless because the shadows were thick.
But there she stood, quite alone upon the edge of
the dais in front of the two thrones, and, oh! she
was different from what they had expected. Thus
now she wore no gorgeous robes, but only a simple
garment of purest white, cut low upon her bosom,
where the red rays of the sinking sun, striking up the
hall, revealed to every eye that dark mole shaped
like the Cross of Life, which was her wondrous birth-
mark. But two ornaments adorned her, the double
snakes of royalty, golden with red eyes, set in front
of her tall white head-dress, which none but she
might wear, the crowns of Upper and of Lower Egypt,

and of all the subject lands, and in her hand a sceptre fashioned of gold, and surmounted by a lotus-bloom of sapphire, that sceptre of which rumour had told the magic tale.

Yes, she was different. They had thought to see a woman weak and pale, her eyes still red with grief, her face still stained with tears, one who had been tamed by misfortune, hunger, and the fear of death, whence she had bought herself by marriage with her conqueror. But it was not so, for never had the Star of Amen shone half so beautiful, never had they seen such majesty in those deep blue eyes that looked them through and through as though they read the secret heart of every one of them. Her tall and lovely form had not wasted, her cheeks were red with the glow of health; power and dignity flowed from her presence, fear seemed beneath her feet.

Now no voice was lifted up; they stared at her, and, smiling a little, she answered them with her calm eyes till their heads sank beneath her gaze. Then at length in the midst of that dead, oppressive silence which none dared to break, she turned, and they heard the sweep of her silken robe upon the alabaster floor.

With an effort two chamberlains stepped forward, their wands of office in their hands, to lead her to her seat, but she waved them back, and said in her clear voice :

" Nay, here I am alone ; of all the millions who serve her, not one is left to lead Amen's daughter and Egypt's Queen to her rightful place. Therefore she takes it of her own strength, now and for evermore."

Then very slowly, still in the midst of silence, she mounted the greater throne that had been prepared for Abi, and there seated herself and waited.

Now murmuring rose among the courtiers and Kaku whispered into Abi's ear, while the multitude held its breath. Abi stamped his foot and issued orders which all seemed to fear to execute. At length he stepped forward, addressing the Queen in a hoarse voice.

" Lady," he said, " doubtless you know it not, but that place is mine; your seat is on my left. Be pleased to take it."

" Why so, Prince Abi ? " she asked quietly.

" Lady," he answered, " because the husband takes precedence of the wife, and," he added with savage meaning, " the conqueror of the conquered."

" The conqueror of the conquered ? " she repeated after him in a musing voice. " Should you not have said—the murderer of the murdered and his seed ? Nay, Prince Abi, you are wrong. The sovereign of Egypt by right divine, takes precedence of her vassal, even though it has pleased the gods, whose will she has come to execute, to command her to give to him the name of husband until that will is more fully known. Come now and do homage to your Queen, and after you these slaves of yours who dared to lift the sword against her."

Then a great tumult arose, a tumult of rage and of dismay, for well nigh all in that vast place were partners in this crime, and knew that if Neter-Tua prevailed death yawned wide for them.

They shouted to Abi to take no heed of her.

They shouted to him to tear her from the throne, to kill her, and seize the crown. They drew their swords and raged like an angry sea. Those who were loyal among them to Pharaoh's House, and those who feared turmoil, began to work their way backwards, and slipped by twos and threes out of the great open doors, till Tua had no friend left in all that hall. But ever as they went, others of the turbulent and the rebellious who had been concerned in the slaughter of Pharaoh's guard, took their place, pouring in from the mob without.

Wild desert-dwellers of the Bedouin tribes, who for thousands of years had been the bitter enemies of Egypt; descendants of the Hyksos, whose fore-fathers had ruled the land for a dozen generations, and at last been driven out; those Hyksos whose blood ran in Abi's veins, and who looked to him to lift them up again; evil-doers who had sought shelter in his regiments; hook-nosed Semites from the Lebanon; black, barbarian savages from the shores of Punt—with such as these was that hall filled.

Abi was the hope of every one of them; to him they looked for the spoils of Egypt, and before them on Abi's throne they saw a woman who stood be-tween them and their ends, who in her ancient pride dared to demand that he, her husband, should do homage to her, and who to-morrow, if she conquered, would give them to the sword.

"Tear her to pieces!" they screamed, "the bastard whom childless Pharaoh palmed off upon the land! She is a sorceress who keeps fat on air—an evil spirit. Away with her! Or if you fear, then let us come!"

At length they had roared themselves hoarse ; at length they grew still.   Then Abi, who all this while had stood there hesitating, and now and again turning to hearken to Kaku who whispered in his ear, looked up at Tua and spoke.

" You see and you hear, Queen," he said.   " My people mistrust you, and they are a rough people, I cannot hold them back for long.   If once they get at you, very soon that sweet body of yours will be in more fragments than was Osiris after Set had handled him."

Now Tua, who hitherto had sat still and in-different, like one who takes no heed, seemed to awake, and answered :

" A bad example, Prince, for Osiris rose again, did he not ? "   Then she leaned back and once more was silent.

" Do you still desire that I should do homage to you, Queen, I, your husband ? " he asked pre-sently.

" Why not ? " she replied.   " I have spoken. A decree of Pharaoh may not be changed, and though a woman, I am—Pharaoh."

Now Abi went white with rage, and turned to his guard to bid them drag her from the throne. But she who was watching him, suddenly lifted her sceptre and spoke in a new voice, a clear, strong voice that rang through the hall, and even reached those who were gathered on the steps without.

" There is a question between you and me, O People," she said, " and it is this—Shall I, your Queen, rule in Egypt, as my fathers ruled, or shall yonder man rule whom by the decree of Amen I have taken for husband ? Now you who for the most part have the Hyksos blood running in your veins, as he has, desire that he should rule, and you have slain the good god, my father, and would make Abi king over you, and see me his handmaid, one to give him children of my royal race, no more. See, you are a multitude and my legions are far away, and I—I am alone, one lamb among the jackals, thousands and thousands of jackals who for a long while have been hungry. How, then, can I match myself against you ? "

" You cannot," shouted a wild-eyed spokesman. " Come down, lamb, and kneel before the lion, Abi, or we, the jackals, will rend you. We will not acknowledge you, we who are of the fierce Hyksos blood. While the obelisks stand without the cedar doors, those obelisks that were set up by the great Hyksos Pharaoh whose descendant was Abi's mother, while the obelisks stand that are set there for all eternity, we will not acknowledge you. Come down and take your place in our lord's harem, O Pharaoh's bastard daughter."

" Ah ! " Tua repeated after him, " while the obelisks stand that the Hyksos thief set up you will not acknowledge me, Pharaoh's bastard daughter ! "

Then she paused and seemed to grow disturbed ; she sighed, wrung her hands a little, and said in a choking voice :

" I am but one woman alone among you. My father, Pharaoh, is dead, and you bid me lay down my rank and henceforth rule only through him who trapped Pharaoh and brought him to his end. What, then, can I do ? "

" Be a good maid and obey your husband,
Bastard," mocked a voice, and during the roar of
laughter that followed Tua looked at the speaker,
an officer of Abi's, who had taken a great part in
the slaughter of their escort.

Very strangely she looked at him, and those
who stood by the man noted that his lips became
white, and that he turned so faint that had it not
been for the press about him he would have fallen.
Presently he seemed to recover, and asked the priests
who were near to let him join their circle, as among
the outer throng the heat was too great for him
to bear. Thereon one of them nodded and made
room for him, and he passed in, which Tua noted
also.

Now she was speaking again.

" Ill names to throw at Egypt's anointed queen,
crowned and accepted by the god himself in the
sanctuary of his most holy temple," she said, her
eyes still resting on the brutal soldier. " Yet it
is your hour, and she must bear them who has no
friends in Memphis. Oh ! what shall I do ? " and
again she wrung her hands. " Good People, it was
sworn to me that Amen, greatest of the gods, set
his spirit within me when I was born, and vowed
that he would help me in the hour of my need. Of
your grace, then, give me space to pray to Amen.
Look," and she pointed before her, " yonder sinks
the red ball of the sun ; soon, soon it will be gone
—give me until it enters the gateways of the West
to pray to Amen, and then if no help comes I will
bow me to your· bidding, and do homage to this
noble Prince of the Hyksos blood, who snared

Pharaoh his brother, and by help of his magicians and of his spy, Merytra, brought him to his end."

" Yes, my people, give her the space she asks," called Abi, who feared nothing from Amen, a somewhat remote personage, and was afraid lest some tumult should happen in the course of which this lovely, new-made wife of his might be slain or injured.

So they gave her the space of time she asked. Standing up, Tua raised her arms and eyes towards heaven, and began to pray aloud :

" Hear me, Amen my Father, in the House of thy Rest, as thou hast sworn to do. O Amen my Father, thou seest my strait. Is it thy will that thy daughter should degrade herself and thee before this man who slew his king and brother, to whom thou hast commanded her to give the name of husband ? If it be so, I will obey ; but if it be not so, then show thy word by might or marvel, and cause him and his folk who mock my majesty and name me bastard, to bow down before me. O Amen, they deny thee in their hearts who worship other gods, as did the barbarians who begat them and threw down thy shrines in Egypt, but I know that thou sentest me forth, and in thee I put my trust, aye, even if thou slay me. Amen my Father, yonder sinks that glory in which thou dost hide thy spirit. Now, ere it be gone and night falls upon the world, declare thyself in such fashion that all men may know that indeed I am thy child; or if this be thy decree, desert me and Egypt, and leave me to my shame."

She ended her prayer and, sinking back upon the throne, rested her chin upon her hand, and gazed

steadily upon the splendour of the sinking sun.
Nor did she gaze alone, for every man in that vast
hall turned himself about, and stared at its departing
glory. There in the red light they stood, and stared,
and since the place was open to the sky, the shadows
of the two towering obelisks without fell on them
like the shadows of swords whereof the points met
together at the foot of Tua's throne. They did not
believe that anything would happen, no, not even
the priests believed it who here at Memphis, the
city of Ptah, thought little of Amen, the god of
Thebes. They thought that this piteous prayer
was but a last cry of dying faith wrung from a
proud and fallen woman in her wretchedness.

And yet, and yet they stared, for she had spoken
with a strange certainty like one who knew the god,
and was she not named Star of Amen, and were there
not wondrous tales as to her birth, and had not a
lotus-bloom seemed to turn to gold and jewels in
the hand of this young, anointed Queen who bore
the Cross of Life upon her breast ? No, nothing
would happen, but still they stared.

It was a very strange sunset. For days the heat
had been great, but now it was fearful, also a marvellous stillness reigned in heaven and earth. Nothing
seemed to stir in all the city, no dog barked, no child
cried, no leaf quivered upon the tall palms ; it might
have been a city of the dead.

Dense clouds arose upon the sky, and moved,
though no wind blew. Where the sun's rays touched
them they were gold and red and purple, but above
these of an inky blackness. They took strange
shapes those clouds, and marshalled themselves

like a host gathering for battle. There were the
commanders moving swiftly to and fro ; there the
chariots, and there the sullen lines of footmen with
their gleaming spears. Now one cloud higher than
the rest seemed to shoot itself across the arch of
heaven, and its fashion was that of a woman with
outspread hair of gold. Her feet stood upon the
sun, her body bent itself athwart the sky, and upon
the far horizon in the east her hands held the pale
globe of the rising moon.

The watchers were frightened at this cloud.
" It is Isis with the moon in her arms," said one.
" Nay, it is the mother goddess Nout brooding
upon the world," answered another. And though
they only spoke softly, in that awful silence their
voices reached Tua on the throne, and for the first
time her face changed, for on it came a cold, curious
smile.

Kaku began to whisper into Abi's ear, and there
was fear in the eyes of both of them. He pointed
with his finger at two stars, which of a sudden shone
out through the green haze above the sunset glow,
and then turned and looked at the Queen, urging
his master eagerly. At last Abi spoke.

" Ra is set," he said. " Come, let us make an
end of all this folly."

" Not yet," answered Tua quietly, " not yet
awhile."

As she said the words, of a sudden, as though
at a given signal, all the long lines of palm trees
that grew in the rich gardens upon the river banks
were seen to bow themselves towards the east, as
though they did obeisance to the Queen upon her

throne. Thrice they bowed thus, without a wind, and then were straight and still once more. Next the clouds rushed together as though a black pall had been drawn across the heavens, only in the west the half-hidden globe of the sun shone on through an opening in them, shone like a great and furious eye. By slow degrees it sank, till nothing was left save a little rim of fire. All the hall grew dark, and through the darkness Neter-Tua could be heard calling on the name of Amen.

" Ra is dead ! " shouted a voice. " Have done, Bastard, Ra is dead ! "

" Aye," she answered in a cold triumphant cry, " but Amen lives. Behold his sword, ye Traitors ! "

As the words left her lips the heavens were cleft in twain by a fearful flash of lightning, and in it the people saw that once again the palm-trees bowed themselves, this time almost to the ground. Then with a roar the winds were loosed, and beneath their feet the solid earth began to heave as though a giant lifted it. Thrice it heaved like a heaving wave, and the third time through the thick cover of the darkness there rose a shriek of terror and of agony followed by the awful crash of falling stones.

Now the whole sky seemed to melt in fire, and in that fierce light was seen Tua, Star of Amen, seated on her throne, holding her sceptre to the heavens, and laughing in triumphant merriment. Well might she laugh, for the two great obelisks without the gate that the old Hyksos lion had set up there to stand " to all eternity," had fallen across the low pylons and the doors and crushed them. On to the heads of those who watched beneath they had fallen, shattering in their fall and carrying death to hundreds. Beneath the electrum cap of one of them that had been hurled from it in its descent right into the circle of the priests, lay a shapeless mass. It was that man who had mocked the Queen and turned faint beneath her gaze.

Through the western ruin of the hall those who were left alive within it fled out, a maddened mob, trampling each other to death by scores, fighting furiously to escape the vengeance of Amen and his daughter. Within the enclosure the priests lay prostrate on their faces, each praying to his god for mercy. In front of the throne, upon his knees, the royal crown shaken from his head, Abi grasped the feet of Neter-Tua and screamed to her to forgive and spare him, whilst above, shining like fire, That which sat upon the throne pointed with her sceptre at the ruin and the rout, and laughed and laughed again.

Soon all were gone save the mumbling priests, the dying, the dead, and Abi with his officers.

The clouds rolled off, the moon and the stars shone out, filling the place with gentle light. Then Tua spoke, looking down at the wretched Abi who grovelled before her.

" Say, now, Husband," she asked, " who is god in Egypt ? "

" Amen your father," he gasped.

" And who is Pharaoh in Egypt ? "

" You, and no other, O Queen."

" Ah ! " she said, " it was over that matter that we quarrelled, did we not ? which forced me, whom you thought so helpless, to find helpers. Look, there are their footsteps; they walk heavily, do they not, my Uncle?" and she nodded towards the huge fragments of the broken obelisks.

He glanced behind him at his ruined hall, at the dying and the dead. "You are Pharaoh and no other," he repeated with a shudder. "Give breath to your servant, and let him live on in your shadow."

"The first is not mine to give," she answered coldly, "though perchance it may please Amen to hold you back a little while from that place where you must settle your account with him who went before me, and his companions who died in your streets. I hope so, for you have work to do. As for the second—arise, you Priests and Officers, and see this Prince of yours do homage to the Queen of Egypt."

They rose, and clung to each other trembling, for all the heart was out of them. Then she pointed to her foot with the sceptre in her hand, and in their presence Abi knelt down and kissed her sandal. After him followed the others, the priests, the captains, the head-stewards, and the butlers, till at length came Kaku, the astrologer, who prostrated himself before her, trembling in every limb. But him she would not suffer even to touch her sandals.

"Tell me," she said, drawing back her foot, "you who are a magician, and have studied the secret writings, how does it chance that you still live on, when for lesser crimes so many lie here dead, you who are stained with the blood of Pharaoh?"

Hearing these words from which he presaged the very worst, Kaku beat his head upon the ground, babbling denials of this awful crime, and at the same time began to implore pardon for what he said he had not committed.

" Cease," she exclaimed, " and learn that your life is spared for a while, yes, and even Merytra's. Also you will retain your office of Vizier—for a while."

Now he began to pour out thanks, but she stopped him, saying :

" Thank me not, seeing that you do not know the end of this matter. Perchance it is hidden from you lest you should go mad, you and your wife, Merytra, she who was Pharaoh's Lady of the Footstool, and sang him to sleep. Look at me, Wizard, and tell me, who am I ? " and she bent down over him.

He glanced up at her, and their eyes met, nor could he turn his away again.

" Come," she said, " as you may have learned to-night, I also have some knowledge of the hidden things. For otherwise, why did the earth shake and the everlasting pillars fall at my bidding ? Now, between two of a trade there should be no secrets, so I will tell you something that perhaps you have already guessed, since I am sure that you will not repeat it even to your master or to Merytra. For I will add this—that the moment you repeat it will be the moment of your death, and the beginning of that punishment which here I withhold. Now, in the Name of the Eater-up of Souls, listen to me, O fashioner of waxen images ! " and, bending down, she whispered into his ear.

Another instant, and, stark horror written on his face, the tall shape of Kaku was seen reeling backward, like to a drunken man. Indeed, had not Abi caught him he would have fallen over the edge of the dais.

"What did she tell you?" he muttered, for the Queen, who seemed to have forgotten all about him, was looking the other way.

But, making no answer, Kaku wrenched himself free and fled the place.

CHAPTER XIII

ABI LEARNS THE TRUTH

A MOON had gone by, and on the first day of the new month Kaku the Vizier sat in the Hall of the Great Officers at Memphis, checking the public accounts of the city. It was not easy work, for during the past ten days twice these accounts had been sent back to him by the command of the Queen, or the Pharaoh as she called herself, with requests for information as to their items, and other awkward queries. Abi had overlooked such matters, recognising that a faithful servant was worthy of his hire—provided that he paid himself. But now it seemed that things were different, and that the amount received was the exact amount that had to be handed over to the Crown, neither more nor less. Well, there was a large discrepancy which must be made up from somewhere, or, in other words, from Kaku's private store.

In a rage he caused the two head collectors of taxes to be brought before him, and as they would not pay, bade the executioners throw them down and beat them on the feet until they promised to produce the missing sums, most of which he himself had stolen.

Then, somewhat soothed, he retired from the hall into his own office, to find himself face to face with Abi, who was waiting for him. So changed

was the Prince from his old, portly self, so aged
and thin and miserable did he look, that in the dusk
of that chamber Kaku failed to recognise him.
Thinking that he was some suppliant, he began to
revile him and order him to be gone. Then the
fury of Abi broke out.

Rushing at him, he seized the astrologer by the
beard and smote him on the ears, saying: "Dog,
is it thus that you speak to your king? Well, on
you at least I can revenge myself."

"Pardon, your Majesty," said Kaku, "I did
not know you in these shadows. Your Majesty is
changed of late."

"Changed!" said Abi, letting him go. "Who
would not be changed who suffers as I do ever since
I listened to your cursed counsel, and tried to climb
into the seat of Pharaoh? Before that I was happy.
I had my sons, I had my wives, as many as I wished.
I had my revenues and armies. Now everything
has gone. My sons are dead, my women are driven
away, my revenues are taken from me, my armies
serve another."

"At least," suggested Kaku, "you are Pharaoh,
and the husband of the most beautiful and the wisest
woman in the world."

"Pharaoh!" groaned Abi. "The humblest
mummy in the common city vaults is a greater
king than I am, and as for the rest——" and he
stopped and groaned again.

"What is the matter with your Majesty?"
asked Kaku.

"The matter is that I have fallen under the
influence of an evil planet."

" The Star of Amen," suggested the astrologer.

" Yes, the Star of Amen, that lovely Terror whom you call my wife. Man, she is no wife to me. Listen—there in the harem I went into the chamber where she was, none forbidding me, and found her sitting before her mirror and singing, clothed only in a thin robe of white, and her dark hair—O Kaku, never did you see such hair—which fell almost to the ground. She smiled on me, she spoke me fair, she drew me with those glittering eyes of hers— yes, she even called me husband, and sighed and talked of love, till at length I drew near to her and threw my arms about her."

" And then——"

" And then, Kaku, she was gone, and where her sweet face should have been I saw the yellow, mummied head of Pharaoh, he who is with Osiris, that seemed to grin at me. I opened my arms again, and lo ! there she sat, laughing and shaking perfume from her hair, asking me, too, what ailed me that I turned so white, and if such were the way of husbands ?

" Well, that was nigh a month ago, and as it began, so it has gone on. I seek my wife, and I find the mummied head of Pharaoh, and all the while she mocks me. Nor may I see the others any more, for she has caused them to be hunted hence, even those who have dwelt with me for years, saying that she must rule alone."

" Is that all ? " asked Kaku.

" No, indeed, for as she torments me, so she torments every other man who comes near to her. She nets them with smiles, she bewitches them with

H

her eyes till they go mad for love of her, and then, still smiling, she sends them about their business. Already two of them who were leaders in the great plot have died by their own hands, and another is mad, while the rest have become my secret but my bitter foes, because they love my Queen and think that I stand between her and them."

" Is that all ? " asked Kaku again.

" No, not all, for my power is taken from me. I who was great, after Pharaoh the greatest in all the land, now am but a slave. From morning to night I must work at tasks I hate ; I must build temples to Amen, I must dig canals, I must truckle to the common herd, and redress their grievances and remit their taxes. More, I must chastise the Bedouin who have ever been my friends, and—next month undertake a war against that King of the Khita, with whom I made a secret treaty, and whose daughter that I married has been sent back to him because I loved her."

" And then ? " asked Kaku.

" Oh ! then when the Khita have been destroyed and made subject to Egypt, then her Majesty purposes to return in state to Thebes ' to attend to the fashioning of my sepulchre ' since, so she says, this is a matter that will not bear delay. Indeed, already she makes drawings for it, horrible and mystic drawings that I cannot understand, and brings them to me to see. Moreover, Friend, know this, out of it opens another smaller tomb for *you*. Indeed, but this morning she sent an expedition to the desert quarries to bring thence three blocks of stone, one for my sarcophagus, one for yours, and one for that

of your wife, Merytra. For she says that after the
old fashion she purposes to honour both of you
with these gifts."

At these words Kaku could no longer control
himself, but began to walk up and down the room,
muttering and snatching at his beard.

"How can you suffer it ?" he said at length,
"You who were a great prince, to become a woman's
slave, to be made as dirt beneath her feet, to be held
up to the mockery of those you rule, to see your wives
and household driven away from you, to be tor-
mented, to be mocked, to look on other men favoured
before your eyes, to be threatened with early death.
Oh ! how can you suffer it ? Why do you not kill
her, and make an end ? "

"Because," answered Abi, "because I dare not,
since if I dreamed of such a thing she would guess
my thought and kill *me*. Fool, do you not remember
the fall of the eternal obelisks upon my captains,
and what befell that man who mocked her, calling
her Bastard, and sought refuge among the priests ?
No, I dare not lift a finger against her."

"Then, Prince, you must carry your yoke until
it wears through to the marrow, which will be when
that sepulchre is ready."

"Not so," answered Abi, shivering, "for I have
another plan ; it is of it that I am come to speak
with you. Friend Kaku, *you* must kill her. Listen :
you are a master of spells. The magic which prevailed against the father will overcome the daughter
also. You have but to make a waxen image or
two and breathe strength into them, and the thing
is done, and then—think of the reward."

"Indeed I am thinking, most noble Prince," replied the astrologer with sarcasm. "Shall I tell you of that reward? It would be my death by slow torture. Moreover, it is impossible, for if you would know the truth, she cannot be killed."

"What do you mean, Fool?" asked Abi angrily. "Flesh and blood must bow to death."

A sickly smile spread itself over Kaku's thin face as he answered:

"A saying worthy of your wisdom, Prince. Certainly the experience of mankind is that flesh and blood must bow to death. Yes, yes, flesh and blood!"

"Cease grinning at me, you ape of the rocks," hissed the enraged Abi, "or I will prove as much on your mocking throat," and snatching out his sword he threatened him with it, adding: "Now tell me what you mean, or——"

"Prince," ejaculated Kaku, falling to his knees, "I may not, I cannot. Spare me, it is a secret of the gods."

"Then get you gone to the gods, you lying cur, and talk it over with them," answered Abi, lifting the sword, "for at least she will not blame me if I send you there."

"Mercy, mercy!" gasped Kaku, sprawling on the ground, while his lord held the sword above his bald head, thinking that he would choose speech rather than death.

It was at this moment, while the astrologer's fate trembled in the balance, that a sound of voices reached their ears, and above them the ring of a light, clear laugh which they knew well. Forgetting

his purpose, Abi stepped to the window-place, and
looked through the opening of the shutters. Presently he turned, beckoning to Kaku, and whispered :
   " Come and look ; there is always time for you
to die."
   The Vizier heard, and, creeping on his hands
and knees to the window-place, raised himself and
peeped through the shutter. This was what he saw.
In the walled garden below, the secret garden of
the palace, stood the queen Neter-Tua, and the
sunlight piercing through the boughs of a flowering
tree, fell in bright bars upon her beauty. She was
not alone, for before her knelt a man wearing the
rich robes of a noble. Kaku knew him at once,
for although still young, he was Abi's favourite
captain, an officer whom he loved, and had raised
to high place because of his wit and valour, having
given him one of his daughters in marriage. Also
he had played a chief part in the great plot against
Pharaoh, and it was he who had dealt the death-
blow to Mermes, the husband of the lady Asti.
   Now he was playing another part, namely that of
lover to the Queen, for he clasped the hem of her
robe in his hands, and kissed it with his lips, and
pleaded with her passionately. They could catch
some of his words.
   He had risked his life to climb the wall. He
worshipped her. He could not live without her.
He was ready to do her bidding in all things—to
gather a band and slay Abi ; it would be easy, for
every man was jealous of the Prince, and thought
him quite unworthy of her. Let her give him her
love, and he would make her sole Pharaoh of Egypt

again, and be content to serve her as a slave. At least let her say one kind word to him.

Thus he spoke, wildly, imploringly, like a man that is drunk with passion and knows not what he says or does, while Neter-Tua listened calmly, and now and again laughed that light, low laugh of hers.

At length he rose and strove to take her hand, but, still laughing, she waved him back, then said suddenly :

" You slew Mermes when he was weak with wounds, did you not, and he was my foster-father. Well, well, it was done in war, and you must be a brave man, as brave as you are handsome, for other-wise you would scarcely have ventured here where a word of mine would give you to your death. And now get you gone, Friend, back to my Lord's daughter who is your wife, and if you dare—tell her where you have been and why, you who are so brave a man," and once more she laughed.

Again he began his passionate implorings, begging for some token, till at length she seemed to melt and take pity on him, for stretching out her hand, she chose a flower from the many that grew near, and gave it to him, then pointed to the trees that hid the wall, among which presently he vanished, reeling in the delirium of his joy.

She watched him go, smiling very strangely, then, still smiling, looked down at the bush whence she had plucked the flower, and Kaku noted that it was one used only by the embalmers to furnish coronals for the dead.

But Abi noted no such thing. Forgetting his quarrel with Kaku and all else, he gasped, and foamed in his jealous rage, muttering that he would kill that captain, yes, and the false Queen, too, who dared to listen to a tale of love and give the lover flowers. Yes, were she ten times Pharaoh he would kill her, as he had the right to do, and, the naked sword still in his hand, he turned to leave the place.

"If that is your will, Lord," said Kaku in a strained voice, "bide here."

"Why, man?" asked Abi.

"Because her Majesty comes," he answered, "and this chamber is quiet and fitting. None enter it save myself."

As he spoke the words the door opened, and closed again, and before them stood Neter-Tua, Star of Amen.

In the dusk of that room the first thing that seemed to catch her eye was the bared blade in Abi's hand. For a moment she looked at it and him, also at Kaku crouching in the corner, then asked in her quiet voice:

"Why is your sword drawn, O Husband?"

"To kill you, O Wife," he answered furiously, for his rage mastered him.

She continued to look at him a little while and said, smiling in her strange fashion:

"Indeed? But why more now than at any other time? Has Kaku's counsel given you courage?"

"Need you ask, shameless woman? Does not this window-place open on to yonder garden?"

"Oh! I remember, that captain of yours—he who slew Mermes, your daughter's husband who made love to me—so well that I rewarded him with a funeral flower, knowing that you watched us. Settle your account with him as you and his wife may wish ; it is no matter of mine. But I warn you that if you would take men's lives for such a fault as this, soon you will have no servants left, since they all are sinners who desire to usurp your place."

Then Abi's fury broke out. He cursed and reviled her, he called her by ill names, swearing that she should die, who bewitched all men and was the love of none, and who made him a mock and a shame in the sight of Egypt. But Neter-Tua only listened until at length he raved himself to silence.

" You talk much and do little," she said at length. " The sword is in your hand, use it, I am here."

Maddened by her scorn he lifted the weapon and rushed at her, only to reel back again as though he had been smitten by some power unseen. He rested against the wall, then again rushed and again reeled back.

" You are a poor butcher," she said at length, " after so many years of practice. Let Kaku yonder try. I think he has more skill in murder."

" Oh ! your Majesty," broke in the astrologer, " unsay those cruel words, you who know that rather than lift hands against you I would die a thousand times."

" Yes," she answered gravely, " the Prince Abi suggested it to you but now, did he not, after you had suggested it to him, and you refused—for your own reasons ? "

Then the sword fell from Abi's hand, and there was silence in that chamber.

" What were you talking of, Abi, before you peeped through the shutters and saw that captain of yours and me together in the garden, and why did you wish to kill this dog ? " she went on presently. " Must I answer for you ? You were talking of how you might be rid of me, and you wished to kill him because he did not dare to tell you why he could not do the deed, knowing that if he did so he must die. Well, since you desire to know, you shall learn, and now. Look on me, wretched Man, whom men name my husband. Look on me, accursed Slave, whom Amen has given into my hand to punish here upon the earth, until you pass to his yonder in the Under-world."

He looked, and Kaku looked also, because he could not help it, but what they saw they never told. Only they fell down upon their faces, both of them, and groaned ; beating the floor with their foreheads.

At length the icy terror seemed to be lifted from their hearts, and they dared to glance up again, and saw that she was as she had been, a most royal and lovely woman, but no more.

" What are you ? " gasped Abi. " The goddess Sekhet in the flesh, or Isis, Queen of Death, or but dead Tua's ghost sent here for vengeance ? "

" All of them, or none of them, as you will, though, Man, it is true that I am sent here for vengeance. Ask the Wizard yonder. He knows, and I give him leave to say."

" *She is the Double of Amen's daughter,*" moaned Kaku. " She is her Ka set free to bring doom upon those who would have wronged her. She is a ghost
н*

armed with the might of the gods, and all we who
have sinned against dead Pharaoh and her and her
father Amen are given into her hand to be tor-
mented and brought to doom."

"Where, then, is Neter-Tua, who was Queen of
Egypt ? " gasped Abi, rolling his great eyes. "Is
she with Osiris ? "

"I will tell you, Man," answered the royal
Shape. "She is not dead—she lives, and is gone to
seek one she loves. When she returns with him and
a certain Beggar, then I shall depart and you will
die, both of you, for such is the punishment decreed
upon you. Until then, arise and do my bidding."

CHAPTER XIV

THE BOAT OF RA

TUA, Star of Amen, opened her eyes. For some
time already she had lain as one lies between sleep
and waking, and it seemed to her that she heard
the sound of dipping oars, and of water that rippled
gently against the sides of a ship. She thought
to herself that she dreamed. Doubtless she was in
her bed in the palace at Thebes, and presently,
when it was light, her ladies would come to waken
her.

In the palace at Thebes! Why, now she remembered that it was months since she had seen
that royal city, she who had travelled far since then,
and come at last to white-walled Memphis, where
many terrible things had befallen her. One by
one they came into her mind; the snare, Pharaoh's
murder by magic, the battle, and the slaughter of
her guards, the starvation in the tower, with death
on one hand, and the hateful Abi in the other;
the wondrous vision of that spirit who wore her
face, and said she was the guardian Ka given to
her at birth, the words it spoke, and her dread
resolve; and last of all Asti and herself standing
in the lofty window niche, then a flame of fire before
her face, and that fearful downward rush.

Oh! without a doubt it was over; she was dead,
and these dreams and memories were such as come

to the dwellers in the Under-world. Only then
why did she hear the sound of lapping water, and
of dipping oars ?

Very slowly she opened her eyes, for Tua greatly
feared what she might see. Light flowed upon her,
the light of the moon which hung in a clear sky
like some great lamp of gold. By it she saw that,
robed all in white, she lay upon a couch in a pavilion,
whereof the silken curtains were drawn back in
front, and tied to gilded posts. At her side, wrapped
in a grey robe, lay another figure, which she knew
for Asti. It was still, so still that she was sure it
must be dead, yet she knew that this was Asti.
Perchance Asti dreamed also, and could hear her
in her dreams ; at least, she would speak to her.

" Asti," she whispered, " Asti, can you hear
me ? "

The grey figure at her side stirred, and the head
turned towards her. Then the voice of Asti, none
other, answered :

" Aye, Lady, I hear and see. But say, where are
we now ? "

" In the Under-world, I think, Asti. Oh ! that
fire was death, and now we journey to the Place
of Souls."

" If so, Lady, it is strange that we should still
have eyes and flesh and voices as mortal women have.
Let us sit up and look."

So they sat up, their arms about each other,
and peered through the open curtains. Behold !
they were on a ship more beautiful than any they
had ever seen, for it seemed to be covered with gold
and silver, while sweet odours floated from its hold.

Their pavilion was set in the centre of the ship and looking aft, they perceived lines of white-clad rowers seated at their oars in the shadow of the bulwarks, and on the high stern—also robed in white—a tall steersman whose face was veiled, behind whom in the dim glimpses of the moon, they caught sight of a wide and silvery river, and on its distant banks palms and temple towers.

" It is the Boat of Ra," murmured Tua, " which bears us down the River of Death to the Kingdom behind the Sun."

Then she sank back upon her cushions, and once more fell into swoon or sleep.

Tua woke again, and lo ! the sun was shining brightly, and at her side sat Asti watching her. Moreover, in front of them was set a table spread with delicate food.

" Tell me what has chanced, Nurse," she said faintly, " for I am bewildered, and know not in what world we wander."

" Our own, Queen, I think," answered Asti, " but in charge of those who are not of it, for surely this is no mortal boat, nor do mortals guide her to her port. Come, we need food. Let us eat while we may."

So they ate and drank heartily enough, and when they had finished even dared to go out of the pavilion. Looking around them they saw that they stood upon a high deck in the midst of a great ship, but that this deck was enclosed with a net of silver cords in which they could find no opening. Looking through its meshes they noted that the oars were inboard, and the great purple sails set upon the mast, also that the rowers were gone, perchance to rest beneath the deck, while on the forecastle of the ship stood the captain, white-robed and masked, and aft the steersman, also still masked, so that they could see nothing of their faces. Now, too, they were no longer sailing on a river, but down a canal bordered by banks of sand on either side, beyond which stretched desert farther than the eye could reach.

Asti studied the desert, then turned and said:

" I think I know this canal, Lady, for once I sailed it as a child. I think it is that which was dug by the Pharaohs of old, and repaired after the fall of the Hyksos kings, and that it runs from Bubastis to that bay down which wanderers sail towards the rising sun."

" Mayhap," answered Tua. " At least, this is the world that bore us and no other, and by the mercy of Amen and the power of my Spirit we are still alive, and not dead, or so it seems. Call now to the captain on yonder deck ; perhaps he will tell whither he bears us in his magic ship."

So Asti called, but the captain made no sign that he saw or heard her. Next she called to the steersman, but although his veiled face was towards them, he also made no sign, so that at last they believed either that these were spirits or that they were men born deaf and dumb. In the end, growing weary of staring at this beautiful ship, at the canal and the desert beyond it, and of wondering where they were, and how they came thither, they returned to the pavilion to avoid the heat of the sun. Here they found that during their absence some hand unseen had arranged the silken bed-clothing on their couches and cleared away the fragments of their meal, resetting the beautiful table with other foods.

"Truly here is wizardry at work," said Tua, as she sank into a leather-seated ivory chair that was placed ready.

"Who doubts it?" answered Asti calmly. "By wizardry were you born; by wizardry was Pharaoh slain; by wizardry are we saved to an end that we cannot guess; by wizardry, or what men so name, does the whole world move; only being so near we see it not."

Tua thought a while, then said:

"Well, this golden ship is better than the sty of Abi the hog, nor do I believe that we journey to no purpose. Still I wonder what that spirit who named herself my Ka does on the throne of Egypt; also how we came on board this boat, and whither we sail."

"Wonder not, for all these things we shall learn in due season, and for my part, although I hate him I am sorry for Abi," answered Asti drily.

So they sat there in the pavilion watching the desert, over the sands of which their ship seemed to move, till at length the sun grew low, and they went to walk upon the deck. Then they returned to eat of the delicious food that was always provided for them in such plenty, and at nightfall sought their couches, and slept heavily, for they needed rest.

When they awoke again, it was daylight, though no sun shone through the clouds, and their vessel rolled onward across a wide and sullen sea out of sight of land. Also the silken pavilion about them was gone, and replaced by a cabin of massive cedar wood, though of this, being sated with marvels, Tua and Asti took little note. Indeed, having neither of them been on an angry ocean before, a strange dizziness overcame them, which caused them to sleep much and think little for three whole days and nights.

At length, one evening as the sun sank, they perceived that the violent motion of the vessel had ceased with the roaring of the gale above, which for all this while had driven them onward at such fearful speed. Venturing from their cedar house, they saw that they had entered the mouth of a great river upon the banks of which grew enormous trees that sent out long crooked roots into the water, and that among these roots crouched crocodiles and other noisome reptiles. Also the white-robed oarsmen had appeared again, and, as there was no wind, rowed the ship up the river, till at length they came to a spit of sand which jutted out into the stream, and here cast anchor.

Now Tua's and Asti's desire for food returned to them, and they ate. Just as they had finished their meal, and the sun was sinking suddenly, there appeared before them two masked men, each of whom bore a basket in his hand. Asti began to question them, but, like the captain and the steersman, they seemed to be deaf and dumb. At least they made no answer, only prostrated themselves humbly, and pointed towards the shore where now Tua saw a fire burning upon a rock, though who had lit it she did not know.

"They mean us to leave the ship," said Asti. "Come, Queen, let us follow our fortunes, for doubtless these are high.

"As you will," answered Tua, "seeing that we should scarcely have been brought here to no end."

So they accompanied the men to the side of that splendid vessel, for now the netting that confined them had been removed, to find that a gangway had been laid from its bulwark to the shore. As they stepped on to this gangway their masked companions handed to each of them one of the baskets, then again bowed humbly and were gone. Soon they gained the bank, and scarcely had their feet touched it when the gangway was withdrawn, and the great oars began to beat the muddy water.

Round swung the ship, and for a minute hung in midstream. There stood the captain on the foredeck, and there was the steersman at the helm, and the red light of the sinking sun turned them into figures of flame. Suddenly with a simultaneous motion these men tore off their masks so that for a moment Asti and Tua saw their faces—and behold! the face of the captain was the face of Pharaoh, Tua's father, and the face of the steersman was the face of Mermes, Asti's husband.

For one moment only did they see them, then a dark cloud hid the dying sun, and when it passed that ship was gone, whither they knew not.

The two women looked at each other, and for the first time were much afraid.

"Truly," said Tua, "we are haunted if ever mortals were, for yonder ship has ghosts for mariners."

"Aye, Lady," answered Asti, "so have I thought

from the first. Still, take heart, for these ghosts once were men who loved us well, and doubtless they love us still. Be sure that for no ill purpose have we been snatched out of the hand of Abi, and brought living and unharmed by the shades of Pharaoh your sire, and Mermes my husband, to this secret shore. See, yonder burns a fire, let us go to it, and await what may befall bravely, knowing that at least it can be naught but good."

So they went to the rock and, darkness being come, sat themselves down by the fire, alongside of which lay wood for its replenishment, and near the wood soft robes of camel-hair to shield them from the cold. These robes they put on with thankfulness, and, having fed the flame, bethought them of and opened the baskets which were given to them when they left the ship. The first basket, that which Asti held, they found to contain food, cakes, dried meats and dates, as much as one woman could carry. But the second, that which had been given to Tua, was otherwise provided, for in the mouth of it lay a lovely harp of ivory with golden strings, whereof the frame was fashioned to the shape of a woman. Tua drew it out and looked at it by the light of the fire.

" It is my own harp," she said in an awed voice, " the harp that the Prince of Kesh, whom Rames slew, brought as a gift to me, to the notes of which I sang the Song of the Lovers but just before the giver died. Yes, it is my own harp that I left in Thebes. Say, now, Nurse, how came it here ? "

" How came *we* here ? " answered Asti shortly. " Answer my question, and I will answer yours."

Then, laying down the harp, Tua looked again into her basket and found that beneath a layer of dried papyrus leaves were hidden pearls, thousands of pearls of all sizes, and of such lustre and beauty as she had never seen. They were strung upon threads of silk, all those of a like size being set upon a single thread, except the very biggest, which were as great as a finger nail, or even larger, that lay wrapped up separately in cloth at the bottom of the basket.

"Surely," said Tua, amazed, "no Queen in all the earth ever had a dower of such priceless pearls. Moreover, what good they and the harp can be to us in this forest I may not guess."

"Doubtless we shall discover in due course," answered Asti ; "meanwhile, let us thank the gods for their gifts and eat."

So they ate, and then, having nothing else to do, lay down by the fire and would have slept.

But scarcely had they closed their eyes when the forest seemed to awake. First from down by the river there came dreadful roarings which they knew must be the voice of lions, for there were tame beasts of this sort in the gardens at Thebes. Next they heard the whines and whimperings of wolves and jackals, and mingled with them great snortings such as are made by the rhinoceros and the river-horse.

Nearer, nearer came these awful sounds, till at length they saw yellow eyes moving like stars in the darkness at the edge of the forest, while across the patch of sand beneath their rock galloped swift shapes which halted and sniffed towards them. Also on the river side of them appeared huge, hog-like beasts, with gleaming tusks, and red cavernous mouths, and beyond these again, crashing through the brushwood, a gigantic brute that bore a single horn upon its snout.

"Now our end is at hand," said Tua faintly, "for surely these creatures will devour us."

But Asti only threw more wood upon the fire and waited, thinking that the flame would frighten them away. Yet it did not, for so curious, or so hungry were they, that the lions crept and crept nearer, and still more near, till at length they lay lashing their tails in the sand almost within springing distance of the rock, while on the farther side of these, like a court waiting on its monarch, gathered the hyenas and other beasts.

"They will spring presently," whispered Tua.

"Did the Spirits of the divine Pharaoh your father, and of Mermes my lord, bring us here in the Boat of Ra that we should be devoured by wild animals, like lost sheep in the desert?" asked Asti. Then, as though by an inspiration, she added, "Lady, take that harp of yours, and play and sing to it."

So Tua took the harp and swept its golden chords, and, lifting up her lovely voice, she began to sing. At first it trembled a little, but by degrees, as she forgot all save the music, it grew strong, and rang out sweetly in the silence of the forest, and the great, slow-moving river. And lo! as she sang thus, the wild brutes grew still, and seemed to listen as though they were charmed. Yes, even a snake wriggled out from between the rocks and listened, waving its crested head to and fro.

At length Tua ceased, and as the echoes died away the brutes, every one of them, turned and vanished into the forest or the river, all save the snake that coiled itself up and slept where it was. So stillness came again, and Tua and Asti slept also, nor did they wake until the sun was shining in the heavens.

Then they arose wondering, and went down over the patch of sand that was marked with the footprints of all the beasts to the river's brink, and drank and washed themselves, peering the while through the mists, for they thought that perchance they would see that golden ship with the veiled crew which had carried them from Memphis, returned and awaiting them in midstream.

But no ship was there; nothing was there except the river-horses which rose and sank, and the crocodiles on the mud-banks, and the wildfowl that flighted inward from the sea to feed. So they went back to the ashes of their fire and ate of the food in Asti's basket, and, when they had eaten, looked at each other, not knowing what to do. Then Tua said:

"Come, Nurse, let us be going. Up the river and down the river we cannot walk, for there are nothing but weeds and mud, so we must strike out through the forest, whither the gods may lead us."

Asti nodded, and, clad in the light warm clothes of camel-hair, they set the baskets upon their heads after the fashion of the peasant women of Egypt and started forward, the harp of ivory and of gold hanging upon Tua's back.

For hour after hour they marched thus through the forest, threading their path between the big boles of the trees, and heading always for the south, for that way ran the woodland glades beyond which was dense bush. Great apes chattered above them in the tree tops, and now and again some beast of prey crossed their path and vanished in the underwood, but nothing else did they see. At length, towards midday, the ground began to rise, and the trees grew smaller and farther apart, till at last they reached the edge of a sandy desert, and walked out to a little oasis, where the green grass showed them they would find water. In this oasis there was a spring, and by the edge of it they sat down and drank, and ate of their store of food, and afterwards slept a while.

Suddenly Tua, in her sleep, heard a voice, and, awaking with a start, saw a man who stood near by, leaning on a thornwood staff and contemplating them. He was a very strange man, apparently of great age, for his long white hair fell down upon his shoulders, and his white beard reached to his middle. Once he must have been very tall, but now he was bent with age, and the bones of his gaunt frame thrust out his ragged garments. His dark eyes also were horny, indeed it seemed as though he could scarcely see with them, for he leaned forward to peer at their faces where they lay. His face was scored by a thousand wrinkles, and almost black with exposure to the sun and wind, but yet of a marvellous tenderness and beauty. Indeed, except that it was far more ancient, and the features were on a larger and a grander scale, it reminded Tua of the face of Pharaoh after he was dead.

"My Father," said Tua, sitting up, for an impulse prompted her to name this wanderer thus, "say whence do you come, and what would you with your servants?"

"My Daughter," answered the old man in a sweet, grave voice, "I come from the wilderness which is my home. Long have I outlived all those of my generation, yes, and their children also. Therefore the wilderness and the forest that do not change are now my only friends, since they alone knew me when I was young. Be pitiful now to me, for I am poor, so poor that for three whole days no food has passed my lips. It was the smell of the meat which you have with you that led me to you. Give me of that meat, Daughter, for I starve."

"It is yours, O——" and she paused.

"I am called Kepher."

"Kepher, Kepher!" repeated Tua, for she thought it strange that a beggar-man should be named after that scarabæus insect which among the Egyptians was the symbol of eternity. "Well, take and eat, O Kepher," she said, and handed him the basket that contained what was left to them of their store.

The beggar took it, and having looked up to heaven as though to ask a blessing on his meal, sat down upon the sand and began to devour the food ravenously.

"Lady," said Asti, "he will eat it all, and then we shall starve in this desert. He is a locust, not a man," she added, as another cake disappeared.

"He is our guest," answered Tua gravely, "let him take what we have to give."

For a while Asti was silent, then again she broke out into remonstrance.

"Peace, Nurse," replied Tua, "I have said that he is our guest, and the law of hospitality may not be broken."

"Then the law of hospitality will bring us to our deaths," muttered Asti.

"If so, so let it be, Nurse; at least this poor man will be filled, and for the rest, as always, we must trust to Amen our father."

Yet as she spoke the words tears gathered in her eyes, for she knew that Asti was right, and now that all the food was gone, on which with care they might have lived for two days or more, soon they would faint, and perish, unless help came to them, which was not likely in that lonesome place. Once, not so long ago, they had starved for lack of sustenance, and it was the thought of that slow pain so soon to be renewed, that brought the water to her eyes.

Meanwhile Kepher, whose appetite for one so ancient was sharp indeed, finished the contents of the basket down to the last date, and handed it back to Tua with a bow, saying:

"I thank you, Daughter; the Queen of Egypt could not have entertained me more royally," and he peered at her with his horny eyes. "I who have been empty for long, am full again, and since I cannot reward you I pray to the gods that they will do so. Beautiful Daughter, may you never know what it is to lack a meal."

At this saying Tua could restrain herself no more.
A large tear from her eyes fell upon Kepher's rough
hand as she answered with a little sob :

" I am glad that you are comforted with meat,
but do not mock us, Friend, seeing that we are but
lost wanderers who very soon must starve, since now
our food is done."

" What, Daughter," asked the old man in an
astonished voice, " what ? Can I believe that you
gave all you had to a beggar of the wilderness, and
sat still while he devoured it ? And is it for this
reason that you weep ? "

" Forgive me, Father, but it is so," answered
Tua. " I am ashamed of such weakness, but re-
cently my friend here and I have known hunger,
very sore hunger, and the dread of it moves me.
Come, Asti, let us be going while our strength remains in us."

Kepher looked up at the name, then turned to
Tua and said :

" Daughter, your face is fair, and your heart is
perfect, since otherwise you would not have dealt
with me as you have done. Still, it seems that you
lack one thing—undoubting faith in the goodness
of the gods. Though, surely," he added in a slow
voice, " those who have passed yonder lion-haunted
forest without hurt should not lack faith. Say,
now, how came you there ? "

" We are ladies of Egypt," interrupted Asti,
" or at least this maiden is, for I am but her old
nurse. Man-stealing pirates of Phœnicia seized us
while we wandered on the shores of the Nile, and
brought us hither in their ship, by what way we

do not know. At length they put into yonder river for water, and we fled at night. We are escaped slaves, no more."

" Ah ! " said Kepher, " those pirates must mourn their loss. I almost wonder that they did not follow you. Indeed, I thought that you might be other folk, for, strangely enough, as I slept in the sand last night, a certain spirit from the Underworld visited me in my dreams, and told me to search for one Asti and another lady who was with her—I cannot remember the name of that lady. But I do remember the name of the spirit, for he told it to me ; it was Mermes."

Now Asti gave a little cry, and, springing up, searched Kepher's face with her eyes, nor did he shrink from her gaze.

" I perceive," she said slowly, " that you who seem to be a beggar are also a seer."

" Mayhap, Asti," he answered. " In my long life I have often noted that sometimes men are more than they seem—and women also. Perhaps you have learned the same, for nurses in great houses may note many things if they choose. But let us say no more. I think it is better that we should say no more. You and your companion—how is she named ? "

" Neferte," answered Asti promptly.

" Neferte, ah ! Certainly that was not the name which the spirit used, though it is true that other name began with the same sound, or so I think. Well, you and your companion, Neferte, escaped from those wicked pirates, and managed to bring certain things with you, for instance, that beautiful

harp, wreathed with the royal *uræi*, and—but what
is in that second basket ? "

" Pearls," broke in Tua quickly.

" And a large basket of pearls. Might I see
them ? Oh ! do not be afraid, I shall not rob
those whose food I have eaten, it is against the
custom of the desert."

" Certainly," answered Tua. " I never thought
that you would rob us, for if you were of the tribe
of thieves, surely you would be richer, and less
hungry than you seem. I only thought that you
were almost blind, Father Kepher, and therefore
could not know the difference between a pearl and
a pebble."

" My feeling still remains to me, Daughter
Neferte," he answered with a little smile.

Then Tua gave him the basket. He opened it
and drew out the strings of pearls, feeling them,
smelling and peering at them, touching them with
his tongue, especially the large single ones which
were wrapped up by themselves. At length, having
handled them all, he restored them to the basket,
saying drily :

" It is strange, indeed, Nurse Asti, that those
Syrian man-stealers attempted no pursuit of you,
for here, whether they were theirs or yours, are
enough gems to buy a kingdom."

" We cannot eat pearls," answered Asti.

" No, but pearls will buy more than you need
to eat."

" Not in a desert," said Asti.

" True, but as it chances there is a city in this
desert, and not so very far away."

" Is it named Napata ? " asked Tua eagerly.

" Napata ? No, indeed. Yet, I have heard of such a place, the City of Gold they called it. In fact, once I visited it in my youth, over a hundred years ago."

" A hundred years ago ! Do you remember the way thither ? "

" Yes, more or less, but on foot it is over a year's journey away, and the path thither lies across great deserts and through tribes of savage men. Few live to reach that city."

" Yet I will reach it, or die, Father."

" Perhaps you will, Daughter Neferte, perhaps you will, but I think not at present. Meanwhile, you have a harp, and therefore it is probable that you can play and sing ; also you have pearls. Now the inhabitants of this town whereof I spoke to you love music. Also they love pearls, and as you cannot begin your journey to Napata for three months, when the rain on the mountains will have filled the desert wells, I suggest that you would do wisely to settle yourselves there for a while. Nurse Asti here would be a dealer in pearls, and you, her daughter, would be a musician. What say you ? "

" I say that I should be glad to settle myself anywhere out of this desert," said Tua wearily. " Lead us on to the city, Father Kepher, if you know the way."

" I know the way, and will guide you thither in payment for that good meal of yours. Now come. Follow me." And taking his long staff he strode away in front of them.

" This Kepher goes at a wonderful pace for an old man," said Tua presently. " When first we saw him he could scarcely hobble."

" Man ! " answered Asti. " He is not a man, but a spirit, good or bad, I don't know which, appearing as a beggar. Could a man eat as much as he did—all our basketful of food ? Does a man talk of cities that he visited in his youth over a hundred years ago, or declare that my dead husband spoke to him in his dreams ? No, no, he is a ghost like those upon the ship."

" So much the better," answered Tua cheerfully, " since ghosts have been good friends to us, for had it not been for them I should have been dead or shamed to-day."

" That we shall find out at the end of the story," said Asti, who was cross and weary, for the heat of the sun was great. " Meanwhile, follow on. There is nothing else to do."

For hour after hour they walked, till at length towards evening, when they were almost exhausted, they struggled up a long rise of sand and rocks, and from the crest of it perceived a large walled town set in a green and fertile valley not very far beneath them. Towards this town Kepher, who marched at a distance in front, guided them till they reached a clump of trees on the outskirts of the cultivated land. Here he halted, and when they came up to him, led them among the trees.

" Now," he said, " drop your veils and bide here, and if any should come to you, say that you are poor wandering players who rest. Also, if it pleases you, give me a small pearl off one of those strings, that

I may go into the city, which is named Tat, and sell
it to buy you food and a place to dwell in."

" Take a string," said Tua faintly.

" Nay, nay, Daughter, one will be enough, for
in this town pearls are rare, and have a great value."

So she gave him the gem, or rather let him take
it from the silk, which he re-fastened very neatly
for one who seemed to be almost blind, and strode
off swiftly towards the town.

" Man or spirit, I wonder if we shall see him
again ? " said Asti.

Tua made no answer—she was too tired, but
resting herself against the bole of a tree, fell into a
doze. When she awoke again it was to see that
the sun had sunk, and that before her stood the
beggar Kepher, and with him two black men, each
of whom led a saddled mule.

" Mount, Friends," he said, " for I have found
you a lodging."

So they mounted, and were led to the gate of
the city which at the word of Kepher was opened
for them, and thence down a long street to a house
built in a walled garden. Into this house they
entered, the black men leading off the mules, to
find that it was a well-furnished place with a table
ready set in the ante-room, on which was food in
plenty. They ate of it, all three of them, and when
they had finished Kepher bade a woman who was
waiting on them, lead them to their chamber, saying
that he himself would sleep in the garden.

Thither then they went without more questions,
and throwing themselves down upon beds which
were prepared for them, were soon fast asleep.

CHAPTER XV

TUA AND THE KING OF TAT

In the morning, after Tua and Asti had put on the clean robes that lay to their hands, and eaten, suddenly they looked up and perceived that Kepher, the ancient beggar of the desert, was in the room with them, though neither of them had heard or seen him enter.

"You come silently, Friend," said Asti, looking at him with a curious eye. "A Double could not move with less noise, and—where is your shadow?" she added, staring first at the sun without, and then at the floor upon which he stood.

"I forgot it," he answered in his deep voice. "One so poor as I am cannot always afford a shadow. But look, there it is now. And for the rest, what do you know of Doubles which those who are uninstructed cannot discern? Now I have heard of a Lady in Egypt who by some chance bore your name, and who has the power, not only to see the Double, but to draw it forth from the body of the living, and furnish it with every semblance of mortal life. Also I have heard that she who reigns in Egypt to-day has such a Ka or Double that can take her place, and none know the difference, save that this Ka, which Amen gave her at her birth, works the vengeance of the gods without pity or remorse. Tell me, Friend Asti, when you were a slave-woman

in Egypt did you ever hear talk of such things as
these ? "

Now he looked at Asti, and Asti looked at him,
till at length he moved his old hands in a certain
fashion, whereon she bowed her head and was silent.

But Tua, who was terrified at this talk, for she
knew not what would befall them if the truth were
guessed, broke in, saying :

" Welcome, Father, however it may please you
to come, and with or without a shadow. Surely
we have much to thank you for who have found us
this fine house and servants and food—by the way,
will you not eat again ? "

" Nay," he answered, smiling, " as you may
have guessed yesterday, I touch meat seldom ; as
a rule, once only in three days, and then take my
fill. Life is so short that I cannot waste time in
eating."

" Oh ! " said Tua, " if you feel thus whose
youth began more than a hundred years ago, how
must it seem to the rest of us ?   But, Father Kepher,
what are we to do in this town Tat ? "

" I have told you, Maiden.   Asti here will deal
in pearls and other goods, and you will sing, but
always behind the curtain, since here in Tat you
must suffer no man to see your beauty, and least
of all him who rules it.   Now give me two more
pearls, for I go out to buy for you other things that
are needful, and after that perhaps you will see
me no more for a long while.   Yet if trouble should
fall upon you, go to the window-place wherever you
may be, and strike upon that harp of yours, and
call thrice upon the name of Kepher.   Doubtless

there will be some listening who will hear you and
bring me the news in the Desert, where I dwell
who do not love towns, and then I may be able to
help you."

"I thank you, my Father, and I will remember.
But pardon me if I ask how can one so——" and she
paused.

"So old, so ragged and so miserable give help to
man or woman—that is what you would say, Daughter
Neferte, is it not? Well, judge not from the outward seeming; good wine is often found in jars
of common clay, and the fire hid in a rough flint
can destroy a city."

"And therefore a wanderer who can swallow his
own shadow can aid another wanderer in distress,"
remarked Tua dryly. "My Father, I understand,
who although I am still young, have seen many
things and ere now been dragged out of deep water
by strange hands."

"Such as those of Phœnician pirates," suggested
Kepher. "Well, good-bye. I go to purchase what
you need with the price of these pearls, and then
the Desert calls me for a while. Remember what
I told you, and do not seek to leave this town of
Tat until the rain has fallen on the mountains,
and there is water in the wells. Good-bye, Friend
Asti, also; when I come again we will talk more
of Doubles, until which time may the great god of
Egypt—he is called Amen, is he not?—have you
and your Lady in his keeping."

Then he turned and went.

"What is that man?" asked Tua when they
had heard the door of the house close behind him.

ɪ

" Man ? " answered Asti. " I have told you that he is no man. Do men unfold their shadows like a garment ?   He is a god or a ghost, wearing a beggar's shape."

" Man or ghost, I like him well for he has befriended us in our need, Nurse."

" That we shall know when he has done with us," answered Asti.

An hour later, whilst they were still talking of Kepher and all the marvels that had befallen them, porters began to arrive, bearing bundles which, when opened, were found to contain silks and broideries in gold and silver thread, and leather richly worked, such as the Arabs make, and alabaster pots of ointments, and brass work from Syria, and copper jars from Cyprus, with many other goods, all very costly, and in number more than enough for a wealthy trader's store.

These goods the porters set out on the mats and shelves of the large front room of the house that opened to the street, which room seemed to have been built to receive them.   Then they departed, asking no fees, and there appeared a man riding a fine white horse, who dismounted, and, bowing low towards the screen of pierced wood-work behind which Tua and Asti were hidden, laid a writing upon a little table, and rode away.   When he had gone Asti opened the door in the screen and took the writing which she found she could read well enough, for it was in the Egyptian character and language.

It proved to be the title-deed of the house and garden conveyed to them jointly, and also of the rich goods which the porters had brought. At the foot of this document was written—

" Received by Kepher the Wanderer in payment of the above house and land and goods, three pearls and one full meal of meat and dates."

Then followed the seal of Kepher in wax, a finely cut scarabæus holding the symbol of the sun between its two front feet.

" A proud seal for a tattered wanderer, though it is but his name writ in wax," said Tua.

But Asti only answered :

" If small pearls have such value in this city, what price will the large ones bring ? Well, let us to our business, for we have time upon our hands, and cannot live upon pearls and costly stuffs."

So it happened that Neter-Tua, Star of Amen, Queen of Egypt, and Asti her Nurse, the Mistress of Magic, became merchants in the town of Tat.

This was the manner of their trade. For one hour in the morning, and one in the afternoon, Asti, heavily veiled, and a woman of the servants whom they had found in the house, would sit on stools amidst the goods and traffic with all comers, selling to those who would buy, and taking payment in gold dust or other articles of value, or buying from those who would sell. Then when the hour drew towards its close Tua would sweep her harp behind the screen that hid her and begin to sing, whereon all would cease from their chaffering and listen, for never before had they heard so sweet a voice. Indeed, at these times the broad street in front of their house was packed with people, for the fame of this singing of hers went through the city and far into the country that lay beyond. Then the traffic came to an end, with her song, and leaving their goods in charge of the servants, Tua and Asti departed to the back rooms of the house, and ate their meals or wandered in the large, walled garden that lay behind.

Thus the weeks went on and soon, although they sold few of the pearls, and those the smallest, for of the larger gems they said little or nothing, they began to grow rich, and to hoard up such a weight of gold in dust and nuggets, and so many precious things, that they scarcely knew what they should do with them. Still that seemed to be a peaceful city, or at the least none tried to rob or molest them, perhaps because a rumour was abroad that these strangers who came out of the Unknown were under the protection of some god.

There was nothing to show how or why this rumour had arisen in the city, but on account of it, if for no other reason, these pearl-merchants, as they were called, suffered no wrong, and although they were only undefended women, whatever credit they might give, the debt was always paid. Also their servants, to whom they added as they had means, were all faithful to them. So there they remained and traded, keeping their secrets and awaiting the appointed hour of escape, but never venturing to leave the shelter of their own walls.

Now, as it happened, when they came thither the King of Tat was away making war upon another king whose country lay upon the coast, but after they had dwelt for many weeks in the place, this King, who was named Janees, returned victorious from his war and prepared to celebrate a triumph.

While he was making ready for this triumph his courtiers told him of these pearl-merchants, and, desiring pearls for his adornment on that great day, he went in disguise to the house of those who sold them. As it chanced he arrived late, and requested to see the gems just as Tua, according to her custom, was playing upon her harp. Then she began to sing, and this King Janees, who was a man of under forty years of age, listened intently to her beautiful voice, forgetting all about the pearls that he had come to buy. Her song finished, the veiled Asti rose, and bowing to all the company gathered in the street, bade her servants shut up the coffers and remove the goods.

" But I would buy pearls, Merchant, if you have such to sell," said Janees.

" Then you must return this afternoon, Purchaser," replied Asti, scanning his pale and haughty face, " for even if you were the King of Tat I would not sell to you out of my hours."

" You speak high words, Woman," exclaimed Janees angrily.

" High or low, they are what I mean," answered Asti, and went away.

The end of it was that this King Janees returned at the evening hour, led thither more by a desire to hear that lovely voice again than to purchase gems. Still he asked to see pearls, and Asti showed him some which he thrust aside as too small. Then she produced those that were larger, and again he thrust them aside, and so it went on for a long while. At length from somewhere in her clothing Asti drew two of the biggest that she had, perfect pearls of the size of the middle nail of a man's finger, and at the sight of these the eyes of Janees brightened, for such gems he had never seen before. Then he asked the price. Asti answered carelessly that it was doubtless more than he would wish to pay, since there were few such pearls in the whole world, and she named a weight in gold that caused him to step back from her amazed, for it was a quarter of the tribute that he had taken from his new-conquered kingdom.

"Woman, you jest," he said, "surely there is some abatement."

"Man," she answered, "I jest not; there is no abatement," and she replaced the pearls in her garments.

Now he grew very angry, and asked:

"Do you know that I am the King of Tat, and if I will, can take your pearls without any payment at all?"

"Are you?" asked Asti, looking at him coolly. "I should never have guessed it. Well, if you steal my goods, as you say you can, you will be King of Thieves also."

Now those who heard this saying laughed, and the King thought it best to join in their merriment. Then the bargaining went on, but before it was finished, at her appointed hour Tua began to sing behind the screen.

"Have done," said the King to Asti, "to-morrow you shall be paid your price. I would listen to that music which is above price."

So Janees listened like one fascinated, for Tua was singing her best. Step by step he drew ever nearer to the screen, though this Asti did not notice, for she was engaged in locking up her goods. At length he reached it, and thrusting his fingers through the openings in the pierced woodwork, rested his weight upon it like a man who is faint, as perhaps he was with the sweetness of that music. Then of a sudden, by craft or chance, he swung himself backward, and with him came the frail screen. Down it clattered to the floor, and lo! beyond it, unveiled, but clad in rich attire, stood Tua sweeping her harp of ivory and gold. Like sunlight from a cloud the bright vision of her beauty struck the eyes of the people gathered there, and seemed to dazzle them, since for a while they were silent. Then one said :

" Surely this woman is a queen," and another answered :

" Nay, she is a goddess," but ere the words had left his lips Tua was gone.

As for Janees the King, he stared at her open-mouthed, reeling a little upon his feet, then, as she fled, turned to Asti, saying :

" Is this Lady your slave ? "

" Nay, King, my daughter, whom you have done ill to spy upon."

" Then," said Janees slowly, " I who might do less, desire to make this daughter of yours my Queen —do you understand, Merchant of Pearls—my Queen, and as a gift you shall have as much gold again as I have promised for your gems."

" Other kings have desired as much and offered

more, but she is not for you or any of them," answered Asti, looking him in the face.

Now Janees made a movement as though he would strike her, then seemed to change his mind, for he replied only :

"A rough answer to a fair offer, seeing that none know who you are or whence you come. But there are eyes upon us. I will talk with you again to-morrow ; till then, rest in peace."

"It is useless," began Asti, but he was already gone.

Presently Asti found Tua in the garden, and told her everything.

"Now I wish that Kepher of the Desert were at hand," said Tua nervously, "for it seems that I am in a snare, who like this Janees no better than I did Abi or the Prince of Kesh, and will never be his Queen."

"Then I think we had better fly to the wilderness and seek him there this very night, for, Lady, you know what chances to men who look upon your loveliness."

"I know what chanced to the Prince of Kesh, and what will chance to Abi at the hands of one I left behind me, I can guess ; perhaps this Janees will fare no better. Still, let us go."

Asti nodded, then by an afterthought went into the house and asked some questions of the servants. Presently she returned, and said :

"It is useless ; soldiers are already stationed about the place, and some of our women who tried to go out have been turned back, for they say that by the King's order none may leave our door."

" Now shall I strike upon the harp and call upon the name of Kepher, as he bade me ? " asked Tua.

" I think not yet awhile, Lady. This danger may pass by or the night bring counsel, and then he would be angry if you summoned him for naught. Let us go in and eat."

So they went in, and while they sat at their food suddenly they heard a noise, and looking up, perceived by the light of the lamp that women were crowding into the room led by two eunuchs.

Tua drew a dagger from her robe and sprang up, but the head eunuch, an old, white-haired man, bowed low before her, and said :

" Lady, you can kill me if you will, for I am unarmed, but there are many more of us without, and to resist is useless. Hearken ; no harm shall be done to you or to your companion, but it is the King's desire that one so royal and beautiful should be better lodged than in this place of traffic. Therefore he has commanded me to take you and all your household and all your goods to no less a place than his own palace, where he would speak with you."

" Sheathe the dagger and waste no words upon these slaves, Daughter," said Asti. " Since we have no choice, let us go."

So after they had veiled and robed, they suffered themselves to be led out and placed in a double litter with their pearls and gold, while the King's women collected all the rest of their goods and took them away together with their servants, leaving the house quite empty. Then, guarded by soldiers,

*t**

they were borne through the silent streets till they came to great gates which closed behind them, and having passed up many stairs, the litter was set down in a large and beautiful room lit with silver lamps of scented oil. Here, and in other rooms beyond, they found women of the royal household and their own servants already arranging their possessions.

Soon it was done, and food and wine having been set for them, they were left alone in that room, and stood looking at each other.

" Now shall I strike and call ? " said Tua, lifting the harp which she had brought with her. " Look, yonder is a window-place such as that of which Kepher spoke."

" Not yet, I think, Lady. Let us learn all our case ere we call for help," and as the words left her lips the door opened, and through it, clad in his royal robes, walked Janees the King.

Now in the centre of this great room was a marble basin filled with pure water which, perhaps, had served as the bath of the queens who dwelt there in former days, or, perhaps, was so designed for the sake of coolness in times of heat. Tua and Asti stood upon one side of this basin, and to the other came the King, so that the water lay between them. Thrice he bowed to Tua, then said :

" Lady, who, as your servants tell me, are known as Neferte, a maiden of Egypt, and for lack of the true name, doubtless this will serve, Lady, I come to ask your pardon for what must seem to you to be a grievous wrong. O Lady Neferte, this must be my excuse, that I have no choice. By

fortune, good or ill, I know not which, this day I
beheld your face, and now but one desire is left to
me, to behold it again, and for all my life. Lady,
the Goddess of Love, she, whom in Egypt you name
Hathor, has made me her slave, so that I no longer
think of pomp or power or wealth, or of other women,
but of you and you only. Lady, I would do you
no harm, for I offer you half my throne. You and
you alone shall be my Queen. Speak now."

" King Janees," answered Tua, " what evil spirit
has entered into you that you should wish to make
a Queen of a singing-girl, the daughter of a merchant
who has wandered to your city ? Let me go, and
keep that high place for one of the great ones of
the earth. Send now to Abi, who I have heard
rules as Pharaoh in Egypt, and ask a daughter of
his blood, for they say that he has several ; or to
some of the princes of Syria, or to the King of Byblos
by Lebanon, or to the lords of Kesh, or across the
desert to the Emperor of Punt, and let this poor
singing-girl go her ways."

" This poor singing-girl," repeated Janees after
her, " who, or whose mother," and he bowed to
Asti with a smile, " has pearls to sell that are worth
the revenue of a kingdom ; this singing-girl, the ivory
figure on whose harp is crowned with the royal
uræi of Egypt ; this singing-girl whose chiselled
loveliness is such as might be found perhaps among
the daughters of ancient kings ; this singing-girl
whose voice can ravish the hearts of men and beasts !
Well, Lady Neferte, I thank you for your warning,
still I am ready to take my chance, hoping that my
children will not be made ashamed by the blood of

such a singing-girl as this, who, as I saw when that screen fell, has stamped upon her throat the holy sign they worship on the Nile."

" I am honoured," answered Tua coldly, " yet it may not be. Among my own humble folk I have a lover, and him I will wed or no man."

" You have a lover ! Then hide his name from me, lest presently I should play Set to his Osiris and rend him into pieces. You shake your head, knowing doubtless that the man is great, yet I tell you that I will conquer him and rend him into pieces for the crime of being loved by you. Listen now ! I would make you my Queen, but Queen or not, mine you shall be who lie in my power. I will not force you, I will give you time. But if on the morning of the third day from this night you still refuse to share my throne, why, then you shall sit upon its footstool."

Now, in her anger, Tua threw back her veil, and met him eye to eye.

" You think me great," she said, " and truly you are right, for whatever is my rank, with me go my gods, and in their strength my innocence is great. Let me be, you petty King of Tat, lest I lift up my voice to heaven, and call down upon you the anger of my gods."

" Already, Lady, you have called down upon me the anger of a goddess, that Hathor of whom I spoke, and for the rest I fear them not. Let them do their worst. On the third night from this night, as Queen or slave, I swear that you shall be mine. This woman here, whom you call your mother, shall be witness to my oath, and to its end."

" Aye, King," broke in Asti, " I will be witness, but as to the end of that oath I do not know it yet. Would you like to learn ? In my own country I was held to have something of a gift, I mean in the way of magic. It came to me, I know not whence, and it is very uncertain—at times it is my servant, and at times I can do nothing. Still, for your sake, I would try. Is it your pleasure to see that end of which you spoke, the end of your attempt to force yonder maiden to be your queen or love ? "

" Aye, Woman," answered Janees, " if you have a trick, show it—why not ? "

" So be it, King ; but, of course, I have your word that you will not blame me if by any chance the trick should not prove to your liking—your royal word. Now stand you there, and look into this water while I pray our gods, the gods of my own country, to be gracious, and to show you what shall be your state at this same hour on the third night from now, which you say and hope shall be the night of your wedding. Sing, my Daughter, sing that old and sacred song which I have taught you. It will serve to while away the tedium of our waiting until the gods declare themselves, if such be their will."

Then Asti knelt down by the pool, and bent her head, and stretched out her hands over the water, and Tua touched the strings of her harp and began to chant very solemnly in an unknown tongue. The words of that chant were low and sweet, yet it seemed to Janees that they fell like ice upon his hot blood, and froze it within his veins. At first he kept his eyes fixed upon her beauty, but by slow

degrees something drew them down to the water
of the pool.

Look! A mist gathered on its blackness. It
broke and cleared and there, as in a mirror, he saw
a picture. He saw himself lying stripped and dead,
a poor, naked corpse with wide eyes that stared
to heaven, and gashed throat and sides whence the
blood ran upon the marble floor of his own great
hall, ruined by fire, with its scorched pillars pointing
like fingers to the moon. There he lay alone, and
by him stood a hound, his own hound, that lifted
up its head and seemed to howl.

The last words of Tua's chant died away, and
with them that picture passed. Janees leapt back
from the edge of the pool, glaring at Asti.

"Sorceress!" he cried, "were you not my guest
who names herself the mother of her who shall be
my Queen, I swear that to-night you should die by
torture in payment of this foul trick of yours."

"Yet as it is," answered Asti, "I think that I
shall not die, since those who call upon the gods
must not quarrel with their oracle. Moreover, I
know not what you saw, and it may be nothing but
a fantasy of your brain or of mine. Now let us sleep,
I pray you, O King, for we are weary, and leave
its secrets to the future. In three days we shall
know what they may be."

Then, without another word, Janees turned and
left them.

"What was it that lay in the pool, Nurse?"
asked Tua. "I saw nothing."

"The shadow of a dead man, I think," answered
Asti grimly. "Some jealous god has looked upon

this poor King whose crime is that he desires you, and therefore he must die. Of a truth it goes ill with your lovers, O Star of Amen, and sometimes I wonder if one who is dear to me will meet with better fortune at those royal eyes of yours. If ill befalls him I think that at the last I may learn to hate you, whom from the first I cherished."

Now at the thought that she might bring death to Rames also, Tua's tears began to gather, and her voice choked in her throat.

" Say not such evil-omened words," she sobbed, " since you know well that if he is taken hence for whose sake I endure all these things, then I must follow him over the edge of the world. Moreover, you are unjust. Did I slay the Prince of Kesh, or was it another ? "

" Another, Queen, but for your sake."

" And would you have had me wed Abi the hog, the murderer of my father, and of your lord ? Again, was it I who but now showed this barbarian chief a shadow in the water, or was it Asti the witch, Asti the prophetess of Amen ? Lastly, will the man die, if die he must, because he loves me, which, being a woman I can forgive him, or because he laid the hands of violence upon me to force me to be his queen or mistress, which I forgive him not ? Oh ! Asti, you know well I am not as other women are. Perchance it is true that some blood that is not human runs in me ; at least I fulfil a doom laid on me before my birth, and working woe or working weal, I go as my feet are led by ghosts and gods. Why, then, do you upbraid me ? " and she ceased and wept outright.

" Nay, nay, be comforted, I upbraid you not,"
answered Asti, drawing her to her breast. " Who
am I that I should cast reproaches at Amen's Star
and daughter and my Queen ? I know well that
the house of your fate is built, that sail you up stream
or sail you down stream, you must pass its gate at
last. It was fear for Rames that made me speak
so bitterly, Rames my only child, if, indeed, he is
left to me, for I who have so much wisdom cannot
learn from man or spirit whether he lives here or
with Osiris, since some black veil hangs between our
souls. I fear lest the gods, grown jealous of that
high love of yours, should wreak their wrath upon
him who has dared to win it, and bring Rames to
the grave before his time, and the thought of it
rends my heart."

Now it was Tua's turn to play the comforter.

" Surely," she said, " surely, my Foster-mother,
you forget the promise of Amen, King of the Gods,
which he made ere I was born, to Ahura who bore
me, that I should find a royal lover, and that from
his love and mine should spring many kings and
princes, and that this being so, Rames must live."

" Why must he live, Lady, seeing that even if
he can be called royal, there are others ? "

" Nay, Asti," murmured Tua, laying her head
upon her breast, " for me there are no others, nor
shall any child of mine be born that does not name
Rames father. Whatever else is doubtful, this is
sure. Therefore Rames lives, and will live, or the
King of the gods has lied."

" You reason well," said Asti, and kissed her.
Then she thought a moment, and added : " Now

to our work, it is the hour. Take the harp, go to the window-place, and call as the beggar-man bade you do in your need."

So Tua went to the window-place and looked down on the great courtyard beneath that was lit with the light of the moon. Then she struck on the harp, and thrice she cried aloud :

" *Kepher ! Kepher ! Kepher !* "

And each time the echo of her cry came back louder and still more loud, till it seemed as though earth and heaven were filled with the sound of the name of Kepher.

CHAPTER XVI

THE BEGGAR AND THE KING

It was the afternoon of the third day. Tua and Asti, seated in the window-place of their splendid prison, looked through the wooden screen down into the great court below, where, according to his custom at this hour, Janees the King sat in the shadow to administer justice and hear the petitions of his subjects. The two women were ill at ease, for the time of respite had almost passed.

"Night draws near," said Tua, "and with it will come Janees. Look how he eyes this window, like a hungry lion waiting to be fed. Kepher has made no sign ; perchance after all he is but a wandering beggar-man filled with strange fancies, or perchance he is dead, as may well happen at his age. At least, he makes no sign, nor does Amen, to whom I have prayed so hard, send any answer to my prayers. I am forsaken. Oh ! Asti, you who are wise, tell me, what shall I do ? "

"Trust in the gods," said Asti. "There are still three hours to sundown, and in three hours the gods, to whom time is nothing, can destroy the world and build it up again. Remember when we starved in the pylon tower at Memphis, and what befell us there. Remember the leap to death and the Boat of Ra, and those by whom it was captained. Remember and trust in the gods."

" I trust—in truth I trust, Asti, but yet—oh !
let us talk of something else. I wonder what has
chanced in Memphis since we left it in so strange a
fashion ? Do you think that awful Ka of mine
queens it there with Abi for a husband ? If so, I
almost grieve for Abi, for she had something in her
eyes which chilled my mortal blood, and yet you
say she is a part of me, a spirit who cannot die, cast
in my mould, and given to me at birth. I would
I had another Ka, and that you could draw it forth
again, Asti, to bewitch this Janees, and hold him
while we fled. See, that case draws to an end at
length. Janees is giving judgment, or rather his
councillor is, for he prompts him all the time. Can
you not hear his whispers ? As for Janees himself,
his thoughts are here, I feel his eyes burn me through
this wooden screen. He is about to rise. Why !
Who comes ? Awake, Nurse, and look."

Asti obeyed. There in the gate of the court
she saw a tall man, white-bearded, yellow-faced,
horny-eyed, ancient, who, clad in a tattered robe,
leaned upon his staff of thornwood, and stared
about him blindly as though the sun bewildered
him. The guards came to thrust him away, but
he waved his staff, and they fell back from him as
though there were power in that staff. Now his
slow, tortoise-like eyes seemed to catch sight of the
glittering throne, and of him who sat upon it, and
with long strides he walked to the throne and halted
in front of it, again leaning on his staff.

" Who is this fellow," asked Janees in an angry
voice, " who stands here and makes no obeisance
to the King ? "

" Are you a king ? " asked Kepher. " I am very blind. I thought you were but a common man such as I am, only clad in bright clothes. Tell me, what is it like to be a king, and have all things beneath your feet. Do you still hope and suffer, and fear death like a common man ? Is the flesh beneath your gold and purple the same as mine beneath my rags ? Do old memories torment you, memories of the dead who come no more ? Can you feel griefs, and the ache of disappointment ? "

" Do I sit here to answer riddles, Fool ? " answered Janees angrily. " Turn the fellow out. I have business."

Now guards sprang forward to do the King's bidding, but again Kepher waved his staff, and again they fell back. Certainly it seemed as though there were power in that staff.

" Business, King," he said. " Not of the State, I think, but with one who lodges yonder," and he nodded towards the shuttered room whence Tua watched him. " Well, that is three hours hence after the sun has set, so you still have time to listen to my prayer, which you will do, as it is of this same lady with whom you have business."

" What do you know of the lady, you old knave, and of my dealings with her ? " asked Janees angrily.

" Much of both, O King, for I am her father, and—shall I tell the rest ? "

" Her father, you hoary liar ! " broke in Janees.

" Aye, her father, and I have come to tell you that as our blood is more ancient than yours, I will not have you for a son-in-law, any more than that daughter of mine will have you for a husband."

Now some of the courtiers who heard these words laughed outright, but Janees did not laugh, his dark face turned white with rage, and he gasped for breath.

" Drag this madman forth," he shouted at length, " and cut out his insolent tongue."

Again the guards sprang forward, but before ever they reached him Kepher was speaking in a new voice, a voice so terrible that at the sound of it they stopped, leaving him untouched.

" Beware how you lay a finger on me, you men of Tat," he cried, " for how know you who dwells within these rags ? Janees, you who call yourself a King, listen to the commands of a greater king, whose throne is yonder above the sun. Ere night falls upon the earth, set that maiden upon whom you would force yourself and her companion and all her goods without your southern gate, and leave them there unharmed. Such is the command of the King of kings, who dwells on high."

" And what if I mock at the command of this King ? " asked Janees.

" Mock not," replied Kepher. " Bethink you of a certain picture that the lady Asti showed you in the water, and mock not."

" It was but an Egyptian trick, Wizard, and one in which I see you had a hand. Begone, I defy you and your sorceries, and your King. To-night that maid shall be my wife."

" Then, Janees, Lord of Tat, listen to the doom that I am sent to decree upon you. To-night you shall have another bride, and her name is Death. Moreover, for their sins, and because their eyes are evil, and they have rejected the worship of the gods, many of your people shall accompany you to darkness, and to-morrow another King, who is not of your House, shall rule in Tat."

Kepher ceased speaking, then turned and walked slowly down the court of judgment and through its gates, nor did any so much as lift a finger to stay him, for now about this old man there seemed to be a majesty which made them strengthless.

" Bring that wizard back and kill him here," shouted Janees presently, as the spell passed off them, and like hounds from a leash they sprang forward to do the bidding of the King.

But without the walls they could not find him. A woman had seen him here, a child had seen him there, some slaves had watched him pass yonder, and ran away because they noted that he had no shadow. At length, after many a false turn, they tracked him to the southern gate, and there the guard said that just such a beggar-man had passed through as they were about to close the gate, vanishing into the sandstorm which blew without. They followed, but so thickly blew that sand that they lost each other in their search, and but just before sundown returned to the palace singly, where in his rage the king commanded them to be beaten with rods upon their feet.

Now the darkness came, and at the appointed hour Janees, hardening his heart, went up into the chamber where dwelt Tua and Asti, leaving his guard of eunuchs at the door. The lamps were lit within that chamber, and the window-places closed, but without the desert wind howled loudly, and

the air was blind with sand. On the farther side
of the marble basin, as once before, Tua and Asti
stood awaiting him.

"Lady," he said, "it is the appointed hour, and
I seek your answer."

"King," replied Tua, "hear me, and for your
own sake—not for mine. I am more than I seem.
I have friends in the earth and air, did not one of
them visit you to-day in yonder court? Put away
this madness and let me be, for I wish you good,
not evil, but if you so much as lay a finger on me,
then I think that evil draws near, or at the best
I die by my own hand."

"Lady," replied Janees in a cold voice, "have
done with threats; I await your answer."

"King," said Tua, "for the last time I plead with
you. You think that I lie to save myself, but it
is not so. I would save you. Look now," and she
threw back her veil and opened the wrappings about
her throat. "Look at that which is stamped upon
my breast, and think—is it well to offer violence
to a woman who bears this holy seal?"

"I have heard of such a one," said Janees hoarsely,
for the sight of her beauty maddened him. "They
say that she was born in Thebes, and of a strange
father, though, if so, how came she here? I am told
that she reigns as Pharaoh in Egypt."

"Ask that question of your oracles, O King, but
remember that rumour does not always lie, and let
the daughter of that strange father go."

"There is another who claims to be your father,
Lady, if by now my soldiers have not scourged him
to his death—a tattered beggar-man."

" Whom those soldiers could not touch or find,"
broke in Asti, speaking for the first time.

" Well," went on Janees, without heeding her,
" whether your father be a beggar or a god, or even
if you are Hathor's self come down from heaven to
be the death of men, know that I take you for
my own. For the third time, answer, will you be
my Queen of your own choice, or must my women
drown yonder witch in this water at your feet, and
drag you hence ? "

Now Tua made no answer. She only let fall
her veil, folded her arms upon her breast, and waited.
But Asti, mocking him, cried in a loud voice, that
he might hear above the howling of the hurricane
without :

" Call your women, King, for the air is full of
sand that chokes my throat, and I long for the
water which you promise me."

Then, in his fury, Janees turned, and shouted :

" Come hither, Slaves, and do what I have
commanded you."

As he spoke the door burst open, and through it,
no longer clad in rags, but wearing a white robe and
head-dress, walked Kepher the Wanderer, while after
him, their red swords in their hands, came savage-
looking chiefs, bearded, black-faced, round-eyed,
with gold chains that clanked upon their mail,
captains of the Desert, men who knew neither fear
nor mercy.

Janees looked and understood. He snatched out
his sword, and for a moment stayed irresolute, while
the great men ringed him round and waited, their
eyes fixed on Kepher's face.

" Spare him, Father, if it may be so," said Tua,
" since love has made him mad."

" Too late ! " answered Kepher solemnly. " Those
who will not accept the warning of the gods must
suffer the vengeance of the gods. Janees, you who
would do violence to a helpless woman, your palace
burns, your city is in my keeping, and the few who
stood by you are slain. Janees, to-morrow another
shall rule in your place. Amen the Father has
decreed your doom."

" Aye," echoed Janees heavily, " too late !
Mortals cannot fight against the gods that make
their sport of them. Some god commanded that I
should love. Some god commands that I shall die.
So be it, I am glad to die ; would that I had not been
born to know grief and death. Tell me, O Prophet,
what evil power is there which ordains that we
must be born and suffer ? "

Kepher beckoned to Tua and to Asti, and they
followed him, leaving Janees ringed round by those
stern-faced men.

" Farewell, Lady," he called to Tua as she passed.
" Here and hereafter remember this of Janees, King
of Tat, that he who might have saved his life chose
to die for love of you."

Then they went and saw him no more.

They passed the door of the great marble chamber
about which they found guards and eunuchs lying
dead ; they passed down the stairways, and through
the tall gates where more soldiers lay dead, and
looking behind them, saw that the palace was in
flames. They reached the square without, and at
the command of Kepher entered into a litter, and

were borne by black slaves whither they knew not.

All that night they were borne, awake or sleeping, till at length the morning came, and they descended from the litter to find themselves in an oasis of the wilderness surrounded by a vast army of the desert men. Of the city of Tat they could see nothing; like a dream it had passed out of their lives, nor did they ever hear of it and its king again. Only in the pavilion that had been provided for them they found their pearls and gold, and Tua's ivory harp.

They laid themselves down and slept, for they were very weary, only to wake when once more the day had dawned. Then they rose and ate of the food that had been placed by them, and went out of the tent. In the shadow of some palm trees stood Kepher, awaiting them, and with him certain of the stern-faced, desert chiefs, who bowed as they advanced.

" Hearken, Lady Neferte, and you, O Asti her companion," said Kepher to them, " I must depart, who, this matter finished, have my bread to beg far from here. Yet, fear not, for know that these Lords of the Desert are your servants, and for this reason were they born, that they may help you on your way. Repeat your orders," he continued, addressing the chiefs.

Then the captain of them all said :

" Wanderer, known to our fathers' grandfathers, Guardian of our race by whom we live and triumph, these are your commands : That we lead this divine Lady and her companion a journey of many moons across the deserts and the mountains, till at length we bring her to the gates of the City of Gold, where our task ends. While one man of us remains alive they shall be obeyed."

" You hear," said Kepher to Tua. " Put your trust in these men. Go in peace in the day time, and sleep in peace at night, for be sure that they shall not fail you. But if they, or any other should perchance bring you into trouble, then strike upon the harp and call the name you know, as you called it in the house of Janees the mad, and I think that one will come to you. Lords of the Desert, whose great grandsires were known to me, and who live by my wisdom, this divine Lady is in your keeping. See that you guard her as you should, and when the journey is done, return and make report to me. Farewell."

Then, lifting his staff, without speaking another word to Tua or to Asti, Kepher strode away from amongst them, walking through the ranks of the Desert men who forced their camels to kneel and saluted him as he passed. Presently they saw him standing alone upon a ridge, and looking towards them for a while. Then of a sudden he was gone.

" Who is that man, O Captain, at whose bidding the wilderness swarms with tribesmen and kings are brought to doom ? " asked Asti when she had watched him disappear.

" Lady," he answered, " I cannot tell you, but from the beginning he has been Master of the Desert, and those who dwell therein. At his word the sand-wind blows as it blew yesterday to cover our advance, at his word the fountains spring and tribes grow great or sink to nothingness. We think that he is a spirit

who moves where he lists, and executes the decrees
of heaven. At the least, though they but see him
from time to time, all the dwellers in the wilderness
obey him, as we do, and ill does it go, as you have
learned, with those dwellers in cities who know not
the power which breathes beneath that tattered robe."

"I thank you," answered Asti. "I think with
you that this Wanderer is a spirit, and a great one,
so great that I will not name his name. Captains,
my Lady is ready to march towards the City of Gold,
whither you will lead us."

For day after day, for week after week, for month
after month, they marched southward and westward
across the Desert, and in the centre of their host,
mounted upon camels, rode Tua and Asti veiled.
Once the hillmen attacked them in a defile of some
rugged mountains, but they beat them back, and
once there was a great battle with other tribes of
the wilderness, who, hearing that they had a goddess
among them, sought to capture her for themselves.
These tribes also they defeated with slaughter, for
when the fight hung in the balance Tua herself headed
the charge of her horsemen, and at the sight of her
in her white robes the enemy fled amazed. Once also
they camped for two whole moons in an oasis, waiting
till rain should fall, for the country beyond lacked
water. At length it came, and they went on again,
on and on over the endless lands, till on a certain
night they pitched their tent upon a hill.

At the first brightening of the dawn Tua and
Asti went out, and there, beneath them, near to the
banks of a great river, which they knew for the Nile,

they saw the pyramids and the temples of Napata
the Golden, the southern city of Amen, and thanked
the gods who had brought them here in safety.

While they still gazed upon its glories in the red
light of the rising sun the captain of the desert
men appeared, and bowed before them.

"Divine Lady," he said, "woman or goddess,
whichever you may be, we have fulfilled the command
given to us by Kepher, the ancient King of the Wilderness. Beneath you lies Napata whither we have
journeyed through so many weary months, but we
would draw no nearer to its walls, who from generation to generation are sworn not to enter any city
save in war. Lady, our task is done, and our men
murmur to be led back to their own place, where
their wives and children await them, ere, thinking
that we are enemies, the people of Napata sally
forth to attack us."

"It is well," answered Tua. "I thank you and
the gods shall give you your reward. Leave us, and
go back to your homes, but before you go, take a
gift from me."

Then she sent for the gold that they had
gathered in their trading in the city of Tat, and gave
it to be divided among them, a great and precious
treasure. Only the pearls she kept, with a little
of the gold. So the captains saluted her, and in the
mists of the morning they and their swarthy host
stole away, and soon were hidden in a cloud of
dust.

From the backs of their camels Tua and Asti
watched them go like a dream of the night. Then
with no word spoken between them, for their lips

were sealed with hope and wonder, wrapping themselves in their dark cloaks, they rode down to the highway by the banks of the Nile, which led to the walls of Napata. Mingling with other travellers, they passed through the Field of Pyramids, and coming to the beautiful northern gate that was covered over with gold, waited there, for this gate was not yet opened. A woman who led three asses laden with green barley and vegetables, which she purposed to sell in the market-place, fell into talk with them, asking them whence they came.

Asti answered, from the city of Meroe, adding that they were singers and dealers in pearls.

" Then you have come to the right place," answered the woman, " for pearls are rare at Napata, which is so far from the sea ; also it is said that the young King loves singing if it be good."

" The young King ? " asked Asti. " What is his name, and where is the old king ? "

" You cannot have dwelt long in Meroe, Strangers," answered the woman suspiciously, " or you would know that the old King dwells with Osiris beneath yonder pyramid, where the general of the Pharaoh of Egypt, he who rules here now, buried him after the great battle. Oh ! it is a strange story, and I do not know the rights of it who sell my stuff and take little heed of such things. But at the last high Nile before one this general came with three thousand soldiers of Egypt, and the body of the Prince of Kesh, whom it seems he had slain somewhere, it is said because both of them sought the favour of the Queen of Egypt. As they tell, this was the command of that Queen—that he should submit himself to the King of Napata to be judged for his crime. This he did, and the King in his fury commanded that he should be hanged from the mast of the sacred boat of Amen. The general answered that he was ready to be hanged if the King could hang him. Then there was a war between the people of Napata and the Egyptians, aided by many of the soldiers of the city who hated their master and rebelled against his rule, which was ever cruel. The end of it was that the Egyptians and the rebels won, and the King having fallen in the fight, they crowned the Egyptian general in his place.

"His name ?—Oh, I forget it, he has so many, but he is a goodly man to look at, and all love him although he is mad. See, the gates are open at last. Farewell," and dragging her asses by the halter, the peasant woman mingled with the crowd and was gone.

Tua and Asti also mingled with the crowd, and rode on up a wide street till they came to a square planted round with trees, on one side of which was built a splendid palace. Here they halted their camels, not knowing whither they should go, and as they stood irresolute the gates of the palace opened and through them came a body of horsemen clad in armour.

" See the writing on their shields," whispered Asti.

Tua looked and read, and lo ! there in the royal cartouche was her own name, and after it new titles—Queen of the Upper and the Lower Land, Opener of the Gates of the South, Divine Lady of Napata by grace of Amen, Father of the Gods.

" It seems that I have subjects here," she murmured, " who elsewhere have none," then ceased.

For now through the gate rode one mounted on a splendid horse, whose shape seemed familiar to her even while he was far away.

" Who is that ? " faltered Tua.

" My heart tells me it is Rames my son," answered Asti, grasping at her saddle-rope.

CHAPTER XVII

TUA FINDS HER LOVER

RAMES it was without a doubt ; Rames grown older and stern and sad of face, but still Rames, and no other man, and oh! their eyes swam and their hearts beat at the sight of him.

" Say, shall we declare ourselves ? " asked Asti.

" Nay," answered Tua, " not here and now. He would not believe, and we cannot unveil before all these men. Also, first I desire to learn more. Let him pass."

Rames rode on till he came opposite to where the two women sat on their white camels beneath a tree, when something seemed to attract his gaze to them. He looked once carelessly and turned his head away. He looked a second time, and again turned his head, though more slowly. He looked a third time, and his eyes remained fixed upon those two veiled women seated on their camels beneath the trees. Then, as though acting upon some impulse, he pulled upon his horse's bit, and rode up to them.

" Who are you, Stranger Ladies," he asked, " who own such fine camels ? "

Tua bowed her head that the folds of her veil might hide her shape, but Asti answered in a feigned voice :

" Sir, both of us are merchants, and one is a

K 277

harper and a singer. We have travelled hither up
the Nile to the Golden City because we understand
that in Napata pearls are rare, and such we have
to sell. Also we were told that the new King of this
city loved good singing, and my companion, who
sings and harps, learned her art in Egypt, even at
Thebes the holy. But who are you, Sir, that question
us ? "

" Lady," answered Rames, " I am an Egyptian
who holds this town on behalf of the Queen of Egypt
whom once I knew. Or perhaps I should say that
I hold it on behalf of the Pharaoh of Egypt, since
my spies tell me that the Star of Amen has taken
Abi, Prince of Memphis, to husband, although they
add that he finds her a masterful wife," and he
laughed bitterly.

" Sir," replied Asti, " it is long since we left
holy Thebes, some years indeed, and we know
nothing of these things, who ply our trade from
place to place. But if you are the governor of this
town, show us, we pray you, as countrywomen of
yours, where we may lodge in safety, and at your
leisure this afternoon permit that we exhibit our
pearls before you, and when that is done, and you
have bought or refused them, as you may wish, that
my companion should sing to you some of the ancient
songs of Egypt."

" Ladies," answered Rames, " I am a soldier
who would rather buy swords than pearls. Also,
as it chances, I am a man who dwells alone, one in
whose household no women can be found. Yet
because you are of my country, or by Amen I know
not why ! I grant you your request. I go out to

exercise this company in the arts of war, but after sundown you shall come to my palace, and I will see your wares and hear your songs. Till then, farewell. Officer," he added to a captain who had followed him, " take these Egyptians and their camels and give them a lodging in the guest-house, where they will not be molested, and at sundown bring them to me."

Then, still staring at them as though they held his eyes in their hearts, Rames departed, and the captain led them to their lodging.

It was the hour of sundown, and Tua, adorned in beautiful white raiment, broidered with royal purple, that she carried in her baggage on the camel, with her long hair combed out and scented, a necklace of great pearls upon her bosom, a veil flung over her head, and her harp of gold and ivory in her hand, waited to be led before Rames. Asti, his mother, waited also, but she was clad in a plain black robe, and over her head was a black veil. Presently that captain who had shown them their lodging, came to them and asked if they were ready to be led before the Viceroy of Napata.

" Viceroy ? " answered Asti, " I thought he was a King."

" So he is, my good Woman," replied the captain, " but it is his fancy to call himself the Viceroy of Neter-Tua, Star of Amen, wife of Abi the Usurper who rules in Egypt. A mad fancy when he might be a Pharaoh on his own account, but so it is."

" Well, Sir," said Asti, " we merchants have nothing to do with these high matters ; lead us to this Pharaoh, or General, or Viceroy, with whom we hope to transact business."

So the captain conducted them to a side gate of the palace, and thence through various passages and halls, in some of which Tua recognised officers of her own whom she had commanded to accompany Rames, to an apartment of no great size, where he bade them be seated. Presently a door opened, and through it came Rames, plainly dressed in the uniform of an Egyptian general, on which they saw he wore no serpent crest or other of the outward signs of royalty. Only on his right hand that lacked the little finger, gleamed a certain royal ring, which Tua knew. With him also were several captains to whom he talked of military affairs.

Seeing the two women, he bowed to them courteously, and asked them to forgive him for having kept them waiting for him. Then he said:

"What was it that you wished to show me, Ladies? Oh! I remember, precious stones. Well, I fear me that you have brought them to a bad market, seeing that although Napata is called the City of Gold, she needs all her wealth for her own purposes, and I draw from it only a general's pay, and a sum for the sustenance of my household, which is small. Still, let me look at your wares, for if I do not buy myself, perhaps I may be able to find you a customer."

Now when they saw the young man's noble face and bearing, and heard his simple words, the hearts of Asti and of Tua, his mother and his love, beat so hard within their breasts that for a while they could scarcely speak. Glad were they, indeed, that the veils they wore hid their troubled faces from his eyes, which, as in the morning, lingered on them curiously.

At length, controlling herself with an effort, Asti answered :

" Perchance, Lord, the Great Lady your wife, or the ladies your companions, will buy if you do not."

" Have I not already told you, Merchant," asked Rames angrily, " that I have no wife, and no companions that are not men ? "

" You said so, Sir," she replied humbly, always speaking in her feigned voice, " yet forgive us if we believed you not, since in our journeyings my daughter and I have seen many princes, and know that such a thing is contrary to their nature. Still we will show you our wares, for surely all the men in Napata are not unmarried."

Then, without more ado, she drew out a box of scented cedar and, opening it, revealed a diadem of pearls worked into the shape of the royal *uræus*, which they had fashioned thus at Tat, and also a few of their largest single gems.

" Beautiful, indeed," said Rames, looking at them, " though there is but one who has the right to wear this crown, the divine Queen of the Upper and the Lower Land," and he sighed.

" Nay, Lord," replied Asti, " for surely her husband might wear it also."

" It would sit but ill on the fat head of Abi, from all I hear, Lady," he broke in, laughing bitterly.

" Or," went on Asti, taking no heed of his words, " a general who had conquered a great country could usurp it, and find none to reprove him, especially if he himself happened to be of the royal blood."

Now Rames looked at her sharply.

" You speak strange words," he said, " but doubtless it is by chance. Merchant, those pearls of yours are for richer men than I am, shut them in the box again, and let the lady, your daughter, sing some old song of Egypt, for such I long to hear."

" So be it, Lord," answered Asti. " Still, keep the diadem as a gift, since it was made for you alone, and may yet be useful to you—who can know ? It is the price we pay for liberty to trade in your dominions. Nay, unless you keep it my daughter shall not sing."

" Let it lie there, then, most princely Merchant, and we will talk of the matter afterwards. Now for the song."

Then, her moment come at last, Tua stood up, and holding the ivory harp beneath her veil, she swept its golden chords. Disguising her voice, as Asti had done, she began to sing, somewhat low, a short and gentle love-song, which soon came to an end.

" It is pretty," said Rames, when she had finished, " and reminds me of I know not what. But have you no fuller music at your command ? If so, I would listen to it before I bid you good-night."

She bent her head and answered almost in a whisper :

" Lord, if you wish it, I will sing you the story of one who dared to set his heart too high, and of what befell him at the hands of an angry goddess."

" Sing on," he answered. " Once I heard such a story—elsewhere."

Then Tua swept her harp and sang again, but this time with all her strength and soul. As the first glorious notes floated from her lips Rames rose from his seat, and stood staring at her entranced. On went the song, and on, as she had sung it in the banqueting hall of Pharaoh at Thebes, so she sang it in the chamber of Rames at Napata. The scribe dared the sanctuary, the angry goddess smote him cold in death, the high-priestess wailed and mourned, the Queen of Love relented, and gave him back his life again. Then came that last glorious burst when, lifted up to heaven, the two lovers, forgiven, purged, chanted their triumph to the stars, and, by slow degrees, the music throbbed itself to silence.

Look! white-faced, trembling, Rames clung to a pillar in his chamber, while Tua sank back upon her chair, and the harp she held slipped from her hand down upon the floor.

" Whence came that harp ? " he gasped. " Surely there are not two such in the world ? Woman, you have stolen it. Nay, how can you have stolen the music, and the voice as well ? Lady, forgive me, I have no thought of evil, but oh ! grant me a boon. Why, I will tell you afterwards. Grant me a boon— let me look upon your face."

Tua lifted her hands, and undid the fastening of her veil, which slipped from her to her feet, showing her in the rich array of a princess of Egypt. His eyes met her beautiful eyes, and for a while they gazed upon each other like folk who dream.

" What trick is this ? " he said angrily at last.
" Before me stands the Star of Amen, Egypt's
anointed Queen. The harp she bears was the royal
gift of the Prince of Kesh, he who fell that night
beneath my sword. The voice is Egypt's voice,
the song is Egypt's song. Nay, how can it be ?
I am mad, you are magicians come to mock me,
for that Star, Amen's daughter, reigns a thousand
miles away with the lord she chose, Abi, her own
uncle, he who, they say, murdered Pharaoh. Get
you gone, Sorceress, lest I cause the priests of Amen,
whereof you also make a mock, to cast you to the
flames for blasphemy."

Slowly, very slowly, Tua opened the wrappings
about her throat, revealing the Sign of Life that
from her birth was stamped above her bosom.

" When they see this holy mark, think you that
the priests of Amen will cast me to the flames, O
Royal Son of Mermes ? " asked Tua softly.

" Why not ? " he answered. " If you have
power to lie in one thing, you have power to lie in
all. She who can steal the loveliness of Egypt's
self, can also steal the signet of the god."

" Say, did you, O Rames, also steal that other
signet on your hand, a Queen's gift, I think, that
once a Pharaoh wore ? Say also how did you lose
the little finger of that hand ? Was it perchance
in the maw of a certain god that dwells in the secret
pool of a temple at holy Thebes ? "

So Tua spake, and waited a while, but Rames
said nothing. He opened his mouth to answer, indeed, but a dumbness sealed his lips.

" Nurse," she went on presently, " I cannot

persuade this Lord that I am Egypt and no other. Try you."

So Asti loosed her black veil, and let it fall about her feet. He stared at her noble features and grey hair, then, uttering a great cry of "Mother, my Mother, who they swore to me was dead in Memphis," he flung himself upon her breast, and there burst into weeping.

"Aye, Rames," said Asti presently, "your Mother, she who bore you, and no other woman, and with her one who because her royal heart loves you now as from the first, from moon to moon for two whole years has braved the dangers of the desert, and of wicked men, till at last Amen her father brings her safely to your side. Now do you believe?"

"Aye," answered Rames, "I believe."

"Then, O faithful Captain," said Tua, "take this gift from Egypt's Queen, which a while ago you thrust aside, and be its Lord and mine," and lifting the diadem of pearls crested with the royal *uræi* she set it on his brow, as once before she had done in that hour of dawn when she vowed herself to him in Thebes.

It was night, and all their wonderful story had been told.

"Such is our tale, Rames my Son," said Asti, "and long may you search before you find another that will match it. Now tell us yours."

"It is short, Mother," he answered. "Obeying the commands of her Majesty yonder," and he bowed towards Tua, who sat at the further side of the table at which they ate, "I travelled up the

K*

Nile to this city. As the old king, the father of the Prince of Kesh, would have slain me I attacked him first by the help of my Egyptians and his own subjects, and—well, he died. Moreover, none regretted him, for he was a bad king, and I stepped into his place, and ever since have been engaged in righting matters which they needed. Long ago I would have returned to Egypt and reported myself, only my spies told me of all that had happened there. They told me, for instance, of the murder of Pharaoh, by the witchcraft of Abi and his companions; and they told me that Pharaoh's daughter, the Star of Amen, forgetting all things and the oath she swore to me, had married her old uncle Abi that she might save her life and power."

"And you believed them, Rames?" asked Tua reproachfully.

"What else could I do but believe, Lady, seeing that those same spies swore that they had seen your Majesty seated upon your throne at Memphis, and elsewhere, and causing Abi to run to and fro like a little dog, and do your bidding in all things? How could I know that it was your Double, and not yourself that married Abi?"

"I think that Abi knows to-day," answered Tua, "since it seems that a Ka makes but a bad wife to any man. But now what shall we do?"

"Will you not first marry me, Lady?" suggested Rames. "Afterwards, we can think."

"Aye," she answered, "I will marry you as I have promised, but in one place only, the temple of Amen in Egypt. First win me back my throne, then ask for my hand."

"It shall be done," he answered, "though how I know not, seeing that another sits upon that throne of yours, who, perhaps, will not be willing to bid it farewell."

"We will send her a message, Son," said Asti. "Now leave us, for we must sleep."

"Where is your messenger, Mother?" asked Rames as he went.

"Have you known me all these years, my Son, and not learned that I have servants whom you cannot see?" answered Asti.

It was midnight, and in their chamber of the palace of Rames, Asti and Tua knelt side by side in prayer to Amen, Father of the Gods. Then, their petitions finished, Asti rose to her feet, and once again, as in the pylon tower at Memphis, uttered the awful words that in bygone days had been spoken to her by the spirit of Ahura the divine in Osiris.

There was a sound as of whispering, a sound as of beating wings. Lo! in the shadow beyond the lamplight a mist gathered that brightened by degrees and took shape, the shape of a royal woman clad in the robes and ornaments of Egypt's Queen, whose face was as the face of Neter-Tua, only prouder and more unearthly. In silence it stood before them, scanning them with its glittering eyes.

"Whence come you, O Double?" asked Asti.

"From that place where your command found me, O Mistress of Secret Things, from the house of Abi at Thebes, wherein he seems to rule as Pharaoh," the Form answered in its cold voice.

"How fares it with Abi and with Egypt, O Double?"

"With Abi it fares but ill; he wastes in toil and fear and longings, and knows no happy hour. But with Egypt it fares well. Never, O Lady of Strength, was she more great than she is to-day, for in all things I have fulfilled·the commandments that were laid upon me, and now I desire to rest in that bosom whence I came," and she pointed to Tua, who stood and watched.

"Not yet, O Double, for there is still work for you to do, and then you shall be at peace till the day of the last Awakening. Hearken: Return to Thebes, and tell a false tale in the ears of Abi and his councillors. Say that Rames the Egyptian, who has seized the rule of Kesh, has declared himself Pharaoh of Egypt by right of race, and your husband by the promise of him who ruled before you whom Abi did to death. Cause this Abi to gather a great army, and to march southward to make an end of Rames. But secretly whisper into the ears of the generals of this army, that it is true the divine Pharaoh who is gone promised you in marriage to Rames with your own consent, and by the command of Amen, Father of the Gods, and of your Spirit. Whisper to them that Amen is wrath with Abi because of his crime, as he will show them in due season, and that those who rebel against him shall have his love and favour. At the Gateway of the South, whence the Nile rushes northward between great walls of rock, Rames shall meet the army of Abi. With him will come her of whom you are, and I whom you must obey; also perchance another who is greater than all of us. There at the Gateway of the South your task shall be accomplished, and you shall find the rest you seek. It is said."

"I hear the command, and it shall be done," answered the Ka in its cold, passionless voice. "Only, Lady of the Secrets, Doer of the Will Divine, delay not, lest, outworn, I should break back like a flame to yonder breast that is my home, slaying as I come, and leaving wreck behind me."

Then as the figure had appeared, so also it disappeared, growing faint by degrees, and vanishing away into the night out of which it came.

It was morning at Thebes, and Abi sat in the great hall of Pharaoh transacting business of the State, while at his side stood Kaku the Vizier. Changed were both of them, indeed, since they had plotted the death of their guest and king at Memphis, for now Abi was so worn with work and fear and wretchedness, that his royal robes hung about him in loose folds, while Kaku had become an old, old man, who trembled as he walked.

"Is the business finished, Officer?" asked Abi impatiently.

"Nay, Mighty Lord," answered Kaku, "there is still enough to keep you sitting here till noon, and after that you must receive the Council and the Embassies."

"I will not receive them. Let them wait till another day. Knave, would you work me to death, who have never known an hour's rest or peace since the happy time when I ruled as Prince of Memphis?"

"Lord," answered Kaku, bowing humbly, "weary

or no you must receive them, for so it has been decreed by her Majesty the Queen, whose command may not be broken."

" The Queen ! " exclaimed Abi in a low voice, rolling his hollow eyes around him as though in fear. " Oh, Kaku, would that I had never beheld the Queen. I tell you that she is not a woman, as indeed you know well, but a fiend with a heart of ice, and the venomous cunning of a snake. I am called Pharaoh, yet am but her puppet to carry out her decrees. I am called her husband, yet she is still no wife to me, or to any, although all men love her, and by that love are ofttimes brought to doom. Last night again she vanished from my side as I sat listening to her orders, and after a while, lo ! there she was as before, only, as it seemed to me, somewhat weary. I asked her where she had been and she answered : Further than I could travel in a year to visit one she loved as much as she hated me. Now who can that be, Kaku ? "

" Rames, I think, Lord, he who has made himself King of Kesh," replied Kaku in an awed whisper. " Without a doubt she loved the man when she was a woman, though whom she loves now the evil gods know alone. We are in her power, and must work her will, for, Lord, if we do not we shall die, and I think that neither of us desires to die, since beyond that gate dead Pharaoh waits for us."

At these words Abi groaned aloud, wiping the sweat from his blanched face with the corner of his robe, and saying :

" There you speak truly. Go, call the scribes, and let us get on with the Queen's business."

Kaku turned to obey, when suddenly heralds entered the empty hall, crying :

" Her Majesty the Queen waits without with a great company, and humbly craves audience of her good lord, the divine Pharaoh of the Upper and the Lower Land."

Abi and Kaku looked at each other, and despair was in their eyes.

" Let her Majesty enter," said the King in a low voice.

The heralds retired, and presently through the cedar doors appeared the Queen in state. She was splendid to behold, splendid in her proud beauty, splendid in her dress, and in her royal ornaments. On she swept up the hall, attended by Merytra, who bore her fan and cushion, for it was her pleasure that this woman should wait upon her day and night without pause or rest, although she who had once been so handsome now was worn almost to nothingness with toil and terror. Behind Merytra came guards and high-priests, and after them the great lords of the Council, who were called the King's Companions and the generals of the army.

On she swept up the hall till reaching the foot of the throne whereon Abi sat, she motioned to Merytra to place the cushion upon its step, and knelt, saying :

" I am come as a loyal wife to make a humble prayer to Pharaoh my Lord in the presence of his Court."

" Rise and speak on, Great Lady," answered Abi. " It is not fit that you should kneel to me."

" Nay, it is most fit that Pharaoh's Queen should

kneel to Pharaoh when she seeks his divine favour."
Yet she rose, and, seating herself in a chair that had
been brought, spoke thus :

"O Pharaoh, last night I dreamed a dream.
I dreamed of the Count Rames, son of Mermes, the
last of that royal race which ruled before our House
in Egypt. I mean that man who slew the Prince
of Kesh in this very hall, and whom, my Father being
sick, I sent to Napata, to be judged by the King of
Kesh, but who, it seems, overthrew that king and
took his kingdom in the name of Egypt.

"I dreamed that this bold and able man, not
satisfied with the rich kingdom of Kesh, has made a
scheme to attack Egypt; to slay you, most glorious
Lord, to proclaim himself Pharaoh by right of
ancient blood, and more—to take me, your faithful
wife, to be his wife, and thereby secure his throne."

"Without doubt, Queen, this turbulent Rames
might think of such things," said Abi, "and so
far your dream may be true ; yet it should be remembered that at present he is at Napata, which
is a very long way off, and has probably only a
small army at his command, so why should you
trouble about what he thinks ? "

"O Pharaoh, that was not all my dream, for
in it I saw two pictures. The first was of this bold
Rames attacking Thebes, and conquering it, yes,
and dragging me away to be his wife over your very
corpse, O Pharaoh. The second was of you and
your army meeting him at the Gate of the South
Land, and slaying him, and taking possession of
the kingdom of Kesh, and its golden city, and ruling
them for Egypt, until you die."

" Here be two dreams, O Queen," said Abi.
" Tell us now, which would you follow, for both
of them cannot be right ? "

" How can I know, Pharaoh, and how can you
know ? Yet by your side stands one who will
know, for he is the first of magicians, and a chosen
interpreter of the heart of the gods. Grant that
he may make this matter clear," and she pointed to
Kaku, who stood by the throne.

" Divine Lady," stammered Kaku, " the thing
is too high for me. I have no message, I cannot
tell you——"

" You were ever over-modest, Kaku," said the
Queen. " Command him, O Pharaoh, to shed the
light of his wisdom on us, for without doubt he knows
the truth."

" Yes, yes," said Abi, " he knows it, he knows
everything. Kaku, delay not, interpret the dream
of her Majesty."

" I cannot, I will not," spluttered the old
astrologer. " Ask my wife, the Lady Merytra there,
she is wiser than I am."

" My good friend Merytra has already told me
her mind," said the Queen, " now we wait for yours.
A prophet must speak when the gods call on him,
or," she added slowly, " he must cease to be a prophet
who betrays the gods by hiding their high counsel."

Now Kaku could find no way of escape, so, since
he feared the very name of Rames, within himself
he determined that he would interpret the dream
in the sense that Pharaoh should await the attack
of this Rames at Thebes, and while every ear listened
to him, thus began his tale. Yet as he spoke he

felt the glittering eyes of that spirit who was called the Queen, fix themselves upon him and compel his tongue, so that he said just what he did not mean to say.

" A light shines in me," he cried, " and I see that the second vision of her Majesty is the true vision. You must go up with your army to the Gate of the South, O Pharaoh, and there meet this usurper, Rames, that these matters may be brought to their appointed end."

" Their appointed end ?   What appointed end ? " shouted Abi.

" Doubtless that which her Majesty dreamed," answered Kaku. " At least, it is laid upon me to tell you that you must go up to the Gate of the South."

" Then I wish that the Gate of the South were laid upon you also, O Evil Prophet," exclaimed Abi.   " For two years only have I ruled in Egypt, and lo ! three wars have been my portion, a war against the people of Syria, a war against the desert men, and a war against the Nine Bow barbarians that invaded the Low Lands. Must I now, in my age, undertake another war against the terrible sons of Kesh also ?   Let this dog, Rames, come, if come he will, and I will hang him here at the gates of Thebes."

" Nay, nay, O Pharaoh," replied Kaku, " it is laid upon me to tell you that you must hang him in the desert hundreds of miles away from Thebes. That is the interpretation of the vision ; that is the command of the gods."

" The gods have spoken by the mouth of their

prophet," cried the Queen in a thrilling, triumphant voice. "Now Pharaoh, Priests, Councillors, and Captains of Egypt, let us make ready to travel to the Gate of the South, and there hang the dog Rames in the desert land, that thus Egypt and Egypt's King and Egypt's Queen may be freed from danger, and rest in peace, and the wealth of the City of Gold be divided amongst you all."

"Aye, aye," answered the Priests, Councillors, and Captains, the shrill voice of Kaku leading the chorus, still against his will, "let us go up at once, and let her Majesty accompany us."

"Yes," said the Queen, "I will accompany you, for though I be but a woman, shall I shrink from what Pharaoh, my dear Lord, dares? We will sail at the new moon."

That night Abi and Kaku stood face to face.

"What is this that you have done?" asked Abi. "Do you not remember the words which dead Pharaoh spoke in the awful vision that came to me that night at Memphis, when he bade me take the Royal Loveliness which I desired to be my wife? Do you not remember that he bade me also reign in her right until I met 'one Rames, Son of Mermes' and with him a Beggar-man who is charged with another message for me?"

"I remember," answered Kaku in a hollow voice.

"What, then, is this message, Man, that will come from Rames or the Beggar? Is it not the message of my death and yours, of us whose tombs were finished but yesterday?"

"It may be so, Lord."

"Then why did you interpret the dream of the Queen in the sense that I must hurry southwards to meet this very Rames—and my doom?"

"Because I could not help it," groaned Kaku. "That spirit who is called a Queen compelled me. Abi, there is no escape for us; we are in the net of Fate—unless, unless you dare——" and he looked meaningly at the sword that hung by Pharaoh's side.

"Nay, Kaku," he answered, "I dare not. Let us live while we may, knowing what awaits us beyond the gate."

"Aye," moaned Kaku, "beyond the Gate of the South, where we shall find Rames the Avenger, and that Beggar who is charged with a message for us."

CHAPTER XVIII

THE JUDGMENT OF THE GODS

THREE more months had gone by, and the great
host of Pharaoh was encamped beyond the Southern
Gate, and the warships of Pharaoh were anchored
thick on either bank of the Nile. There they lay
prepared for battle, for spies had reported to them
that the general, Rames, Lord of Kesh, was advancing
northward swiftly, though with so small an army
that it could easily be destroyed. Therefore Abi
waited there to destroy it without further toil, nor
did his terrible Queen gainsay him. She also seemed
content to wait.

One evening as the sun sank it was told to them
that the troops of Rames had appeared, and occupied
the mountains on the right bank of the Nile, being
encamped around that temple of Amen which had
stood there for thousands of years.

" Good," said the Queen. " To-morrow Pharaoh
will go up against him and make an end of this
matter. Is it not so, Pharaoh ? " and she looked
at him with her glittering eyes.

" Yes, yes," answered Abi, " the sooner the better,
for I am worn out, and would return to Thebes.
Yet," he added in a weak, uncertain voice, " I
misdoubt me of this war, I know not why. What
is it that you stare at in the heavens so fixedly,
O Kaku ? "

Now the eyes of the Council were turned on
Kaku the Vizier, and they perceived that he was
much disturbed.

" Look," he said, pointing with a trembling
finger towards the skies.

They looked, and saw hanging just above the
evening glow a very bright and wonderful star,
and near to it another, paler star which presently it
seemed to cover.

" The Star of Amen," gasped Kaku in a voice
that shook, " and your star, O Pharaoh. The
Star of Amen eats it up, your star goes out, and
will never be seen again by living man. Oh! Abi,
that which I foresaw years and years ago has come
to pass. Your day is done, and your night is at
hand, O Abi."

" If so," shouted Abi in his rage and terror,
" be sure of this, Dog—that you shall share it."

As he spoke a sound of screams drew near, and
presently into the midst of them rushed Merytra,
the wife of Kaku.

" The vengeance of the gods," she screamed,
" the vengeance of the gods! Listen, Abi. But
now this very evening as I slept in my pavilion,
who can never sleep at night, there appeared to
me the spirit of dead Pharaoh, of Pharaoh whom
we slew by magic, and he said : ' Tell the murderer,
Abi, and the wizard-rogue, Kaku, your husband, that
I summon both of them to meet me ere another sun
be set, and Woman, come you with them.' Death
is at our door, Abi, death and the terrible vengeance
of the god!" and Merytra fell down foaming in a
fit

Now Abi went mad in the extremity of his fear.

"They are sorcerers," he shouted, "who would bewitch me. Take them and keep them safe, and let Kaku be beaten with rods till he comes to his right mind again. To-morrow, when I have slain Rames, I will hang this magician at my mast-head."

But the Queen only laughed and repeated after him :

"Yes, yes, my good Lord, to-morrow, when you have killed Rames, this magician shall hang at your mast-head. Fear not, whatever chances I will see that it is done."

Merytra, recovered from her madness, lay upon a bed, when a woman entered and stood over her. Looking up she saw that it was the Queen.

"Hearken to me," said the Queen in an icy voice, "and tell the words I speak to Abi. The time is accomplished, and I leave him. If he would look again upon Neter-Tua, Morning Star of Amen, the Great Lady of Egypt, let him seek her in the camp of Rames. There he shall find her in the temple of Amen, which is set upon the mountain in the midst of the camp."

Then she was gone.

Merytra rose from the bed, and called to the guards to lead her to Abi. So loudly did she call, saying that she had a message for him which must not be delayed, that at length one went and told him of her words, and he came to her.

"What is it now, Sorceress ? " he asked. " Have you dreamed more ill-omened dreams ? "

"Nay, Pharaoh," she answered, " but the Queen

has fled to Rames," and word for word she repeated what had been said to her.

"It is a lie," said Abi. "How can she have fled through a triple line of guards?"

"Search, then, and see, O Pharaoh."

So Abi searched, but though none had seen her pass, and none had gone with her, the Queen could not be found.

It was midnight, and while they still searched, by the light of the moon a tall figure clad in tattered robes, who bore a thornwood staff in his hand, and had a white beard that fell down below his middle, was perceived walking to and fro about the camp.

"Who is that fellow?" asked Abi, and as he spoke the figure cried aloud in a great voice:

"Listen, Councillors, Captains, and Soldiers of Egypt, to the command of Amen, spoken by the lips of his messenger, Kepher the Wanderer. Lift no sword against Rames, Lord of Kesh, for he is my servant, and shall be Pharaoh over you, and husband of your Queen, and father of kings to come. Seize Abi the usurper, the murderer of Pharaoh, his brother, and Kaku the sorcerer, and Merytra the traitress, and lead them at the dawn to my temple upon yonder hill, where I will declare my commands to you in the sanctuary of the temple. So shall peace be upon you and all Egypt, and the breath of life remain in your nostrils."

Now hearing these fearful words, and remembering dead Pharaoh's prophecy of a Beggar who should bring a message to him, Abi drew his sword and rushed at the man. But ere ever he came there, the Wanderer was gone, and lo! they heard him

repeating his message far away. Thither they ran
also, but now the words of doom were being called
upon the ships, and on their prows they saw his
tall shape stand—first on this and then on that.

" It is the gods who speak," cried the priests,
" let us obey the gods ! " and suddenly they flung
themselves upon Abi and bound him, and Kaku
and Merytra they bound also, waiting for the dawn.
But of the tall, white-bearded man in beggar's robes
they saw and heard no more.

At that same hour Tua slept in a chamber of
the temple upon the hill, while Asti watched her.
Presently a wind blew in the chamber, and Asti,
looking up, became aware of a Shape that she knew
well, the very shape of Tua who slept upon the bed.

" What is your will, O Double ? " asked Asti.

" My will is that you give me rest," answered the
Ka. " My task is accomplished, I am weary.
Speak the secret words of power that you have,
and let me return to her from whom I came, and
in her bosom sleep till the great Day of Awakening."

So Asti, knowing that she was commanded so
to do, uttered those secret words, and as she spoke
them the glorious Shape seemed to grow faint and
fade away. Only Tua rose upon her bed, stretched
out her arms and sighed, fell back again and slept
heavily until the morning. Then she awoke, asking
what had befallen her, for she was changed.

" This has befallen, Queen. That which went
forth from you by the command of Amen has
returned to you again, its duty done. Rise up now

and adorn yourself, for this is your day of victory and marriage."

As the sun rose Tua went forth more beautiful than the morning, and at the gates of the temple found Rames awaiting her, clad in his armour, while from the mists below came a sound as of an army marching.

" What passes ? " asked Tua, looking at him, and there was more love in her blue eyes than there is water in the Nile at flood.

" I think that Abi attacks us, Lady," he said, bowing the knee to her, " and I am fearful for you, for our men are few, and his are many."

" Be not afraid of Abi, or of anything, O Rames, though it is true that this day you must lose your liberty," she answered with a sweet and gentle smile, and he wondered at her words.

Then, before he could speak again, two of the captains of his outposts ran in and reported that without were priests and heralds, who came in peace from the army of Abi.

" Summon the officers, and let them be admitted," said Rames, " but be careful, all of you, lest this embassy should hide some trick of war. Come, Queen, it is to you that they should speak, and not to me, who am but a general of your province, Kesh," and he followed her to the inner court, where, in front of the sanctuary, was a chair, on which, at his prayer, she seated herself, as a mighty Queen should do.

Now, conducted by his own officers, the embassy entered, bearing with them three closed litters, and Tua and Rames noted that among that embassy were the greatest generals, and the most holy priests of Egypt. At a given sign they prostrated themselves before the glory of the Queen, all save the soldiers who bore the litters. Next, from among their ranks out stepped the venerable High-Priest of Amen at Thebes, and stood before Tua with bowed head till, with a motion of her hand, she commanded him to speak.

" O Morning-Star of Amen," he began, " after you left our camp last night a messenger came to us from the Father of the Gods——"

" Stay, O High-Priest," broke in Tua. " I did not leave your camp who never tarried there, and who for two long years have set no foot upon the holy soil of Egypt. No, not since I fled from Memphis to save myself from death, or what is worse—the defilement of forced marriage with Abi, my Uncle, and Pharaoh's murderer."

Now the High-Priest turned and stared at those behind him, and all who were present stared at the Queen.

" Pardon me," he said, " but how can this thing be, seeing that for those two years we have seen your Majesty day by day living among us as the wife of Abi."

Now Tua looked at Asti, who stood at her side, and the tall and noble Asti looked at the High-Priest, saying :

" You know me, do you not ? "

" Aye, Lady," he answered, " we know you. You were the wife of Mermes, the last shoot of a royal tree, and you are the mother of the Lord Rames yonder, against whom we came out to make war.

We know you well, O greatest of all the seers in Egypt, Mistress of Secret Things. But we believed that you had perished in the temple of Sekhet at Memphis, that temple where Pharaoh died. Now we understand that, being a magician, you only vanished thence."

" What bear you there ? " asked Asti, glancing at the litters.

" Bring forth the prisoners," said the High-Priest.

Then the curtains were drawn, and the soldiers lifted from the litters Abi, Kaku, and Merytra, who were bound with cords, and stood them on their feet before the Queen.

" These are the very murderers of Pharaoh, my Father, who would have also brought me to shame. Why are my eyes affronted with the sight of them ? " asked Tua indignantly.

" Because the Messenger of the Gods, clothed as a Beggar-man, commanded it, your Majesty," answered the High-priest. " Now we understand that they are brought hither to be judged for the murder of Pharaoh, the good god who was your father."

" Shall a wife sit in judgment on her husband ? " broke in Abi.

" Man," said Tua, " I never was your wife. How can I have been your wife, who have not seen you since the death of Pharaoh ? Listen, now, all of you, to the tale of that marvel which has come to pass. At my birth—you, O High-Priest, should know it well—Amen gave to me a Ka, a Self within myself, to protect me in all dangers. The dangers came upon me, and Asti the Magician, my foster-

mother, speaking the words that had been taught
to her by the spirit of the divine Ahura who bore
me, called forth that Ka of mine, and left it where
I had been, to be the wife of Abi, such a wife, I
think, as never man had before. But me, Amen,
my father, rescued, and with me Asti, bearing
us in the Boat of the Sun to far lands, and protecting
us in many perils, till at length we came to the city
Napata, where we found a certain servant of mine
whom, as it chances, I—love," and she looked at
Rames and smiled.

" Meanwhile, my Shadow did the work to which
it was appointed, ruling for me in Egypt, and
drawing on Abi to his ruin. But last night It
returned to me, and will be seen no more by men, except, perchance, in my tomb after I am dead. Judge
you if my tale be true, and whether I am indeed
Neter-Tua, Daughter of Amen," and opening the
wrappings about her throat, she showed the holy
sign that was stamped above her breast, adding :

" The High-Priest yonder should know this mark,
for he saw it at my birth."

Now the aged man drew near, looked, and said :

" It is the sign. Here shines the Star of Amen
and no other. Still we do not understand. Tell
us the tale, O Asti."

So Asti stood forward, and told that tale, omitting
nothing, and then Rames told his tale, whereto
Tua the Queen added a little, and, although ere they
finished the sun was high, none wearied in listening
save only Abi, Kaku, and Merytra, who heard
death in every word.

It was done at length, and a great silence fell

upon the place, for the tongues of men were tied. Presently, the High-Priest, who all this while had stood with bent head, lifted up his eyes to heaven, crying :

" O Amen, Father of the Spirit of this Queen, show now thy will, that we may learn it and obey."

For a while there was silence, till suddenly a sound was heard in the dark sanctuary where stood the statue of the god, a sound as of a stick tapping upon the granite floor. Then the curtains of that sanctuary were drawn, and standing between them there appeared the figure of an ancient, bearded man, with stony eyes, who was clad in a beggar's robe. It was he who had met Tua and Asti in the wilderness and eaten up their food. It was he who had saved them in the palace of the desert king. It was he who but last night had walked the camp of Abi.

" I am that Messenger whom men from the beginning have called Kepher," he said. " I am the Dweller in the wilderness whom your fathers knew, and your sons shall know. I am he who seeks for charity and pays it back in life and death. I am the pen of Thoth the Recorder, I am the scourge of Osiris. I am the voice of Amen, god above the gods. Hearken you people of Egypt—not for a little end have these things come to pass, but that ye may learn that there is design in heaven, and justice upon earth, and, after justice, judgment. Pharaoh, the good servant of the gods, was basely murdered by his own kin whom he trusted. Neter-Tua, his daughter, and daughter of Amen, was condemned to shame, Rames of the royal race was sent forth to danger or to death, far from her he loved, and who loved him by that divine command which rules the hearts of men. This is the command of the gods—Let these twain be wed and take Egypt as their heritage, and call down upon it peace and greatness. But as for these murderers and wizards "—and he pointed to Abi, to Kaku, and to Merytra—" let them be placed in the sanctuary of Amen, to await what he shall send them."

So spoke Kepher the Messenger, and departed whence he came, nor in that generation did any see him more.

Then they took up Abi, Kaku, and Merytra, and cut their bonds. They threw them into the dark sanctuary before the great stone image of the god. They shut the electrum doors upon them, and left them there wailing and cursing, while the High-Priest of Amen joined the hands of Rames and of Tua, and declared them to be man and wife for ever.

Now, after these things were done, the Pharaoh and his Queen drove through the hosts of Egypt in their golden chariot, and received the homage of the hosts ere they departed northwards for Thebes. At nightfall they returned again and sat side by side at the marriage feast, and once more Tua swept her harp of ivory and gold, and sang the ancient song of him who dared much for love, and won the prize.

So in the dim, forgotten years, their joy fell on Rames and on Tua, Morning-Star of Amen, which still with them remains in the new immortal kingdom that they have won long and long ago.

But when in the morning Asti the wise dared to open the great doors and peer into the sanctuary of Amen, she saw a dreadful sight. For there at the feet of the effigy of the god lay Abi, who slew his brother, and Kaku the sorcerer, and Merytra the traitress, dead, slain by their own or by each other's hand, and the stony eyes of the god stared down upon them.

THE END